BEST DETECTIVE STORIES
OF THE YEAR—1977
31st Annual Collection

BEST DETECTIVE STORIES OF THE YEAR 1977

31st Annual Collection

Edited by
Edward D. Hoch

E.P. Dutton | New York, N.Y.

Library of Congress Catalog Card Number: 46-5872

ISBN: 0-525-06436-2

Published simultaneously in Canada
by Clarke, Irwin & Company
Limited, Toronto and Vancouver

10 9 8 7 6 5 4 3 2 1

First Edition

For Eleanor Sullivan

CONTENTS

INTRODUCTION

The very first attempt to collect the year's best mystery short stories into an annual volume was made almost fifty years ago when *The Best Detective Stories of 1928,* edited by Ronald A. Knox and H. Harrington, was published in London in 1929 (an American edition, *The Best English Detective Stories of 1928,* appeared in New York the same year). The contents included Agatha Christie's first Miss Marple story, but the book is remembered today mainly for Monsignor Knox's superlative introduction in which he listed his "Ten Commandments" for the writing of detective stories.

Unfortunately, the British series survived for only two annual volumes, but it was immediately replaced in the United States by *The Best American Mystery Stories of the Year,* edited by Carolyn Wells (New York, 1931). Miss Wells, who is all but forgotten today, was then a popular mystery writer and produced two volumes in her series before it too ceased publication. After that there were no annual "Best" volumes until Dutton launched the present series in 1946 under the able editorship of David C. Cooke.

It's interesting to examine the first of Miss Wells's volumes, since it appeared at the peak of the so-called Golden Age of the detective story and the mystery pulp magazine, when Hollywood was beginning to produce real detective stories as contrasted with the thrillers of the silent screen. The book reprinted twenty stories from 1929 and 1930, but only two were drawn from mystery magazines—a Dashiell Hammett story from *Black Mask* and a MacKinlay Kantor tale from *Real Detective Stories.* Three stories (including Lawrence G. Blochman's classic "Red Wine") were from *Adventure* and the remaining fifteen were from such slick magazines as *The Saturday Evening Post, Collier's, Ladies' Home Journal, Red Book, Cosmopolitan,* and *The American.*

If they were still alive and writing today, most of these slick writers—authors like Ben Hecht and Melville Davisson Post—would be more likely to appear in mystery magazines. While slick magazine markets for suspense fiction continue to shrink, the leading mystery magazines are becoming publishing institutions. The oldest and best of them, *Ellery Queen's Mystery Magazine,* celebrated its 36th anniversary and 400th issue in March 1977. *Alfred Hitchcock's Mystery Magazine* and *Mike Shayne Mystery Magazine* have both passed the twenty-year mark. A newcomer, *Mystery Monthly,* published seven issues during 1976, and another new magazine is promised for '77.

A glance at the Yearbook section at the back of this book shows that publication of mystery collections and anthologies continues to increase, which is certainly one healthy sign for the field. You will note also that two publishers, Garland and Arno Press, have reprinted expensive sets of mystery classics designed mainly for libraries, and The University of California at San Diego has launched its ambitious *Mystery Library* classic reprint series, which will serve as the basis for future creative writing courses.

In all, it was a good year for the mystery story, as the following selected stories will demonstrate. Though only about one-third are formal detective stories, I've tried again this year to include a sampling of series characters—Joyce Porter's Inspector Dover and S.S. Rafferty's Captain Cork are both new to these pages. I've included two stories inspired by our nation's bicentennial and two others in what might be called a "New Wave" of mystery writing.

My thanks to all who helped in the preparation of this volume, and especially to Bill Pronzini, Jon L. Breen, and my wife, Patricia.

EDWARD D. HOCH

BEST DETECTIVE STORIES
OF THE YEAR—1977
31st Annual Collection

No publication, over the years, has been more receptive to the new writer than Ellery Queen's Mystery Magazine. By the end of 1976 it had published 454 "first stories" in its thirty six-year history, introducing such writers as Stanley Ellin, Harry Kemelman, Robert L. Fish, Lillian de la Torre, and Henry Slesar, among others. The story that follows, Etta Revesz's powerful emotional drama of one family's tragedy, was a "first story" in the May 1976 issue of EQMM. *At year's end the Mystery Writers of America voted to award it their Edgar as the finest mystery short story of the year. My special thanks to Fred Dannay of* EQMM *for allowing us to reprint it here, even though it's also scheduled to appear in the next Ellery Queen annual anthology.*

ETTA REVESZ
Like a Terrible Scream

Me, I just sit here and wait until the man outside push the little button and the door open with a small click and the Father walk out. The Father, I know him since I be five, which is now eight years. I bet he never think he come to see me in lockup. Kid lockup they call it but look like real grown-up jail to me.

I look out the little window for two days now. All I see is sky and maybe a airplane go by. The bed is clean but the floor is cement stone and hard on my leg. It is the door that I hate with much feeling. It is gray and iron, like the brace I wear on my leg. The little square window is high and I am yet too little to see out it and down the hall. I know a man sits there by a high desk and pushes buttons for many doors like I have to my cell. Yesterday I push up tight against the door because I am afraid. I think maybe I am the only one left here. But all I see is the ceiling of the hall and it is gray and not so clean.

It is hard to sit here and see the Father leave. He try. He try hard to make me tell why I do it.

"Confess, my son," Father Diaz say. "Tell me why did you do that terrible thing? You could not have realized. You were not thinking right!"

The good Father he lean his head way down and I think he cry, but I shake my head. How can I tell him? If I tell him the reason why I have done this it would be all for nothing. So I let him put his hand on my head and I say nothing.

"Kneel, my son," the Father say. "If you cannot tell me, tell God. It will help."

"No, Father," I say. "I cannot kneel."

He look very unhappy then, almost I think he will slap me when he take his hand away from my head. But he does not.

"A boy that cannot kneel and ask forgiveness from God is lost," he say and then go to my iron door and punch the little black button that tell the man at the desk to open up.

Now I sit here on my cot and wait for the Father to leave. My leg is out straight with my iron brace beginning to hurt me. Always at this time when night sounds start, Rita come home and take it off for me and rub my leg. Her hands, always so soft, rub away the stiffness. She talk to me about things outside. Always she ask to see my picture that I make that day. It was Rita that buy the paper and black crayon for me to draw. And last Christmas she bring me a box of paints! How much I do not guess it cost, but I know it cost much.

I feel in my eyes the water begin, but I want not to cry. I look again at Father Diaz's black suit. Like a crow he looks, standing with his arms folded close to his side like wings. I cannot stop my eyes from making tears. I pretend it is because my leg hurts and I try not to think of Rita.

I decide to tell Father Diaz that I cannot kneel because my iron brace does not bend. Then he would not think that all his teaching about God and the Blessed Virgin was for nothing. But it is too late. I hear the click and the door pop open and I am alone again.

Soon they will bring me food. I do not like noodles and cheese. Cheese should be on enchiladas. Noodles and cheese and maybe wheat bread with edges curled up like a dried leaf. Next to it a spoonful of peanut butter which I hate. It glues my tongue to my teeth. I think back to what Rita always bring to me.

Every night before she go to her job she come by the house with a surprise. First she take off my iron brace and rub my leg and then she put the brown bag in my lap and we stick both our heads close to see what big pleasure is there. Sometimes I look up and see her eyes big on me and smiling when I find a bag of candy or a pomegranate or even a new paint brush. At such time I feel a big pain over my heart and my jaw hurt from not crying. Rita she hate for me to cry. How can she know that it is for love of her that I cry?

Sometimes when only Mama and I are home I stop my painting and look out the window. We are high, two stairs up, but I can see the branches of the tree growing from the brown square of land in our sidewalk. It is not very healthy this poor tree, and has dry brown limbs with no leaves much. But still I watch the sun on what leaves are still there. It is when the sun is low and shines even with my tree that I like it best. Long fingers of white light run sharp from the center and when the wind blows everything shoots gold and shining. It is like a sign from God that the day is gone and Rita will run soon into the room and call out.

"Pepito," she calls, "I am here again. Your ugly old sister is here again!"

I pretend I do not hear her and then she come and put her hands around to cover my eyes from behind.

"Guess who it is?" she ask in make-believe man voice.

"My ugly old sister!" I say and then we both laugh. My sister Rita is not ugly. Sometimes she have a day off and she let me draw her picture. She sit by the window quiet while I look at her and put my markings on my paper. Sometimes I forget to move my hand when I look at her. Rita have long black hair and she tie it back so her neck looks very thin. Her mouth is still but when she think I am not watching, her lips move a little and I think she is telling secrets to herself. It is her eyes that I cannot draw so well.

When I look once they are laughing and show a joke ready to be said, but when I look again, I feel I must weep. Once I really start to cry at least a year ago when I was only twelve. Rita rush over and hug me.

"My little Pepito." She touch my cheek. "Does your leg hurt? I will work hard and save—oh, I will save so and will take you to a big hospital where the finest doctors will make a miracle on your leg."

"No," I tell her. I can never lie to Rita even when I want pity. "It is my love for you that make me cry. You are like Sunday music."

She just laugh then and the next day when she come she say, "Here is your Sunday music for your ears to hear on Wednesday!"

I love my Mama and Papa almost as much as I love Rita. But Mama sigh often as she count her beads and wears black instead of colors bright and gay like Rita. I remember long time before, when we first come to city, Mama sing always. Sometimes she dance with Papa when Papa say about the big job he going to get.

"No more driving the junk truck for me," say Papa. "Lucerno family will be on easy street soon."

When Papa finish driving truck for Mr. George Hemfield he go to night school. When I wake up at night from the couch where I sleep because my leg hurt, I see Papa sitting at the kitchen table with books. All is quiet. Only sleeping sounds and the tick-ting of the wake-up clock and the hush sound of the books when Papa close them. Then I hear him push the chair and walk to his bed.

Carlos and Mikos, my big brothers, sleep in the bedroom. They have the big bed and Rita sleep with little Rosa in the little bed. Rosa is very small, only three years, and Rita call her Little Plum. Mama and Papa have the back porch for them. Papa fix it up and when Mama say, "What about the heat, my husband, when the winter come?" Papa he laugh and grab Mama as she pass him to the stove and say, "I will keep you warm—like always!"

"You crazy fellow, not before the children!" And Mama push his hand away like she is mad but I see her lips smile. Mama think I know nothing about life because I stay at home, because I do not run the streets and only walk outside for special days like Easter and Christmas and Cinque de Mayo when the world is spinning to guitar music.

At first when we come to city I go to school but after a while the stairs and long walk is too much. Rita try to carry me but the iron prison on my leg make her tired and once she drop me and the iron bend and cut into my leg. I learn, but not very much. It is hard for me to read the words and the teacher do not call my name very often.

Rita try to help. She is in the high school and she show me to make my letters. But I cannot do well. At my desk I draw pictures of what I want to say. It is much easier and soon the school hall show them on the walls.

One day the Principal give Rita a note for Mama to come and talk with him. Papa he go instead and after a long time in the Principal's office he come out and we walk home. Papa walk very small steps and not even holds my hand from sidewalk to car street. When we get to house Papa pick me up and carry me up to Mama. He hold me very tight and push my face to look behind him but I know he angry, sad angry. He tell Mama that a special teacher is going to teach me at home because they have no place for me at my school.

The teacher come but not for long. After a while another lady come to talk to Mama about budget and say that if Mama bring me to Down-Town I go to special school. Papa get mad and go Down-Town but come back soon. He say nothing and now I stay home and draw much.

I hear the pop of my iron door and a kid like me come in. He is an old one in experience at this place and they let him bring the food. He push open my door with a foot and carry in the tray. I watch him look where to put it.

"Here's your supper, Crip," he say. "Where d'ya want it?"

I sit up and look at what there is to eat. But all I see is red Jello and two pieces of brown bread poked into a sauce of broken meat. I take off the square paper box of milk and tell him to take the tray. He looks worried at me.

"Look, Mex," he speak low. "Not eating won't help."

I shake my head and lean back on my cot and he leaves. It is almost dark now in my little gray room. I can put on a light. It is held away from me in a wire basket like a muzzle for a dog, but I have nothing to look at anyway. So I stand and press against the stone wall so I see up and out the window into the soon night.

In the sky is fuzzy lines of color, like the cotton when you pull it out of the box and it spread fine in your hand. Somewhere I hear a noise and the red and green light of a airplane pass my eyes. So small it is, like a ladybug. So far away and such a small spot, much bigger looks the bird that flies closer to my window, not knowing that night is close and he should be in his nest. I am all alone now in my darkness.

It is like the darkness that came to our house the day Papa come home from new job hunting. For long days Papa try for new job, after he come home from school and hold high his beautiful piece of paper with gold words saying he is a educated man.

"This is just the beginning," say Papa. "I am just the number one to bring home the High School Certificate. Look, kids," say Papa, "this little piece of paper will be our passport to a new life."

We have a good dinner that night and Mama make a toast. "My man, with all this education, will be *Presidenti* yet!" Papa kiss Mama then and she let us all watch. Rita dance that day. She was fifteen and the next one who would bring home such a paper. But it was not to be.

Papa's paper was only words and no one pull Papa in by the arm and give him a good job. Each day it was harder and harder to see his face at night and each night he have more and more red wine. At last Papa go back to his old job. It was a big truck and Papa was very tired at night after filling it with broken cars and iron and rusty pipes. Soon Mama cry all the time and then Rita stop her school. She come home one day and say she have a fine job that pay much money but she have to work at night. Papa ask who boss is, but Rita say he is Up-Town man and that Papa would not know him.

Rita sleep late now every morning and sometimes she look sad at me when she say goodbye to go for job. Always she look tired and one day she and Mama have big fight. Rita say she move out nearer her job and Mama say, "No," but Rita go anyway. She tell Mama she come every day to see me and bring money every week. The house seem so still now and Mama sit long times with little Rosa on her lap and I hear her say "Little Plum" over and over.

Now for me the day begins when Rita come, for Rita keep her promise. One day she come and after we eat the caramel corn she bring, Rita tell me of a secret she and I will have. It is a plan to make me walk straight without iron brace.

"Pepito," Rita say and put three dollars in my hand, "I want you to hide this and every week I will give you more until there is enough and then we will visit the doctor who fixes legs."

We find empty box that oatmeal come in and cut a hole in the round top big enough to fold money into. It is our secret hiding place and I push the box under the couch where I sleep. Each week Rita add more money, sometimes even more at one time.

Our home is not very happy now. With Rita the smiles have gone. Carlos and Mikos are big now. Carlos is in the high school but want to stop and he and Papa fight now. Carlos say to Papa, "Old man, you live on your daughter's hustling!"

I watch as he pull himself up and like a bear try to squeeze the words back into Carlos's mouth. Papa's big hand slaps out at Carlos but he is quick and runs out and down the steps to the street. For the first time I see Papa cry, and when Mama come in and ask, he will not tell her what hurts him.

I cannot sleep that night. I know what hustling is. It is the walking of the streets that a woman does to offer her body to any man who will pay. I have hear Carlos and Mikos talk when they think I sleep. I hear the names of some girls and then rough words and then small swallowed laughter. I am much older than the pain in my legs. I am as old as the new leaves on my poor tree on the sidewalk.

My pillow is hard that night and I close my eyes against my fear. It is then that Rita's face come before my mind. I see her smooth skin and the quick way her body moves and the softness of her breast. I have watched her grow more beautiful in form as in heart. I have made the curve of her with my crayon on white paper. Do not think I look upon her with more than a brother should. But is it wrong to see beauty when it grows before your eyes? Her name is really Margarita, like the white flower with the golden center.

I cannot bear the evil pictures that pass before my eyes, and I cross myself and insist to my mind that Carlos spoke in anger and said a lie. I prefer it so.

When Rita come that next evening I want to tell her what Carlos say so we could laugh about it together and she could slap his face. But I keep silent. When she ask me why I do not smile I tell her a lie. I say my foot hurt.

"Come," she say, "get our box and let us count the money."

We open the top and count it in her lap. "We need more," Rita say. "I will work overtime."

I nod for I am afraid to ask and afraid not to ask. For the first time I want Rita to leave.

It is weeks before I sleep well and I blame it on my leg but I know it is Rita that worry me. Now I look at her more closely as if I expect to see a sign that all was a lie. Once I start to say something.

"A woman that sells her body." I stutter over the words. "What would one call her?"

Rita look at me quick and pulls her lips tight, then smiles. "Don't tell me that my little Pepito is growing up!"

She put her hand on my head and push my hair off my face.

"You do not answer me," I say.

"A prostitute." She turn away from me and her hand drop.

"That is an evil thing for a woman to do, isn't it?" I say.

"It all depends."

She turns and picks up a big bag. "Look what I brought you tonight."

After we eat the big oranges she lean her head against mine and speaks into the room.

"You must not concern yourself with ugly things. You must see only beauty and put it on paper. I do not know any prostitutes and neither do you."

She leave soon after and before I sleep that night I curse my brother Carlos and his vile tongue.

It goes on as before now with Rita and me. Soon it is her birthday. She is to be eighteen in a week and I decide to buy her a present. Mama has said that eighteen is a special age for a girl and I want to make it fine for her birthday. The only money I have is under my couch in the oatmeal box. I decide within myself that it would not be wrong to use some of it for Rita's birthday present.

Mama is surprised when I tell her I will go down the stairs and on the street until I explain to her what I want to do. I tell her I have saved some money and I show her the twenty dollars I have in my pocket. She helps me down the first steps and watches me as I walk down the street to where the stores are.

The stores are filled with fine things and I move slowly from one window to the other. Before one I stop a long time and almost decide to buy a small radio. But I think maybe a pretty dress would be better for Rita. A white dress to make her hair blacker than the midnight and the white like snow against her golden skin.

Now I look for a dress shop. Across the street is a large store with dresses like a flower garden. At the corner I stand waiting for the streetlight to change when I hear voices behind me. It is what they say that makes me turn and follow them instead of crossing the street.

I do not know all of them but one boy is Luis. He is older than Rita but was in school with her and sometimes Carlos bring him to the house. It is when I hear him say the name Rita that I decide to follow them.

"Yeah, that damn Rita," one boy say. "Since she move Up-Town into the big time, you can't even touch her any more."

"I hear she's hooked up with some pimp who is really rolling in clover." They all laugh.

My blood! I feel it leave my body and sink to the sidewalk. Surely the earth will open up and these boys will fall into hell! I cannot walk any more. They turn the corner and disappear. My heart is dead inside of me. No longer can I doubt what I feared. No longer can I doubt.

I feel people shove at me as they pass me and still I cannot move. Long later I take steps, slowly down the sidewalk. All the time in the center of my throat is a sore spot I cannot swallow away. Like a terrible scream that has no sound.

It was when my leg hurt so much that I stop and lean my face against the smooth glass of a store window. Cool it feels on my hot cheeks. My eyes I close tight—so tight it hurt. Colors dance in my head and run to stab my heart. My leg beats out the music of pain.

No longer can I stand the ache so I open my eyes again. There, under my look, I see the guns. Like soldiers ready to march when the general shout out a command. They wait quietly, these black snails that carry death inside a shell.

For a long time I look at these guns. Has not Father Diaz said that death is only another life? And a better one?

I move to the store door. It is glass with a wire across it, like the knitting Mama does, all looped together. I put two hands on the door handle. It is stiff and cold like a gun, I think. Down I push and shove open the door. I stumble on a mat and my iron brace rips at the rubber as I pull my leg free. A small bell shakes and makes a ringing. I walk in.

When the police ask me I shake my head and when Mama and Papa cry in the courtroom for children and the judge ask me why I kill my sister on her birthday I still am quiet. They would not understand how hard a thing it was to do. To lose your star when you are thirteen is to walk blind on the earth. Better this way than to see your star fall from the heavens and end in mud. Always to me Margarita will be like her name, pure white on the outside and golden in the center.

And that is why I lie here on this cot with the black of my little room hiding me from the night of nothingness and I am called a murderer.

With fifteen novels and a collection of short stories, all published since 1964, Ruth Rendell has established herself as one of the leading British mystery writers of the new generation. An Edgar winner two years ago for her short story "The Fallen Curtain," she has been nominated for the award each year since. We welcome her first appearance in BEST with this year's Edgar nominee–about a man who read detective stories.

RUTH RENDELL
People Don't Do Such Things

People don't do such things.

That's the last line of *Hedda Gabler,* and Ibsen makes this chap say it out of a sort of bewilderment at finding truth stranger than fiction. I know just how he felt. I say it myself every time I come up against the hard reality that Reeve Baker is serving fifteen years in prison for murdering my wife, and that I played my part in it, and that it happened to us three. People don't do such things. But they do.

Real life had never been stranger than fiction for me. It had always been beautifully pedestrian and calm and pleasant, and all the people I knew jogged along in the same sort of way. Except Reeve, that is. I suppose I made a friend of Reeve and enjoyed his company so much because of the contrast between his manner of living and my own, and so that when he had gone home I could say comfortably to Gwendolen, "How dull our lives must seem to Reeve!"

An acquaintance of mine had given him my name when he had got into a mess with his finances and was having trouble with the Inland Revenue. As an accountant with a good many writers among my clients, I was used to their irresponsible attitude to money—the way they fall back on the excuse of artistic temperament for what is, in fact, calculated tax evasion—and I was able to sort things out for Reeve and show him how to keep more or less solvent. As a way, I suppose, of showing his gratitude, Reeve took Gwendolen and me out to dinner, then we had him over at our place, and after that we became close friends.

Writers and the way they work hold a fascination for ordinary chaps like me. It's a mystery to me where they get their ideas from, apart from constructing the thing and creating characters and making their characters talk and so on. But Reeve could do it all right, and set the whole lot at the court of Louis Quinze or in medieval Italy or what not. I've read all nine of his historical novels and admired what you might call his virtuosity. But I only read them to please him really. Detective stories were what I preferred and I seldom bothered with any other form of fiction.

Gwendolen once said to me it was amazing Reeve could fill his books with so much drama when he was living drama all the time. You'd imagine he'd have got rid of it all on paper. I think the truth was that every one of his heroes was himself, only transformed into Cesare Borgia or Casanova. You could see Reeve in them all, tall, handsome, and dashing as they were, and each a devil with the women. Reeve had got divorced from his wife a year or so before I'd met him, and since then he'd had a string of girlfriends—models, actresses, girls in the fashion trade, secretaries, journalists, schoolteachers, high-powered lady executives, and even a dentist. Once when we were over at his place he played us a record of an aria from *Don Giovanni*—another character Reeve identified with and wrote about. It was called the "Catalogue Song" and it listed all the types of girls the Don had made love to—blonde, brunette, redhead, young, old, rich, poor—ending up with something about as long as she wears a petticoat you know what he does. Funny, I even remember the Italian for that bit, though it's the only Italian I know: *Purche porti la gonella voi sapete quel che fa.* Then the singer laughed in an unpleasant way, laughed to music with a seducer's sneer, and Reeve laughed too, saying it gave him a fellow-feeling.

I'm old-fashioned, I know that. I'm conventional. Sex for marriage, as far as I'm concerned, and what sex you have before marriage—I never had much—I can't help thinking of as a shameful, secret thing. I never even believed that people did have much of it outside marriage. All talk and boasting, I thought. I really did think that. And I kidded myself that when Reeve talked of going out with a new girl he meant "going out with." Taking out for a meal, I thought, and dancing with and taking home in a taxi, and then maybe a goodnight kiss on the doorstep. Until one Sunday morning, when Reeve was coming over for lunch, I phoned him to ask if he'd meet us in the pub for a pre-lunch drink. He sounded half asleep and I could hear a girl giggling in the background. Then I heard him say, "Get some clothes on, lovey, and make us a cup of tea, will you? My head's splitting."

I told Gwendolen.

"What did you expect?" she said.

"I don't know," I said. "I thought you'd be shocked."

"He's very good-looking and he's only thirty-seven. It's natural."
But she had blushed a little. "I am rather shocked," she said. "We
don't belong in his sort of life, do we?"

And yet we remained in it, on the edge of it. As we got to know
Reeve better, he put aside those small prevarications he had
employed to save our feelings. And he would tell us, without shy-
ness, anecdotes of his amorous past and present. The one about the
girl who was so possessive that even though he had broken with her,
she had got into his flat in his absence and been lying naked in his
bed when he brought his new girl home that night; the one about the
married woman who had hidden him for two hours in her wardrobe
until her husband had gone out; the girl who had come to borrow a
pound of sugar and had stayed all night; fair girls, dark girls, plump,
thin, rich, poor. . . . *Purche porti la gonella voi sapete quel che fa.*

"It's another world," said Gwendolen.

And I said, "How the other half lives."

We were given to clichés of this sort. Our life was a cliché, the
commonest sort of life led by middle-class people in the Western
world. We had a nice detached house in one of the right suburbs,
solid furniture, and lifetime-lasting carpets. I had my car and she
hers. I left for the office at half past eight and returned at six.
Gwendolen cleaned the house and went shopping and gave coffee
mornings. In the evenings we liked to sit at home and watch television, generally going to bed at eleven. I think I was a good husband. I
never forgot my wife's birthday or failed to send her roses on our
anniversary or omitted to do my share of the dishwashing. And she
was an excellent wife, romantically inclined, not sensual. At any rate,
she was never sensual with me.

She kept every birthday card I ever sent her, and the Valentines I
sent her while we were engaged. Gwendolen was one of those
women who hoard and cherish small mementoes. In a drawer of her
dressing table she kept the menu card from the restaurant where we
celebrated our engagement, a picture postcard of the hotel where we
spent our honeymoon, every photograph of us that had ever been
taken, our wedding pictures in a leather-bound album. Yes, she was
an arch-romantic, and in her diffident way, with an air of daring, she
would sometimes reproach Reeve for his callousness.

"But you can't do that to someone who loves you," she said when he had announced his brutal intention of going off on holiday without telling his latest girlfriend where he was going or even that he was going at all. "You'll break her heart."

"Gwendolen, my love, she hasn't got a heart. Women don't have them. She has another sort of machine, a combination of telescope, lie detector, scalpel, and castrating device."

"You're too cynical," said my wife. "You may fall in love yourself one day and then you'll know how it feels."

"Not necessarily. As Shaw said. . . "—Reeve was always quoting what other writers had said—" 'Don't do unto others as you would have others do unto you, as we don't all have the same tastes.' "

"We all have the same taste about not wanting to be ill-treated."

"She should have thought of that before she tried to control my life. No, I shall quietly disappear for a while. I mightn't go away, in fact. I might just say I'm going away and lie low at home for a fortnight. Fill up the deep freeze, you know, and lay in a stock of liquor. I've done it before in this sort of situation. It's rather pleasant and I get a hell of a lot of work done."

Gwendolen was silenced by this and, I must say, so was I. You may wonder, after these examples of his morality, just what it was I saw in Reeve. It's hard now for me to remember. Charm, perhaps, and a never-failing hospitality; a rueful way of talking about his own life as if it was all he could hope for, while mine was the ideal all men would aspire to; a helplessness about his financial affairs combined with an admiration for my grasp of them; a manner of talking to me as if we were equally men of the world, only I had chosen the better part. When invited to one of our dull, modest gatherings, he would always be the exciting friend with the witty small talk, the reviver of a failing party, the industrious barman, above all, the one among our friends who wasn't an accountant, a bank manager, a solicitor, a general practitioner, or a company executive. We had his books on our shelves. Our friends borrowed them and told their friends they'd met Reeve Baker at our house. He gave us a cachet that raised us enough centimeters above the level of the bourgeoisie to make us interesting.

Perhaps, in those days, I should have asked myself what it was he saw in us.

It was about a year ago that I first sensed a coolness between Gwendolen and Reeve. The banter they had gone in for, which had consisted in wry confessions or flirtatious compliments from him

and shy, somewhat maternal reproofs from her, stopped almost
entirely. When we all three were together they talked to each other
through me, as if I were their interpreter. I asked Gwendolen if he'd
done something to upset her.

She looked extremely taken aback. "What makes you ask?"

"You always seem a bit peeved with him."

"I'm sorry," she said. "I'll try to be nicer. I didn't know I'd
changed."

She had changed to me too. She flinched sometimes when I
touched her, and although she never refused me, there was an
apathy about her lovemaking.

"What's the matter?" I asked her after a failure which disturbed
me because it was so unprecedented.

She said it was nothing, and then: "We're getting older. You can't
expect things to be the same as when we were first married."

"For God's sake," I said, "you're thirty-five and I'm thirty-nine.
We're not in our dotage."

She sighed and looked unhappy. She had become moody and
difficult. Although she hardly opened her mouth in Reeve's pre-
sence, she talked about him a lot when he wasn't there, seizing upon
almost any excuse to discuss him and speculate about his character.
And she seemed inexplicably annoyed when, on our tenth wedding
anniversary, a greetings card arrived addressed to us both from him.
I, of course, had sent her roses. At the end of that week I missed a
receipt for a bill I'd paid—as an accountant, I'm naturally cir-
cumspect about these things—and I searched through our waste-
paper basket, thinking I might have thrown it away. I found it, and I
also found the anniversary card I'd sent Gwendolen to accompany
the roses.

All these things I noticed. That was the trouble with me—I noticed
things but I lacked the experience of life to add them up and make a
significant total. I didn't have the worldly wisdom to guess why my
wife was always out when I phoned her in the afternoons, or why she
was forever buying new clothes. I noticed, I wondered, that was all.

I noticed things about Reeve too. For one thing, that he'd stopped
talking about his girlfriends.

"He's growing up at last," I said to Gwendolen.

She reacted with warmth, with enthusiasm. "I really think he is."

But she was wrong. He had only three months of what I thought of
as celibacy. And then when he talked of a new girlfriend, it was to me
alone. Confidentially, over a Friday-night drink in the pub, he told

me of this "marvelous chick," twenty years old, he had met at a party
the week before.

"It won't last, Reeve," I said.

"I sincerely hope not. Who wants it to *last*?"

Not Gwendolen, certainly. When I told her, she was incredulous,
then aghast. And when I said I was sorry I'd told her, since Reeve's
backsliding upset her so much, she snapped at me that she didn't
want to discuss him. She became even more snappy and nervous and
depressed too. Whenever the phone rang she jumped. Once or twice
I came home to find no wife, no dinner prepared, then she'd come
in, looking haggard, to say she'd been out for a walk. I got her to see
our doctor and he put her on tranquilizers, which just made her
more depressed.

I hadn't seen Reeve for ages. Then, out of the blue, he phoned me
at work to say he was off to the south of France for three weeks.

"In your state of financial health?" I said. I'd had a struggle getting
him to pay the January installment of his twice-yearly income tax,
and I knew he was practically broke till he got the advance on his new
book in May. "The south of France is a bit pricey, isn't it?"

"I'll manage," he said. "My bank manager's one of my fans and
he's let me have an overdraft."

Gwendolen didn't seem very surprised to hear about Reeve's
holiday. He'd told me he was going on his own—the "marvelous
chick" had long disappeared—and she said she thought he needed
the rest, especially as there wouldn't be any of those girls to bother
him, as she put it.

When I first met Reeve he'd been renting a flat but I persuaded
him to buy one, for security and as an investment. The place was
known euphemistically as a garden flat but it was in fact a basement,
the lower ground floor of a big Victorian house in Bayswater. My
usual route to work didn't take me along his street, but sometimes
when the traffic was heavy I'd go through the back doubles and pass
his house. After he'd been away for about two weeks I happened to
do this one morning and, of course, I glanced at Reeve's window.
One always does glance at a friend's house, I think, when one is
passing, even if one knows that friend isn't at home. His bedroom
was at the front, the top half of the window visible, the lower half
concealed by the rise of lawn. I noticed that the curtains were drawn.
Not particularly wise, I thought, an invitation to burglars, and then I
forgot about it. But two mornings later I passed that way again,

passed very slowly this time as there was a traffic holdup, and again I glanced at Reeve's window. The curtains were no longer quite drawn. There was a gap about six inches wide between them. Now, whatever a burglar may do, it's very unlikely he'll pull back drawn curtains. I didn't consider burglars this time. I thought Reeve must have come back early.

Telling myself I should be late for work anyway if I struggled along in this traffic jam, I parked the car as soon as I could at a meter. I'll knock on old Reeve's door, I thought, and get him to make me a cup of coffee. There was no answer. But as I looked once more at that window I was almost certain those curtains had been moved again, and in the past ten minutes. I rang the doorbell of the woman in the flat upstairs. She came down in her dressing gown.

"Sorry to disturb you," I said. "But do you happen to know if Mr. Baker's come back?"

"He's not coming back till Saturday," she said.

"Sure of that?"

"Of course I'm sure," she said rather huffily. "I put a note through his door Monday, and if he was back he'd have come straight up for this parcel I took in for him."

"Did he take his car, d'you know?" I said, feeling like a detective in one of my favorite crime novels.

"Of course he did. What is this? What's he done?"

I said he'd done nothing, as far as I knew, and she banged the door in my face. So I went down the road to the row of lock-up garages. I couldn't see much through the little panes of frosted glass in the door of Reeve's garage, just enough to be certain the interior wasn't empty but that that greenish blur was the body of Reeve's Fiat. And then I knew for sure. He hadn't gone away at all. I chuckled to myself as I imagined him lying low for these three weeks in his flat, living off food from the deep freeze and spending most of his time in the back regions where, enclosed as those rooms were by a courtyard with high walls, he could show lights day and night with impunity. Just wait till Saturday, I thought, and I pictured myself asking him for details of his holiday, laying little traps for him, until even he with his writer's powers of invention would have to admit he'd never been away at all.

Gwendolen was laying the table for our evening meal when I got in. She, I'd decided, was the only person with whom I'd share this joke. I got all her attention the minute I mentioned Reeve's name, but when I reached the bit about his car being in his garage she stared at me and all the color went out of her face. She sat down, letting the bunch of knives and forks she was holding fall into her lap.

"What on earth's the matter?" I said.

"How could he be so cruel? How could he do that to anyone?"

"Oh, my dear, Reeve's quite ruthless where women are concerned. You remember, he told us he'd done it before."

"I'm going to phone him," she said, and I saw that she was shivering. She dialed his number and I heard the ringing tone start.

"He won't answer," I said. "I wouldn't have told you if I'd thought it was going to upset you."

She didn't say any more. There were things cooking on the stove and the table was half laid, but she left all that and went into the hall. Almost immediately afterwards I heard the front door close.

I know I'm slow on the uptake in some ways but I'm not stupid. Even a husband who trusts his wife like I trusted mine—or, rather, never considered there was any need for trust—would know, after that, that something had been going on. Nothing much, though, I told myself. A crush perhaps on her part, hero worship, which his flattery and his confidences had fanned. Naturally, she'd feel let down, betrayed, when she discovered he'd deceived her as to his whereabouts when he'd led her to believe she was a special friend and privy to all his secrets. But I went upstairs just the same to reassure myself by looking in that dressing table drawer where she kept her souvenirs. Dishonorable? I don't think so. She had never locked it or tried to keep its contents private from me.

And all those little mementoes of our first meeting, our courtship, our marriage were still there. Between a birthday card and a Valentine I saw a pressed rose. But there too, alone in a nest made out of a lace handkerchief I had given her, were a locket and a button. The locket was one her mother had left to her, but the photograph in it, that of some long-dead unidentifiable relative, had been replaced by a cutout of Reeve from a snapshot. On the reverse side was a lock of hair. The button I recognized as coming from Reeve's blazer, though it hadn't, I noticed, been cut off. He must have lost it in our house and she'd picked it up. The hair was Reeve's, black, wavy, here and there with a thread of gray, but again it hadn't been cut off. On one of our visits to his flat she must have combed it out of his hairbrush and twisted it into a lock. Poor little Gwendolen. . . .

Briefly, I'd suspected Reeve. For one dreadful moment, sitting down there after she'd gone out, I'd asked myself, could he

have. . . ? Could my best friend have. . . ? But no. He hadn't even
sent her a letter or a flower. It had been all on her side, and for that
reason—I knew where she was bound for—I must stop her reaching
him and humiliating herself.

I slipped the things into my pocket with some vague idea of using
them to show her how childish she was being. She hadn't taken her
car. Gwendolen always disliked driving in Central London. I took
mine and drove to the tube station I knew she'd go to.

She came out a quarter of an hour after I got there, walking fast
and glancing nervously to the right and left of her. When she saw me
she gave a little gasp and stood stock still.

"Get in, darling," I said gently. "I want to talk to you."

She got in but she didn't speak. I drove down to the Bayswater
Road and into the park. There, on the Ring, I parked under the
plane trees, and because she still didn't utter a word, I said, "You
mustn't think I don't understand. We've been married ten years and
I daresay I'm a dull sort of chap. Reeve's exciting and different
and—well, maybe it's only natural for you to think you've fallen for
him."

She stared at me stonily. "I love him and he loves me."

"That's nonsense," I said, but it wasn't the chill of the spring
evening that made me shiver. "Just because he's used that charm of
his on you . . ."

She interrupted me. "I want a divorce."

"For heaven's sake," I said, "you hardly know Reeve. You've never
been alone with him, have you?"

"Never been alone with him?" She gave a brittle, desperate laugh.
"He's been my lover for six months. And now I'm going to him. I'm
going to tell him he doesn't have to hide from women any more
because I'll be with him all the time."

In the half-dark I gaped at her. "I don't believe you," I said, but I
did. I did. "You mean you along with all the rest. . . ? My wife?"

"I'm going to be Reeve's wife. I'm the only one that understands
him, the only one he can talk to. He told me that just before—before
he went away."

"Only he didn't go away." There was a great redness in front of my
eyes like a lake of blood. "You fool," I shouted at her. "Don't you see
it's you he's hiding from, *you*? He's done this to get away from you
like he's got away from all the others. Love you? He never even gave
you a present, not even a photograph. If you go there, he won't let
you in. You're the last person he'd let in."

"I'm going to him," she cried, and she began to struggle with the car door. "I'm going to him, to live with him, and I never want to see you again!"

In the end I drove home alone. Her wish came true and she never did see me again.

When she wasn't back by eleven I called the police. They asked me to go down to the police station and fill out a Missing Persons form, but they didn't take my fear very seriously. Apparently when a woman of Gwendolen's age disappears they take it for granted she's gone off with a man. They took it seriously all right when a park keeper found her strangled body among some bushes in the morning.

That was on Thursday. The police wanted to know where Gwendolen could have been going so far from her home. They wanted the names and addresses of all our friends. Was there anyone we knew in Kensington or Paddington or Bayswater, anywhere in the vicinity of the park? I said there was no one. The next day they asked me again and I said, as if I'd just remembered, "Only Reeve Baker. The novelist, you know." I gave them his address. "But he's away on holiday, has been for three weeks. He's not coming home till tomorrow."

What happened after that I know from the evidence given at Reeve's trial, his trial for the murder of my wife. The police called on him on Saturday morning. I don't think they suspected him at all at first. My reading of crime fiction has taught me they would have asked him for any information he could give about our private life.

Unfortunately for him, they had already talked to some of his neighbors. Reeve had led all these people to think he had really gone away. The milkman and the paper boy were both certain he had been away. So when the police questioned him about that, and he knew just why they were questioning him, he got into a panic. He didn't dare say he'd been in France. They could have shown that to be false without the least trouble. Instead, he told the truth and said he'd been lying low to escape the attentions of a woman. Which woman? He wouldn't say, but the woman in the flat upstairs would. Time and time again she had seen Gwendolen visit him in the afternoons, had heard them quarreling, Gwendolen protesting her love for him and he shouting that he wouldn't be controlled, that he'd do anything to escape her possessiveness.

He had, of course, no alibi for the Wednesday night. But the judge and the jury could see he'd done his best to arrange one. Novelists are apt to let their imaginations run away with them; they don't realize how astute and thorough the police are. And there was firmer evidence of his guilt even than that. Three main exhibits were produced in the court: Reeve's blazer with a button missing from the sleeve; that very button; a cluster of his hairs. The button had been found beside Gwendolen's body and the hairs on her coat. . . .

My reading of detective stories hadn't been in vain, though I haven't read one since then. People don't, I suppose, after a thing like that.

A relatively new writer, Barbara Callahan is getting better with each story. This one, about a Presidential candidate and his wife, could furnish some writers with the plot for a lengthy novel. But Barbara Callahan says it all very well in just a few thousand words.

BARBARA CALLAHAN
November Story

For a long time I've been searching for a ladder out of limbo. I always knew a ladder would be necessary because as a child I visualized limbo as a deep shaft bounded on four sides by concrete. There was no lid on limbo, no covering to block out the view of the sky or of the people who skipped over the opening on their way to joys and sorrows.

In limbo there are no joys or sorrows. There is only a numbness, as if each soul lowered into the shaft, existing somewhere between heaven and hell, had been "novocained" before being dispatched there. I am always asked how I manage to sit so still and stare so intently when I am onstage where my husband, Senator Flip Morley, is delivering a speech I've heard at least a hundred times. It's easy, I tell a reporter or the frightened wife of a young man newly lighting the political horizon—my husband is the most brilliant man I've ever met. His words never fail to mesmerize me.

His words mesmerize me into limbo. I sit on the stage and I can't move because four concrete gray walls have been dropped around my chair. There's a portable limbo that follows me wherever I go. I stare intently because I am hoping that a ladder will appear on one of the walls and that I will become sufficiently unanesthetized to grab at it and pull myself up and out of my concrete pit.

Once I almost caught the ladder. Before sitting down on a chair, I bumped my ankle against a hard metal rung. The pain, unwelcome to most, animated me. For a moment I was a live, feeling human being. I even experienced tears stinging my eyes. I was so alive that I heard an official who was of the same party as my husband introduce Flip Morley as the "man who will save us all, the man who will be the next President of the United States."

His words were the signal for all the faithful gathered in the

audience to leap to their feet and shreik, "Flip! Flip! Flip!" As I sat
there, blinking away the tears of pain, I saw a ladder. It wasn't
distinct. It was wavy and insubstantial, but it would have to do. I
lunged for it. It felt cold in my hand. One side of it had slipped away.
I blinked again and saw that I was gripping a microphone. I had
come too far to let go, and I heard myself saying, "If he is the man to
save us, God save us all."

A hand thrust itself over mine. Once again I felt pain. The hand
belonged to the former champion discus thrower and current
champion senator from Pennsylvania, Flip Morley. "I'm sure you
didn't hear what my wife said because of all the noise. Please permit
an unsolicited testimonial from an unbiased voter who couldn't
contain her enthusiasm. Please be quiet." The crowd laughed de-
lightedly and then settled down. Crowds have always responded
obediently, in fact almost reverently, to Flip.

The hand that threw the discus was about to rule the world and
that hand never left mine as I spoke clearly into the microphone. "If
you look to any other man to save us, then God save us all." The
crowd roared, a high-school band crashed into "The Pennsylvania
Polka," and Flip kissed me on the cheek, a kiss that was forever
frozen into a wire-service photo that flashed around the world.

The next day's headlines on the women's pages read, "Liz Morley
Checks into Arizona beauty spa." A lie. A person looking very much
like me checked into an Arizona beauty spa, courtesy of party
funds. "Mrs. Morley wants to lose eight pounds before purchasing a
chic campaign wardrobe," bubbled the article.

"Take your medicine like a good girl," bubbled the nurse in the
sanatorium in Upper New York State where I was driven immediately after I had grabbed at the elusive ladder.

After three days I was allowed busywork, not basket weaving or
moccasin sewing like the other Limbo Ladies who swished by my
room in shrouds of high-priced bathrobes. My therapy had to be
solitary lest a drug-fogged brain in a moment of lucidity recognize
the wife of the strongest contender for the Presidency. My husband's
secretary, my only visitor, brought me a manila envelope. Briskly she
opened it and told me to get to work. She loathes me and loves my
husband. I am the fly in her ointment. I am the fly that must be
swatted every so often in its erratic flight to the White House. She has
her eye on a desk in a room next to the Oval Office, just as I have my
eye on a ladder which must exist somewhere.

"Liz Morley's Handbook for Political Wives" read the first page in the envelope. "A Lady in every sense of the word," read page two, "a Lady whose grace, charm, and loyalty have assisted her husband in his twenty-two-year ascent to the leadership of our party." The lovely blurb came from Bert Dooley, a raucous political figure whose acquaintance with ladies was limited to those of the night.

The handbook came as an order from Dooley headquarters. "Get your wife to write a book for some of those broads who're coming on the scene with their husbands. Loud-mouthed radical bunch who'll say whatever pops into their heads. And their clothes! One of those dolls came to a rally dressed in jeans—jeans, for Pete's sake!"

I skimmed through the pages, stopping to smile at the chapter on "How to Sit, Smile, and Speak Correctly Onstage." "Don't go looking for ladders, they're really microphones," I penciled in at the top of the page. Then I dropped the sixty-two pages into a waste basket. My husband's secretary has a carbon copy. In fact, she is a carbon copy. Of me. She read my book before I wrote it. Since she was surpassing me in lady-ness, she could finish it.

When I arrived home, the chic campaign wardrobe was waiting for me, along with a reporter from *Lib Magazine*. She had been given permission by my husband and his staff of advisors to stay with me for a day and a half to gather material for an article. The Morley think tank was delighted that a feminist magazine thought me worthy of attention. Before meeting the reporter I was briefed by my husband's secretary.

"This is a unique opportunity for Flip Morley to enter into the consciousness of those women's libbers. They're too chauvinistic to interview him, so you'll have to get him across to their readers. Don't let him down. He's very concerned about you."

"So concerned," I answered, "that he sent me a vase of flowers with a beautiful card signed by you."

"He's busy, you know," she snapped.

"Of course," I said. "With you."

Flashing me a murderous glance, she admitted the reporter. Her name was Molly Schwenker. She was about twenty-eight years old. She had red hair, freckles, an excess of twenty pounds, and spots on her pants suit. She carried a tape recorder in a shoulder bag. Endowed with a strong sense of integrity, she announced, whenever she pressed a button on the machine, "This is for the record, Mrs. Morley."

Our first venture together was to an outing for handicapped children. The Morley team arranged many such appearances for me. Since Flip and I were childless, I had to be seen as often as possible with children. The image to be projected was that of Mrs. Earth, mother of all, rather than mother of none. Our only child had been stillborn.

"This is for the record, Mrs. Morley. Do you really like these visits with kids?" Molly asked after I had been photographed sitting on a motionless carousel horse with a three-year-old boy on my lap.

"I love them," I answered fiercely. "Why do you ask?"

"Because you look so sad when you see them, except when you're being photographed. Then you beam like a movie star. Afterward you hand them right back to their mothers."

We were walking along the fairgrounds, hurrying to keep on schedule so that we could be seen with all the age groups and with all the personnel who cared for them. The bright cotton-candy day suddenly became colorless. I saw a gray Ferris wheel, a gray hot-dog stand, and a gray funhouse. The walls of the funhouse advanced toward me until they enclosed me in their grayness. I didn't have to reach out to know that the walls were made of concrete. I was standing in limbo, in familiar limbo.

A whirring noise invaded my limbo. It came from Molly's tape recorder.

"That question is off the record, Mrs. Morley. I erased it."

She pulled at my arm and led me to a bench.

"I'm sorry," she said. "I did do my homework. I just forgot that you lost your only child. Forgive me."

A face as pretty and vivacious as Molly's should not look pained. I smiled at her and squeezed her hand. The grayness faded from her face and from the fairgrounds.

"Just ask me about my husband and we'll do fine," I told her.

"It's a deal," she promised, and turned on the tape recorder.

For the record I told her about Flip, the star athlete, president of his class, and Phi Beta Kappa, courting me. I told her about our marriage in an army chapel in Georgia. I told her about our neophyte political days when we drove through the gorgeous Pennsylvania countryside in an old jeep, a laughing loving couple on more of a lark than on an earnest foray into the battlefield of politics. When Flip unseated the incumbent in the state legislature, the lark ended.

As I related the story of our early days in Washington, I noticed that Molly hadn't once turned off the tape recorder. Apparently my recitation, polished to perfection from years of performance, enchanted her. She was a thrilled listener to a monologue that I had delivered many times. She believed that the actress loved her lines. An actress, poor Molly, can do a beautiful job even in a role she hates.

When I finished, Molly sighed. "I know we at *Lib Magazine* aren't supposed to be turned on by romantic stories, but I am. You must love your husband so much, Mrs. Morley, that you would die for him."

"I did die for him," I responded. "I went into limbo."

The whirring noise returned. "I'll erase that, Mrs. Morley," Molly said. "That's off the record."

"Thank you," I said.

As we drove back to my home in Virginia, I almost reached into Molly's bag to take the recorder. I wanted to pick up the little microphone and tell it many things. Off-the-record things. Like the night I waited and waited for Flip to come home from a rally so he could drive me to the hospital to have the baby. I needed him badly at that time. When he didn't come, I called a cab. The baby who had needed expert care was delivered in the emergency room by an intern who was plainly scared.

The first gray stone of limbo descended. Whenever I tried to get out of bed to look through the window at the azaleas in our yard, the beautiful flowers were blocked by the image of a gray concrete stone that bore the name of our child. The stone grew larger and larger until it became a wall.

After the baby's death, while I lay wrapped tightly in a quilt of depression, a quilt too heavy to push away, Flip sat with me and read to me. Then as the weeks slipped into a month, his bedside visits became less frequent. A young senator on the rise had to be seen in the right places with the right people.

"Where to tonight, Mrs. Morley?" Molly asked.

"A cocktail party at the State Department," I answered.

Molly didn't bring the tape recorder to the cocktail party. "Too many background noises," she told me. I enjoyed watching her balance a martini glass while nibbling on a miniature quiche Lorraine. I laughed aloud when she shook hands with a distinguished-looking gentleman who walked away from her wiping bits of pie crust from his fingers. Some of the cotton-candy day drifted into the evening until I saw Greta Ferguson.

Greta walked by me without speaking. She hasn't spoken to me since Flip assumed the chairmanship of the committee her husband used to head.

Although her husband had ostensibly resigned because of ill health, Greta and I knew the real reason. Flip had assembled enough damaging information on Senator Ferguson to send him to prison. In exchange for the chairmanship, Flip promised to destroy all the data. He didn't. On the day Flip, as an unnamed source, released the evidence to the press, Senator Ferguson jumped to his death from the twentieth floor of his gray apartment building.

When I went to pay a condolence visit to Mrs. Ferguson, she told me everything. The gray wall of the Ferguson's apartment building became the second wall of my limbo.

After the cocktail party Flip flew to Indianapolis. I insisted that Molly spend the night at our house. We sat at the kitchen table and sipped hot chocolate. Molly did a humorous, nonstop commentary on the people she had met at the party. I squealed with laughter at her recital. The tape recorder stayed inside her shoulder bag. Nothing was on the record. That night I slept without help from pills. Laughter had loosened all my tight muscles.

In the morning Molly accompanied me to a breakfast for senators' wives. Her dexterity with a Danish equaled her finesse with a miniature quiche Lorraine. Her comments about the breakfast centered on Lisa Van Ecklin, the wife of the senator from New York. "Did you see those jewels she was wearing, and to breakfast yet?" she squeaked. "She must have worn a quarter of a million dollars' worth of jewels."

"They're imitations," I told her.

"Are you a connoisseur of jewels?" she asked.

"Only of her jewels."

The real Van Ecklin jewels lay coldly glittering in a safe-deposit box. Our safe-deposit box. I saw them when I went to the bank to secure documents I needed for a trip. When I asked Flip about them, he shrugged and said, "Call them a little insurance for our old age. Van Ecklin's kid is in jail in Mexico for possession of narcotics. The story the esteemed senator from New York gives out is that the kid is on an archeological expedition. The only digging Junior will do, if he's lucky, is tunneling. I got the information from a reporter who owed me a favor. When I confronted Van Ecklin with the scoop, he literally shoved the jewels in my pocket."

The gray door of a bank vault became the third wall of my limbo.

After the breakfast Molly had to catch a plane. I volunteered my driver for the trip to the airport. On the way she said, "You've been very kind, Mrs. Morley, so kind that I have a confession to make. *Lib Magazine* wanted me to do a scathing article about you as a plastic person. They consider you the epitome of passive womanhood, of the woman who rode to fame on her husband's coattails. I can't write about you that way. I see you as a person who formed a partnership and worked actively to keep that partnership alive. You've participated in the electoral process by sacrificing everything to help your husband, a fine man, get to the top. I'm not going to knock that. I'm going to write an article based on the talk we had at the fairgrounds. Nothing else is going into the article. I think you're a beautiful person, Mrs. Morley, but you're very sad. Your sadness is a mystery to me and it's strictly your business. It's no material for an article."

Deeply touched by her remarks, I felt the same kind of stinging in my eyes that I had experienced when my ankle bumped the metal chair—alive once more.

"Your editors aren't going to like that, Molly."

"There are other jobs," she answered.

"What would keep you in your job?" I asked.

"A scoop. Some kind of fantastic scoop. I'd have it made for the rest of my life."

"When you land tonight, wish on a star. Maybe you'll get your scoop."

As I watched her board the plane, I had a sense of loss. I focused on the plane until I could see nothing but the grayness of the November sky.

Driving home, the image of the colorless sky stayed with me. I tried to hold onto the image of Molly's rust-colored freckles and her green eyes, but my mind continued to gravitate toward the absence of color, to the sky.

I remembered standing at a window and looking out at a gray sky for signs of salvation when Flip told me we would not be receiving any more letters from a stewardess who wrote us threatening to expose Flip's affair with her. I could not take my eyes off that gray sky because I had just finished reading a newspaper account of the strangulation of a twenty-five-year-old airline stewardess, the apparent victim of a robbery-slaying.

"She's taking a job overseas," he said. "We'll never hear from her again."

When the hand of the discus thrower touched my shoulder as a prelude to a kiss, I stood rigid, never lifting my eyes from the gray slab of sky formed by my window.

The slab of gray sky became the fourth wall of my limbo. I was sealed inside.

There is not only an absence of color in limbo but also an absence of feeling. It's like being in a full-length cast with only one's head poking out. The head sticks out because there is no lid on limbo. Anyone can look down into limbo. But until Molly came, no one ever did.

When I got home from the airport, I went into Flip's study and sat for a long time in his leather armchair. Dozing, I saw Molly leaning over a concrete shaft. She had something in her hand, something she was unwinding. She lowered it slowly down to me. I reached for it and found that it was tape from a tape recorder. As I grabbed hold of it, Molly pulled me up out of limbo.

When I awoke I realized I had been searching for the wrong thing. It wasn't a ladder that would lift me out of limbo; it was a tape recorder. Flip had a recorder in his desk. I took it out of the drawer. I pressed a button and said, "This is Liz Morley and everything I say on this tape is for the record, Molly. You must have wished on a star tonight because here is your scoop."

The first gray wall, the grave marker, did not go on the tape. I helped construct that wall myself. I should have known that Flip would not leave a rally because I had called. His eye was on the political prize, not on me. I should have known that.

But I did tell the little machine about Senator Ferguson. "Flip Morley was the unnamed source who released the damaging information that sent Senator Ferguson plummeting to his death."

And I told the machine about the jewels in our safe-deposit box, without saying who gave them to Flip. And I told the machine who had ordered the strangling of the airline stewardess a few years ago. As I spoke, my voice became a trumpet and the gray walls came tumbling down.

When I finished making the tape, I put it in a box and wrapped it in brown paper. I addressed it to Molly in care of *Lib Magazine*. It was four o'clock, an hour before the post office closed. I slipped into my coat and hurried downstairs. I wanted to walk to the post office so that I could look at people on the street without the hindrance of the gray cataracts that had clouded my vision for so long.

The first person I saw as I walked down the front steps was Flip. He had stepped out of a cab. I dropped the small package and it bounced crookedly toward his feet. He picked it up and turned it over in his hand.

"What's this?"

"A tape that Molly the reporter from *Lib Magazine* made. She left it here," I lied. "I'm going to mail it to her."

"I hope there's nothing in it that would offend the party," he said.

"Nothing at all," I said.

"Good girl," he said and leaned down to kiss me. As his head neared mine, I noticed the lines of fatigue etched in his face.

"Don't be long," Flip called as I started down the street. "I'm giving a speech tonight."

"I won't be long," I answered.

The people on the street looked so colorful to me. I noticed the ruddiness of their cheeks and the brightness of their eyes. Then for some reason I stopped looking at the women and looked only at the men. And all the men had Flip's face. One man had Flip's face contorted with pain—the pain of my betrayal. Another man had Flip's face twisted with hatred—hatred of me. Still another had Flip's face consumed with despair—the despair at ever being a free man again. Each of the men looked to me as Flip would look when he read Molly's scoop in print.

I had to get away from those faces. Those faces were doing something to me. They were creating a sensation in me that I hadn't experienced for years. Those faces were causing me pain. I was feeling a desperate kind of pain, Flip's future pain.

Holding tightly to the package in my pocket, I started to run. When I reached the post office, I stood outside, breathless, hoping that I could rid myself of the pain as easily as I could rid myself of the box. But I knew that if I mailed the box the pain would never leave me.

In limbo there are no pleasures, but there are also no pains. I put the box into my pocket and walked away from the post office. I walked for a long while until I reached the river. I stood on a bridge and dropped the little package into the river's gray swirling currents. At that moment I knew I had put a lid on my limbo, a fluid gray lid that would ebb and flow over me as long as I lived. No one would ever peer down into the shaft at me again.

That night Flip received a standing ovation for his speech. Then the M.C. worked the audience into a sustained frenzy of whistling and applause. After the tumult subsided, the M.C. wouldn't quit. He solicited more acclaim for his speaker. "Let's hear it for Flip Morley. Let's hear it for the senator from Pennsylvania. Let's hear it for the next President of the United States!" he shouted.

The noise of the crowd was so deafening that I could barely hear a small voice that seemed to be speaking under water, a voice that seemed to be saying, "Let's hear it for limbo."

We've all read a great many mysteries dealing with the heirs to large estates, but none are quite like Jack Ritchie's latest offering, with the traditional Ritchie touch.

JACK RITCHIE
Next in Line

Four of my cigarettes were missing.

Ordinarily, I would not have noticed the loss at all. However, I had been attempting to give up smoking and, as a starter, had rationed myself to one pack a day.

This morning I had broken open a new pack and placed the twenty cigarettes inside my silver case. I had then gone downstairs and breakfasted.

I then retired to the library, lighted my first cigarette of the day, and read my daily two pages of *The Mill on the Floss.* As a test of determination, I am determined to finish that damn book if it kills me. At present I have reached page 171.

I had finished the cigarette and the two pages and then crossed the hall to the drawing room where I worked the crossword puzzle in yesterday's newspaper and kept one eye on the grandfather clock, waiting for nine-thirty and time for my second cigarette.

At the half-hour chime, I reached for my cigarette case and realized that I must have left it back in the library. I found the cigarette case on the table beside the easy chair I'd occupied earlier. When I opened the case, I discovered that instead of nineteen cigarettes waiting to be smoked, there were now only fifteen.

My first thought had been of Edwards. Had he taken the cigarettes? But then I remembered that Edwards did not smoke.

What about Henrietta and Cyrus? No, immediately after breakfast they had driven off together in Cyrus's car to see that attorney in Chicago again about breaking the will.

Except for Edwards, I was the only other person in this huge house at the moment.

I rubbed my jaw.

While I had been seated in the drawing room occupied with the crossword puzzle, I had been facing the open doorway. I had had a clear view of the closed library door across the hall. I was positive that if anyone had entered the library, the movement would have caught my eye. But there had been none.

Was it possible that someone had entered the library through one of the windows and stolen my cigarettes?

Absurd as the sole motive for breaking and entering, of course. However, taking the cigarettes might simply have been a reflex action on the part of the burglar who had larger things on his mind.

I examined the high windows bordering the north and west sides of the room. Every one of them was securely bolted from the inside.

On the other hand, had one of them been open, and had the burglar bolted it *after* him when he entered the room?

In that case, he must still be in this very room, since I would surely have noticed if he had left the library.

I experienced a sense of proprietary outrage, even though I had been a resident of O'Reilly Oaks no more than two weeks.

I armed myself with one of the fireplace pokers and proceeded to search the large room.

I found no one.

I lit my nine-thirty cigarette.

The thief had to be Edwards. He was the only other person in this house. A true burglar would have pocketed the entire case. But only four cigarettes were missing, very likely because Edwards did not believe that I would notice their disappearance.

Was Edwards one of those souls who convince themselves that they are not really smokers if they do not actually buy their cigarettes? Begging or stealing was another matter.

The loss of the cigarettes in themselves was trivial. What intrigued me was how Edwards got into the library without my seeing him and how he managed to leave.

I could think of only one possibility. Ridiculously gothic, and yet in these old houses. . .

I went about the room pressing knobs, protuberances, and carved wooden grapes in search of the device which activated the secret passageway that must be the answer to the mystery.

I had no success.

I pulled the bell rope vigorously.

When Edwards entered the library—by legitimate means—I said, "Edwards, I understand that you do not smoke."

"That's true, sir."

Edwards was tall, in his fifties, and he had served in this house all his life, as had his father and his grandfather.

"Edwards," I said, "has this house ever had any ghosts wandering about the corridors at night? Or possibly even during the day?"

His eyes flickered. "What kind of ghosts, sir?"

"The usual kind," I said. "Headless ghosts, wailing ghosts, ghosts rattling chains, ghosts who smoke cigarettes?"

He thought about that. "In a house this size and age, sir, every creak of a floorboard can rouse the imagination. But I assure you that there are no ghosts in this house." He cleared his throat. "Have you heard . . . or seen . . . anything, sir?"

I smiled enigmatically. "How old is this house?"

"General Horatio Bolivar O'Reilly declared it complete in 1842, sir."

"When General Horatio Bolivar O'Reilly built this place, did he whimsically include a few secret passages? I understand such things were popular at the time."

Edwards shifted slightly. "I wouldn't know, sir."

It appeared that further questioning on the existence of the secret passageway—at this time, at least—would be futile. And in the matter of the disappearing cigarettes, I decided that a warning—of sorts—might be sufficient.

I elaborately studied the contents of my cigarette case. "Hm. I could have sworn that I smoked only two cigarettes so far today. And yet now I have only fourteen left. From now on I intend to keep an exact count of my cigarettes, Edwards. I am trying to give up smoking, you know, and I'm rationing myself to exactly twenty cigarettes a day."

"Yes, sir," Edwards said. "I believe I did hear you mention something to that effect several days ago."

O'Reilly Oaks consists of some forty-five rooms, give or take a few. The present acreage of the estate is one hundred and eighty, most of which is either wooded or rented to neighboring farmers. Only the four or five acres immediately about the house are landscaped.

General Horatio Bolivar O'Reilly, tavern keeper and victualer to the army, attained his rank when he raised a battalion of militia during the Black Hawk War. In the course of the campaign, his unit lost over three hundred men—two hundred of them through desertion, one hundred by way of various fevers, and eight through acute alcoholism. No Indian was ever sighted.

Returning from the war a somewhat richer man, General O'Reilly selected this site some fifteen miles from the town of Green River Falls, which in those days had a population of some three thousand souls. Today the population is still under four thousand.

In the days when servants were plentiful and cheap, a veritable army of them attended O'Reilly Oaks. But time, the rising cost of labor, and attrition on the O'Reilly capital took its toll, so that at the death, earlier this year, of Terrence O'Reilly—General O'Reilly's great-great-grandson, the only occupants of the house were Terrence himself and his man of all parts, Edwards.

When Terrence expired, only three direct, though remote, descendants of General O'Reilly still remained in this world—Cyrus O'Reilly, a certified public accountant in Chicago; Henrietta O'Reilly, who presided over a pool of typists at a mail-order firm in Boston; and myself, Wilbur O'Reilly, who am employed by the Gailliard Steamship Lines, which is based in San Francisco.

None of the three of us had ever met before and we were only vaguely aware of each other's existence. We gathered in the library at O'Reilly Oaks where Amos Keller, attorney and executor of Terrence O'Reilly's estate, read us the will.

It provided that O'Reilly Oaks remain in a trust under Keller's supervision. Any direct descendant of General O'Reilly was welcome to use the house and grounds for his home as long as he wished. The trust also established a fund to cover the real estate taxes and minimal maintenance of the building and grounds.

It further provided that Edwards had the right to remain at O'Reilly Oaks for as long as he chose and that he be paid his regular monthly salary for as long as he lived there.

At the death of the last O'Reilly, the entire estate was to be liquidated and the money realized be distributed to a number of charities.

When Keller finished reading, there was a long minute of silence.

Henrietta, a robust, grim-visaged woman, spoke up first. "Let me get this straight. You mean to say that none of us gets a piece of the estate?"

"I'm afraid not," Keller said. "Though, as mentioned, any or all of you may regard O'Reilly Oaks as your home for as long as you live. I am authorized to provide each of you with a monthly allotment to cover food, clothing, and incidentals."

Cyrus O'Reilly was a small man, balding, and wore rimless glasses. "In terms of cash, how much is the estate worth?"

Keller shrugged. "That is difficult to say. There are so many variables. It all depends upon the buyer, the market, the time, and so forth."

"Has it ever been put up for sale?" Cyrus asked.

"No."

"No offer was ever made?"

"Well, yes," Keller admitted. "A group of businessmen did approach Terrence some years ago. They made him a rather handsome offer, but he turned them down."

Cyrus pursued the point. "Why would a group of businessmen want O'Reilly Oaks? I'd think that in this day and age, a house this size would be a drug on the market."

"Possibly," Keller said. "But they intended to turn the estate into a golf course. They seemed to believe that the main building would make an ideal clubhouse."

"How much did they offer?" Henrietta asked.

"I don't know exactly," Keller said. "But I understand it was in the neighborhood of a million." He looked over his glasses. "Do any of you intend making O'Reilly Oaks your home?"

Cyrus studied his fingernails. "I think I'll give it a try."

I smiled. "Frankly, it sounds ideal to me."

The three of us—Henrietta, Cyrus, and I—spent the next few days wandering independently about the house and grounds, assessing the situation.

I found the building quite to my taste. The furniture was a bit dated, but in excellent condition, though a bit dusty on the second and third floors. I selected a second-floor suite which caught the morning sun, did a bit of tidying, and moved in.

At breakfast at the end of the week, Henrietta surveyed the old-fashioned room without approval. "I'd prefer a smaller, newer place. Especially one that I could call my own."

Cyrus crunched into his toast. "I have an office and a clientele in Chicago. I don't see how I can seriously consider giving that up for subsistence living."

Edwards had done the cooking and now served.

"Edwards," I said, "the scrambled eggs were delicious. Did I detect paprika?"

"Yes, sir. Mild paprika for interesting color and vitamin C."

"What about you, Wilbur?" Cyrus demanded. "I understand that you have a responsible position for some steamship line. Do you intend to give that up for free room and board?"

I sipped coffee. "I have enough time in with my company to qualify for a half-pay pension. I believe the time has come for me to retire."

After my graduation from college some twenty years ago, I went to sea. Not out of a spirit of adventure, but for the solid economic reason that it was the only job I could find at the time.

I signed on as an assistant to the purser of the *Polylandia* of the Gailliard Line. The *Polylandia,* a new luxury liner based at San Francisco, made most of the ports of the Far East. As of my present leave, I had spent all of my working life on the *Polylandia* in the purser's department.

Henrietta put down her knife and fork. "I'm positive we can break the will."

"Oh?" I said. "On what grounds?"

"I found out that Terrence lived here for the last fifteen years as a recluse and everybody knows that recluses aren't normal. He couldn't have been in his right mind when he made out that will. We three are the only blood relatives he had in the world and by all rights we should inherit what he left and split it three ways."

Cyrus concurred emphatically. "We simply can't waste our lives sitting here in this monstrous house. There's a lawyer I know in Chicago who specializes in this type of thing. Will breaking, you know. He's expensive, but we'll split his fee among the three of us and still have plenty left."

I declined to join them. "Personally, I prefer the situation just as it is. I am by nature sedentary. In my entire service on the *Polylandia,* I went ashore less than a dozen times and then only for souvenir shopping. I even had my appendix removed while aboard the *Polylandia.*"

Cyrus crumpled his napkin. "Well, I'm driving to Chicago to see that lawyer. If either of you want to come along, I've got room in my car."

When Cyrus left, Henrietta rode beside him.

I spent the morning evaluating the kitchen garden area and the greenhouse. The latter had a few broken panes but otherwise seemed in serviceable condition.

I returned to the house and found Edwards in the kitchen preparing lunch. "Edwards," I said, "do we have anything like a Rototiller on the premises?"

"Yes, sir. All of the gardening machinery and implements are in the shed next to the greenhouse. Do you intend to garden?"

"Yes. For twenty years I have been priming myself with garden magazines. It is now time to give it all a practical try."

Edwards trimmed some scallions. "The late Terrence O'Reilly was quite a gardener himself. He leaned toward vegetables on the premise that if you couldn't eat it, it wasn't worth growing, though he did have a soft spot for iris, moss rose, and heart's ease."

"I am rather inclined that way myself," I said. "I understand that Uncle Terrence was a recluse."

"Not precisely, sir. He did prefer his own company, but he left the grounds now and then, principally for the monthly meeting of the Green River Falls Garden Club. Local gardeners get together on the second Wednesday of every month at the public library and I understand that new members are welcome."

"I never met Uncle Terrence in the flesh," I said, "though I do vaguely remember sending him some duty Christmas cards as a boy. He never married, did he?"

"He did, sir. Mrs. O'Reilly died thirty years ago."

"They had no children?"

"They had a son, sir. Robert."

"Dead, I suppose—or else Terrence would probably have left him the estate."

"Yes, sir. Dead. These last fifteen years."

"Then he died fairly young? An accident?"

"Yes, sir. I suppose you could call it that."

"Edwards," I said, "I have the distinct suspicion that there is a family skeleton involved here. What about Robert?"

"He was killed when his automobile plunged through a bridge railing and into the Mississippi River."

"Speeding? A few drinks under his belt?"

"No liquor was involved, sir. But he was speeding."

"Edwards," I said, "I am still pulling teeth. Why was he speeding?"

"Well, sir, he was speeding because the police were pursuing him. He had just escaped from the state prison."

"Why was he in prison?"

Edwards sighed. "Robert was a quiet sort of person, but with a strong sense of justice. A straight A student at the university. Or nearly so. In the final semester of his senior year, he received a B in ethics instead of the A he felt he honestly deserved. He lost his head and shot his professor."

I felt a twinge of sympathy. The only blot on my own academic career had been a C in physical education, a subject which has no place in a true university.

Edwards sliced tomatoes. "Robert was sentenced to life imprisonment, but he tired of life in confinement and managed to escape. For a short while, anyway."

"And now he is dead and buried?"

"Not exactly, sir. Dead, yes. But his body was never recovered from the river."

Henrietta and Cyrus returned in time for dinner that evening.

Cyrus rubbed his hands. "Well, Wilbur, we've seen McCardle. He's the lawyer I told you about. He's positive that we can break the will. He suggests that we do a bit of research and gather evidence about Uncle Terrence. When a man is a recluse for fifteen years, he's bound to develop a few idiosyncracies—items which, with the proper handling, we can build into a strong case showing that Uncle Terrence's mind wasn't exactly what it should have been."

He turned to Edwards, who was serving dessert. "Edwards, you were with Uncle Terrence all your life, weren't you?"

"Yes, sir."

"Then you must remember certain incidents, certain circumstances, when you might have called his behavior a little peculiar?"

"No, sir. I do not."

Cyrus smiled thinly. "You have a bad memory—is that it?"

"No, sir," Edwards said, "I have a very good memory." He left the room with the empty tray.

"That was clumsy of you, Cyrus," Henrietta said. "After all, Edwards stands to lose something when we break the will. If we want his cooperation, we will probably have to make some kind of a deal with him."

Cyrus nodded. "Well, Wilbur, are you with us?"

"How much does McCardle expect for his legal services?" I asked.

"Twenty-five percent of the estate," Cyrus said.

I smiled. "So each of us, including our attorney, would get one-fourth of what might or might not amount to a million dollars? Minus, of course, whatever it takes to get Edwards to cooperate and minus the inheritance taxes, which I understand are horrendous these days." I shook my head. "No, I don't consider it at all worth contesting the will. Suppose I did manage to clear one hundred and fifty thousand? If I chose to spend it gloriously, it would be gone before very long and I would be left with nothing. Or even if I invested it wisely, how much could I expect as a return? Twelve thousand a year?" I helped myself to another slice of cottage-cheese torte. "No, at this moment I am living in greater comfort and security than I could possibly expect with one hundred and fifty thousand. I am well fed, live in ease, get to pull the bell rope when so inclined, and how could I possibly afford a servant and superb cook such as Edwards on twelve thousand dollars a year?"

"I'd prefer one hundred and fifty thousand in cold hard cash," Henrietta said firmly.

Cyrus nodded. "The hell with security."

During the next week—interspersed with unsuccessful efforts to get Edwards to cooperate with them—Henrietta and Cyrus traveled to Chicago twice more for conferences with the lawyer.

On the evening of the day Edwards had filched my cigarettes, I sought him out. "Does that station wagon in the garage belong to you or was it Uncle Terrence's?"

"It was your uncle's, sir."

"I don't suppose there would be any objection if I borrow the wagon tonight. This is the second Wednesday of the month, isn't it? I thought I'd drop in at the garden club meeting."

"I'm certain you will enjoy it, sir. Your uncle did." He found the keys to the station wagon and handed them to me.

When I returned from Green River Falls that night after ten o'clock, I found flashing red lights and several State Patrol cars parked in the driveway in front of O'Reilly Oaks.

When I entered the house, a solid, uniformed man appeared in the hallway. "Mr. Wilbur O'Reilly?"

"Yes. What is this all about?"

"I am Lieutenant Stafford," he said. "State Patrol. I would like to ask you a few questions."

We joined Henrietta and Edwards in the drawing room.

Stafford studied me. "Your cousin Cyrus O'Reilly was found shot to death beside the road to Green River Falls about a half mile from here. Can you account for your time this evening?"

"Of course," I said. "I attended a meeting of the Green River Falls Garden Club. The subject was roses. Now what is this again about Cyrus?"

"His body was discovered in front of his automobile parked on the shoulder of the road at approximately eight-thirty this evening. We are fairly certain that he must have been killed within minutes of that time because the road is well traveled and his body lay in the beam of his headlights."

I rubbed my chin. "Cyrus probably made the mistake of picking up a hitchhiker."

"Possibly," Stafford said. "However, in cases like this hitchhikers almost invariably take the car along with them. Also Cyrus O'Reilly's wallet was intact in his pocket and contained several hundred dollars. I doubt that any hitchhiker murderer would have overlooked something like that."

"Undoubtedly the hitchhiker panicked and fled after the murder," I said. "What was Cyrus doing out this evening anyway?"

"No one seems to know," Stafford said. "He left without telling anyone and no one saw him leave. What time did you leave here this evening?"

"About seven-thirty."

"How many people were at this garden club meeting?"

"About twenty-five, possibly thirty. The meeting broke up at about a quarter to ten."

"These people would be able to verify that you were there the entire evening?"

"I was a stranger there. It was my first meeting. Probably no one even noticed me except the secretary when I signed up as a new member at the end of the meeting."

Stafford shook his head. "When you are a stranger in a small town, everybody notices you. So you were there from the time the meeting started until nearly ten?"

I coughed. "Well . . . actually I arrived at the meeting a bit late."

"How late?"

I smiled quickly. "There seems to be a fork in the road to Green River Falls and I took the wrong turn. I traveled some distance before I realized that I was on the wrong road and turned back. I arrived at the Green River Falls Library at about nine."

Henrietta smiled.

I glared at her. "And where were you at the time Cyrus met his death?"

"In my bedroom reading a book."

"Ha," I said. "And is there anyone who can verify that?"

"Of course not," she said coldly.

"And you, Edwards," I said. "Where were you at eight-thirty?"

He seemed surprised at the question. "I was in the kitchen preparing marinade for sauerbraten."

Stafford's eyes went to Henrietta and me. "I understand that the two of you and Cyrus O'Reilly inherited Terrence O'Reilly's estate. Is the probate complete? What I mean is, will the estate now be divided between the two of you instead of three?"

"I'm afraid your information about the estate is wrong," I said. "We did not inherit Terrence O'Reilly's estate. According to the terms of the will, we are merely allowed to remain here as guests for as long as we choose. We do not ourselves own one inch of the property."

Henrietta hastily backed me up. "Not one inch. So you see, officer, there isn't any possible reason in the world why either one of us might have wanted Cyrus dead. We have absolutely nothing to gain by his death."

"Lieutenant," I said, "I believe that there is a nitrate test or something of that nature for detecting gun-powder grains on the hands of persons who have recently fired guns? That ought to settle this matter once and for all."

Stafford nodded. "Our technician is waiting in the next room. But murderers are getting more sophisticated these days. Especially where premeditation might be involved. They usually take precautions like wearing gloves or some type of wrapper around their hands and arms when they fire a gun. I won't be surprised if I don't find a thing."

He didn't.

Stafford continued to question Henrietta, Edwards, and me until eleven-thirty before giving up for the evening.

The next morning I met Henrietta at breakfast. "Well, Wilbur, now that Cyrus isn't with us any more, we stand to get larger shares of the estate, don't we?" she asked, pouring coffee.

"Henrietta, I still haven't the slightest intention of contesting the will."

She smiled thinly. "Of course not, Wilbur. And neither have I. At least not right now. We'll wait a while, won't we? Six months? A year? After all, even though the police apparently can't prove a thing about Cyrus's death, it isn't wise to appear so greedy." The smile disappeared. "It's got to be either you or me, and it certainly isn't me."

"What isn't you?"

"You understand perfectly well what I mean, Wilbur. One of us murdered Cyrus and I know it isn't me. You're a lot deeper and cleverer than I thought. That innocent expression doesn't fool me for a moment. I intend to keep an eye on you and I shall take precautions."

"Precautions? What precautions?"

"I shall send a sealed letter to a friend of mine with instructions that it is not to be opened unless I meet death under mysterious circumstances."

"Henrietta, I simply don't follow you."

She smiled grimly. "In my letter, I shall accuse you of murdering Cyrus."

I stared at her coldly. "You have absolutely no proof."

"Of course I haven't. If I had, I would most certainly have turned it over to the police. However, in my letter I shall say that both you and I conspired to murder Cyrus for bigger shares in the estate, and that now I suspect that you have plans to kill me too and take over everything. I think that would make the police sit up and take notice if something should happen to me, don't you, Wilbur? The confession of one of two conspirators would make quite a bit of trouble for you."

"Henrietta," I said, "has it ever occurred to you that there is a third person in this house who might want to see Cyrus dead?"

"Edwards?"

"Of course. After all, if you and Cyrus had broken the will, he would stand to lose his home and job."

"But we offered to cut him in."

"Yes, but your offer may not have been enough. Or he may prefer the status quo. He might regard O'Reilly Oaks as his home as much as Terrence O'Reilly did—certainly more than you or I do."

I finished my coffee. "I am now going to send a sealed letter to a friend in which I state flatly that the three of us—Edwards, you, and I—conspired to murder Cyrus for fun and profit and that I now strongly suspect that the two of you are about to murder me too." I smiled. "I will also state that you and Edwards have been having an outrageously erotic love affair."

She flushed. "Me? With a servant?"

"My dear Henrietta," I said. "It's been done before."

As it turned out, neither of us ever sent those letters.

I went to the library, lit my first cigarette of the day, and picked up *The Mill on the Floss*.

When I dispatched the obligatory two pages, I searched for yesterday's newspaper and the crossword puzzle.

Where had I left the paper? Oh, yes—in the sunny alcove at the first-floor landing.

I left the room, found the newspaper, and paused there to read an article I'd missed yesterday. When I finished, I went back down the stairs to the library.

I had finished approximately half the crossword puzzle when the grandfather clock across the hall chimed the half hour.

Time for my second cigarette. I reached for my case on the table beside me and opened it.

Five of my cigarettes were missing. When I had left the room I had not taken the case with me and evidently while I was gone. . .

I went to the bell rope and pulled vigorously.

Edwards appeared. "Yes, sir?"

"Edwards," I said, "I am missing five cigarettes."

He frowned thoughtfully.

"Edwards," I said. "Do you agree that there are only three people in this house?"

"Absolutely, sir."

"Good. I know positively that I did not smoke those five cigarettes, and I also know that the very odor of tobacco makes Henrietta ill. What does that leave us with, Edwards?"

He evaded my eyes. "I don't know, sir."

"It leaves us with the inescapable conclusion that the person who stole those cigarettes is you, Edwards."

Edwards rubbed his neck. "Yes, sir. I confess. I took the cigarettes."

I regarded him sternly. "Edwards, aren't you ashamed of yourself? After all, your salary is quite generous. I should think that you would be able to buy your cigarettes, it shouldn't be necessary to steal them. Do you have an explanation?"

He hung his head. "Sir, when I stopped smoking, I swore never to buy another cigarette. However. . . "

"Ah," I said. "You left yourself a loophole. You did not foreswear to beg or steal cigarettes, did you?"

He looked away. "I think steal is too harsh a word, sir. Filch, perhaps. . . "

"Edwards," I said, "above and beyond the filching, there is one other thing about the incident which bothers me. How the devil did you get into the library? There must be some secret passage. When I left this room, I walked up to the alcove at the first landing to retrieve the paper. I was up there for perhaps two or three minutes, reading, but I faced the open library door down below me. While I did not actually stare at it, it was within the periphery of my attention. I am certain that I would have caught the movement of anyone entering the library."

Edwards chewed his lips for a moment. "As you went up the stairs to the landing, sir, your back was toward the library door. I took that moment to slip into the library."

"Very well," I said. "Then how did you get out of the library? You surely wouldn't have had enough time to enter it, steal the cigarettes, and leave during the relatively short time my back was turned."

Edwards rubbed his jaw. "I hid behind the door, sir. As you reentered the library and walked toward your chair, your back was again turned. I darted out of the door."

I sighed. "Then there is no secret passage?"

"No, sir. No secret passage."

"Edwards," I said, "I admire your timing, but this filching of cigarettes has got to stop."

"Yes, sir," Edwards said firmly. "I'll see that it doesn't happen again."

The weeks passed rather quietly and the second Wednesday of another month appeared.

I borrowed the keys to the station wagon from Edwards.

"The garden club again, sir?" he asked.

"Yes," I said. "This month we have a vegetable gardener as guest speaker. Hungarian wax peppers are his specialty."

"I'm certain it will be interesting, sir. I do hope you don't take the wrong fork in the road again, sir."

"Not very likely. I know my way around by now."

At slightly after nine o'clock that evening, as I sat in the audience in the lecture room of the Green River Falls Library, I felt a tap on my shoulder.

It was Lieutenant Stafford of the State Patrol accompanied by another uniformed officer. Stafford beckoned and I followed him outside, acutely aware that I was the cynosure of all eyes.

On the steps outside the building, he said, "Were you in there all this evening?"

"Since eight o'clock. Why?"

"Would the people in there be willing to swear that you were?"

"You'll have to ask them. But I assure you that I did not leave the room. As a matter of fact, I occupied the seat next to the mayor. His field is geraniums. Frankly, I've never cared about geraniums. All the ones I've seen appear to be perpetually dusty. What is this all about?"

"Your cousin Henrietta was found shot to death beside her car on the road to Green River Falls by a passing motorist at eight-thirty."

I frowned. "Henrietta shot beside the road? The same as Cyrus?"

He nodded. "Same road, same place, same time. Probably the same gun. We'll establish that later. Now let's go back inside."

I balked. "You mean you're going back in there and break up the meeting just to ask if anybody remembers me?"

"Exactly."

We marched back inside, where Lieutenant Stafford mounted the podium and took command of the meeting.

It was most embarrassing, but he found a number of people, including the mayor, who were willing to swear that I had been in my seat in the audience when the meeting began at eight and had not left it until called outside by Stafford. I had the feeling that my new notoriety would either get me expelled from the club or nominated for its presidency at the next election.

Stafford took me to State Patrol headquarters, where I was given another nitrate test, which, of course, proved to be negative.

Nevertheless, I was then taken into a small interrogation room for further questioning.

"Frankly," I said, "outside of some psycho lurking beside the roadway and killing without reason, I think your only bet as the killer is Edwards."

"Edwards? That butler, or whatever?"

"Why not?" I said. "Where was he at the time Henrietta was

murdered?"

"In the kitchen grinding dry bread for wiener schnitzel."

Weiner schnitzel? I considered that tenderly. Usually it also meant cucumber slices in thick cream.

"What possible reason would Edwards have to kill your cousins?" Stafford asked.

"They were planning to break Uncle Terrence's will and convert the estate into cash. Without my cooperation, I assure you. Nevertheless, if they had succeeded, it would have meant that Edwards would lose his job and domicile."

"You think he'd kill two people just to keep his job?"

"If one also considers room and board, I would say that we are talking about a package deal which exceeds fifteen thousand dollars a year. Giving Edwards a conservative additional twenty years of life, that could amount to something over three hundred thousand dollars. Surely something worth killing for."

Stafford did not seem impressed with a motive stretching over twenty years. He regarded me thoughtfully. "Now that your cousins are dead, that leaves only you. The last of the O'Reillys. Is that the way you planned it all along? Eliminate them first and then step up and break the will? There's no point in dividing the spoils three ways if you can hog it all."

I shed the accusation with dignity. "I have a perfect alibi."

He grunted. "I always distrust perfect alibis and I always break them. Do you have a twin brother by any chance?"

I smiled. "I am one of a kind. I would not have it any other way."

It was after midnight before Stafford released me and had me driven back to my car.

In the station wagon, I hesitated.

I most certainly did not murder either Cyrus or Henrietta, though, frankly, I did not mourn their passing.

But that left only Edwards. He had to be the murderer. After all, who else was there? I did not really put much stock in the roadside-psychotic theory.

But if Edwards was the murderer, was it safe for me to return to O'Reilly Oaks?

I pondered that.

Edwards had killed Henrietta and Cyrus because they were intent on breaking the will. But I had no such intention. Besides, I was, after all, the last of the O'Reillys. If anything happened to me, the estate would be liquidated, leaving Edwards homeless and without a job.

No, it might be a bit sticky living in the same house with a murderer, but my life was his life. If he harmed me, he would be cutting his own throat, so to speak. I should be perfectly safe at O'Reilly Oaks.

In time Stafford would undoubtedly gather enough evidence to arrest Edwards, but until then there was no point in my moving to some wretched motel. I drove back to O'Reilly Oaks and had a good night's sleep.

In the morning, after showering and dressing, I went to the bureau drawer where I kept my cigarettes.

I frowned as I looked down at the opened carton. I had purchased it yesterday and removed one pack. There should now be nine packs left. But there were only six.

Damn Edwards. First four cigarettes. Then five. And now three whole packs. And after he had firmly promised that he would stop. . .

I stared down at the cigarettes for perhaps a full minute.

Of course, I thought. Of course. That would explain everything. I filled my case and went downstairs.

I waited in the breakfast room until Edwards appeared.

"Edwards," I said, "I have been putting two and two together. Rationally it would appear that we two are the only people in the world who have motives for the deaths of both Henrietta and Cyrus."

"It appears so, sir."

"However, Edwards, I know that I did not kill either Henrietta or Cyrus. And I have the strange suspicion that neither did you. And neither, Edwards, do I now believe that you stole those cigarettes. Any of them."

Edwards coughed slightly.

I smiled. "I put this to you, Edwards. When Robert O'Reilly's automobile plunged over that Mississippi River bridge, he did not drown, but managed to crawl out of the water and make his way back home. And once here, he concealed himself somewhere in this house and has been hiding here ever since."

Edwards avoided my eyes.

"Edwards," I said, "he must have needed the assistance and connivance of another party or parties to survive here. After all, he had to be provided with food, drink, and whatever." I smiled again. "Edwards, why don't you just supply him with cigarettes too? Why does he find it necessary to steal them?"

Edwards sighed heavily. "Actually Robert was a nonsmoker until recently. But he has begun to acquire the habit."

I helped myself to the platter of browned sausages and delicately fried potatoes. "I assume that Robert killed Cyrus and Henrietta because if they had managed to break the will, he would have lost his sanctuary?"

"Yes, sir. The house would have been sold and the new owner would in time have become aware of Robert's existence. So Robert forced both of your cousins to drive to the spot where their bodies were found, shot them, and then walked back across the fields to the house."

Edwards poured coffee into my cup. "What do you intend to do now, sir?"

"I will have to inform the police, of course, and have them root out Robert."

"Sir, do you enjoy living in this house?"

"Certainly."

"Sir, Robert O'Reilly is the son of Terrence O'Reilly. As such, he has a perfectly legitimate and primary claim to his father's estate. He could go to court and easily break the will and its provisions for your occupancy here."

"But Robert is a murderer and a murderer cannot legally profit from his murders."

"True, sir. But Robert did not murder his father, and the date of his father's natural death is the point from which he would lay claim to the estate. As for your cousins, they did not own any part of the estate nor have a natural claim to it greater than Robert's. In other words, he may have murdered them, but it was not to gain control of the estate. He felt he already had that legally, whenever he chose to make himself known."

Edwards returned the coffeepot to its trivet. "Besides, sir, are you quite positive that the police could successfully prove that Robert murdered your cousins?"

"Well...no. But still, Robert is an acknowledged murderer. There is that matter of the ethics professor. Shouldn't he be returned to prison for that?"

"Possibly, sir. However, if you were responsible for sending him back, he might be inclined to a bit of vindictiveness and pursue his claim to the estate. He might be a felon, sir, but he would become a rich felon and your landlord. Undoubtedly he would evict you and perhaps even charge you room and board for the time you have spent here."

I sipped my coffee slowly while Edwards waited.

"Edwards," I said, "suppose Robert takes it into his head to murder me too?"

"Sir," Edwards said earnestly, "when the last O'Reilly dies—which for all practical purposes means you—the estate will be liquidated. Robert might forestall that by emerging from his hiding place and laying claim to the estate, but that would mean he would be sent back to prison. That is the very last thing in the world he wants. He would not dream of harming you, sir. I'm sure he wishes you a long life."

I sighed. "Edwards, there is a secret passage into the library, isn't there?"

"Yes, sir. From inside the library it is revealed by pressing the posterior of the cherub blowing the trumpet on the wainscoting to the right of the fireplace."

"And the passage leads to where?"

"A bedroom on the third floor."

"Is that where Robert keeps himself?"

"No, sir. His quarters are behind false walls."

I quickly held up a hand. "Never mind. The less I know about his exact whereabouts, the better. And, Edwards, perhaps it might also be wiser if Robert did not know that I am aware of his existence."

"I understand, sir."

After breakfast, I retired to the library. I lit a cigarette and picked up *The Mill on the Floss.*

Was Robert watching me at this very moment? There obviously had to be some type of peephole. Was he waiting for me to leave my cigarette case behind again? But why should he? After all, he had those three packs he'd taken from my bureau drawer. At this moment he was more than likely in his hiding place contentedly puffing tobacco.

I put down the book, rose, and examined the wainscoting. I found the cherub with the worn posterior.

Gingerly I pressed it.

The wainscoting slid noiselessly back, revealing an opening somewhat narrower and shorter than a normal doorway.

I hesitated at the darkness within, but then pulled out my cigarette lighter. Using its flickering light, I stepped cautiously into the opening.

I noticed a small knob just inside. Evidently it opened and closed the passage from the inside.

I left the passage door open and slowly made my way up the narrow stone stairs. There was the smell of dampness and mold, but there were no cobwebs. After all, they couldn't exist long if Robert kept tramping up and down all the time.

I ascended past what I estimated to be the second floor and continued upward until I faced a blank wooden wall.

I found a small knob similar to the one downstairs and turned it until the panel in front of me slid to one side. Whatever one could say about Robert, he certainly kept the mechanism of these doors well oiled.

I entered a small bedroom stale with the smell of disuse. Very likely long ago it had been occupied by one of the maids.

Footmarks, grimed from the passageway, faded to the hallway door.

In the hall they seemed to disappear entirely—however, when I got down on my hands and knees I could just barely make them out again. I trailed them to a doorway down the hall.

Was this Robert's hiding place? Not exactly, I supposed. Edwards had mentioned that Robert's haven was concealed behind a false wall, though probably this door was one way of getting to that false wall.

I hesitated between caution and curiosity and then edged the door open slightly. The medium-sized room appeared to be well lighted and it was empty of human life.

I stepped quietly inside and glanced about.

Where might this walled-off compartment be? Not that I had any intention of disturbing Robert. I simply wanted to know where it could be found.

Certainly not on the east and north sides of the room. They were thoroughly windowed. And not the south either. That bordered the corridor.

I studied the plastered west wall. There had to be some indication of the secret entrance, but there seemed to be none. Not even a hairline crack.

I opened the doors of a free-standing wardrobe and found neatly hung clothes.

But of course! This must be Edwards's room. I had never been inside it before, but now I recognized some of his clothes.

I should have realized at once that this room was lived in. Not a mote of dust anywhere. A clean-smelling comfortable room that I myself might occupy, except that I would add ashtrays.

My eyes went to the wastebasket. It contained a discarded magazine and. . .

I peered closer and lifted the periodical.

There—amid various debris—lay three unopened packs of cigarettes. My brand.

I thoughtfully returned to the wardrobe and examined the soles of Edwards's shoes. Yes, one pair of them bore traces of the unmistakable grime of the secret passageway.

Discarded cigarettes? Grime on the bottoms of Edwards's shoes? A smooth plastered wall that showed absolutely no signs of any entrance to a hideaway. A *supposed* hideaway?

My mouth dropped.

I had been flimflammed. Yes, that was the only word for it. Flimflammed.

Robert was unequivocally dead. He died when his automobile went off that bridge—body recovered or not. He was not lurking in the walls of this house nor had he stolen a single one of my cigarettes.

Edwards had cleverly reanimated him solely for my benefit.

Why?

I saw it all now.

With the deaths of Henrietta and Cyrus, I became the sole surviving O'Reilly and, as such, had to be preserved.

I had declared that I had no intention of challenging Uncle Terrence's will, yet there ever remained the danger to Edwards that someday in the future I might change my mind. After all, a million-dollar estate could be a constant temptation, especially now that I would have to share it with no one.

No, Edwards had to meet that hanging threat by creating, or recreating, Robert.

If Robert existed—or at least if I believed that he did—it was pointless for me to ever consider contesting the will. Robert had a prior claim and would step forward if I tried.

Yes, Edwards had been clever, but the charade was over with now and I would tell him so. It would undoubtedly destroy his sense of security, but the truth must out.

I stalked downstairs and found Edwards in the kitchen doing the breakfast dishes.

He wiped his hands and turned. "Yes, sir?"

Edwards had been born in this house, as had his father, and his grandfather. He belonged here as much as any O'Reilly. He loved it, he served it, he killed to protect it.

I rubbed my jaw. He had also been so considerate as to commit the murders at a time when he thought I would have a perfect alibi—though, of course, he could not have anticipated that I would take the wrong turn in the road on the night Cyrus met his death.

Edwards waited.

I cleared my throat. "Edwards, about this business of Robert filching my cigarettes. Perhaps you'd better see to it that he is regularly supplied. At least a pack a day."

He nodded eagerly. "Yes, sir. I'll put Robert's cigarettes on the master shopping list immediately."

The wiener schnitzel that evening was absolutely delicious.

It's been twenty years since Avram Davidson won first prize in an EQMM *contest with a story titled "The Necessity of His Condition." He has continued to produce memorable stories, winning a science fiction writer's Hugo award and an MWA Edgar award along the way. This story about today's urban criminals who prey on the elderly was another of the year's Edgar nominees.*

AVRAM DAVIDSON
Crazy Old Lady

Before she became the Crazy Old Lady she had been merely the Old Lady and before that Old Lady Nelson and before that (long, long before that) she had been Mrs. Nelson. At one time there had also been a Mr. Nelson, but all that was left of him were the war souvenirs lined up on the cluttered mantelpiece that was never dusted now—the model battleship, the enemy helmet, the enemy grenade, the enemy knife, and some odd bits and pieces that had been enemy badges and buttons.

The enemy had seemed a lot farther away in those days.

But the shopping had been a lot closer.

Of course it was still the same in miles—well, blocks, really—it just seemed like miles now. It had been such a nice walk, such a few blocks' walk, under the pleasant old trees, past the pleasant old family homes, and down to the pleasant old family stores. Now not much was left of the way it had been.

For one thing, the trees had not had sense enough to adjust to changing times. Their branches had interfered with the electric power lines and their roots had interfered with the sewer lines and their trunks had interfered with the sidewalks.

So most of the old trees had been cut down.

That was quite a shock and no one had prepared the Old Lady for it. One day the old trees had been there as always and then the next day there were only stumps and branches, bruised twigs, and leaves and sawdust. And the next day not even that.

A lot of the old family homes had been, so to speak, cut down too, and most of those that had not been cut down had been cut up and converted into multiple dwelling units. It is odd that somehow families do not seem to feel the same about dwelling units as they do about homes.

And as for the pleasant old family stores, what had happened to them? Mr. Berman said, "There's hardly anything I sell today that they don't sell for less in the supermarket, Mrs. Nelson. The kids don't come in the way they used to with a note from their parents, they just come in to steal. I used to think my boy would take over when I'm gone but he came back from Vietnam in a box, so what's the use of talking."

Where there had been a lot of storefronts with either changing displays, which were interesting, or the same familiar old displays, which were comforting, now the storefronts were all boarded over.

The supermarket was where there hadn't been a supermarket—strange that it wasn't built where all the boarded-up stores were; strange that the pleasant old empty lot with its wild flowers had to give way to the supermarket, and now the children played in the street instead.

But that was the way it was. Prices may have been cheaper in the supermarket in the long run, but the prices had to be paid in cash and there were no deliveries, no monthly bills, no friendly delivery boy who thanked you for a fresh-baked cookie.

Often after Mr. Nelson passed away, the delivery boy—or was it his brother?—would mow the small lawn for a quarter. Now no one would mow the small lawn for a quarter or even for two quarters. No boys were interested in collecting empty bottles for the deposits, the way they used to be. Strange, if they were poor, why they would prefer to smash the bottles on the sidewalk and against the lampposts. The yard was a thicket now and not even a clean thicket.

"What is the world coming to?" the Old Lady used to ask.

By and by she stopped asking and started screeching. "Don't think I don't see you there!" she would screech. That was around the time they started calling her the Crazy Old Lady. She said the bigger boys had thrown rocks at her and the bigger boys denied this and the police said they could do nothing.

It wasn't the police who laughed when she took to wearing the military helmet whenever she did her shopping. She had to go out to do her shopping because it was a thing of the past to phone the store and say, "Now before I even ask about Esther and the new baby, don't let me forget the quarter pound of sweet butter for my pastry crust." Sometimes she would forget and call the old number which now belonged to some other people and after a while they weren't nice about it, not nice at all.

There were, of course, still some other old ladies and old gentlemen around in the old neighborhood, although she didn't at first
think of them as old. "Now my Grandmother Delehanty, she was old
and she had seen the soldiers marching off to remember the Maine
and she never forgot anyone's birthday to the last day she lived, but I
don't suppose you would remember her."

"Listen to the Crazy Old Lady talking to herself," some girls would
say very loud and not nicely at all.

"There, never mind, Mrs. Nelson, pay no attention and we'll
pretend we didn't notice, shhh," Mrs. Swift would say, hobbling up.

"Why, Mrs. Swift. Your arm! Your poor arm. What happened?"

"Let's just walk along together and I'll tell you when they aren't
listening."

Mrs. Swift, what a fine-looking woman she had been in her time!
Why would anyone want to knock her down so badly that she broke
her arm?

"My grocery money was in my purse. I don't know what to do. I
can't afford to live anywhere else."

"Oh dear, oh dear."

It just went to prove how necessary it was to wear the war helmet.
If Mr. Schultz had been wearing one, would they have been able to
fracture his skull?

They who?

"Why don't you catch them? What are the police for?"

The policemen said that the descriptions would fit half of the
hoodlums in the neighborhood. "More than half," they said. The
policemen said that about the ones who killed Mr. Schultz. The
policemen said that about the ones who had just grabbed her and
pulled the war helmet off her head and then shoved her and had
hardly bothered to run away very fast, just half looking back and half
laughing. "You got off lucky," the policeman said to her. "Don't go
out at night if you can help it."

"It was broad daylight!" she screeched.

And then someone threw a rock through her window. No, it
wasn't a rock, it was the war helmet, her husband's souvenir from the
mantelpiece. How hard they must have worked to dent it and bash it
and cave it in so that no one could wear it now. And what was she to
do about protection now when she had to go out for the quarter
pound of bacon and the box of oatmeal and the three eggs? Where
were the police?

"Sorry, lady, sorry," the policeman said. "You can't carry no knife
this size. It's against the law." The knife was her husband's war

souvenir of the enemy, but the police took it away from her anyway.

She wanted to tell Mrs. Swift—what a fine-looking woman she was in her time—and she called out, "Oh, Mrs. Swift," but her voice didn't carry. No one heard her over the street noises and the noises of all the radios and record players from every window and all the television sets on full blast. How fast the man was running when he grabbed Mrs. Swift's purse as though he had practiced and practiced, and he knock :d her down as before and kicked her as she started to get up, and then he ran away laughing and laughing with the purse held high up, shielding his face.

What could she do then? No helmet. No knife. And she had to go out shopping. She couldn't carry much at one time. She looked for the old coat with the inside pocket so she could keep the money in that, but somehow she couldn't find it and so she had to carry a purse after all.

Carrying the purse with the few dollars in it when the man came running up. She could hear him running and she started screeching when he grabbed her purse, just as she knew he would some day, and he tugged hard and the string broke. The Crazy Old Lady, had she thought tying something with a string to her scrawny old arm would help?

Then something fell to the sidewalk and jangled, a metal ring or pin, and he ran off laughing and faster than she could ever run, the purse held high to shield his face from passers by as the Crazy Old Lady screeched after him. And he must have got almost half a block away when the enemy grenade went off.

It was well known, of course, that she was crazy, and really they take good care of her where she is, and anyway she can do her little bit of shopping in the canteen, as they call it, and nobody bothers her now at all.

It's not surprising that Bill Pronzini, a collector of mysteries, is well aware of the classic affinity between railroads and the suspense story. His 1977 anthology, Midnight Specials *(Bobbs-Merrill), contains railroad mysteries by a number of famous writers. You'll find more about Pronzini in the biographical feature at the back of this book. But first read his own contribution to the literature of suspense on the rails.*

BILL PRONZINI
Sweet Fever

Quarter before midnight, like on every evening except the Sabbath or when it's storming or when my rheumatism gets to paining too bad, me and Billy Bob went down to the Chigger Mountain railroad tunnel to wait for the night freight from St. Louis. This here was a fine summer evening, with a big old fat yellow moon hung above the pines on Hankers Ridge and mockingbirds and cicadas and toads making a soft ruckus. Nights like this, I have me a good feeling, and I know Billy Bob does too.

They's a bog hollow on the near side of the tunnel opening, and beside it a woody slope, not too steep. Halfway down the slope is a big catalpa tree and that was where we always set, side by side with our backs up against the trunk.

So we come on down to there, me hobbling some with my cane and Billy Bob holding onto my arm. That moon was so bright you could see the melons lying in Ferdie Johnson's patch over on the left, and the rail tracks had a sleek oiled look coming out of the tunnel mouth and leading off toward the Sabreville yards a mile up the line. On the far side of the tracks, the woods and the run-down shacks that used to be a hobo jungle before the county sheriff closed it off thirty years back had them a silvery cast, like they was all coated in winter frost.

We set down under the catalpa tree and I leaned my head back to catch my wind. Billy Bob said, "Granpa, you feeling right?"

"Fine, boy."

"Rheumatism ain't started paining you?"

"Not a bit."

He give me a grin. "Got a little surprise for you."

"The hell you do."

"Fresh plug of blackstrap," he said. He come out of his pocket with it. "Mr. Cotter got him in a shipment just today down at his store."

I was some pleased. But I said, "Now you hadn't ought to go spending your money on me, Billy Bob."

"Got nobody else I'd rather spend it on."

I took the plug and unwrapped it and had me a chew. Old man like me ain't got many pleasures left, but fresh blackstrap's one; good corn's another. Billy Bob gets us all the corn we need from Ben Logan's boys. They got a pretty good sized still up on Hankers Ridge, and their corn is the best in this part of the hills. Not that either of us is a drinking man, now. A little touch after supper and on special days is all. I never did hold with drinking too much, or doing anything too much, and I taught Billy Bob the same.

He's a good boy. Man couldn't ask for a better grandson. But I raised him that way—in my own image, you might say—after both my own son Rufus and Billy Bob's ma got taken from us in 1947. I reckon I done a right job of it, and I couldn't be less proud of him than I was of his pa, or love him no less either.

Well, we set there and I worked on the chew of blackstrap and had a spit every now and then, and neither of us said much. Pretty soon the first whistle come, way off on the other side of Chigger Mountain. Billy Bob cocked his head and said, "She's right on schedule."

"Mostly is," I said, "this time of year."

That sad lonesome hungry ache started up in me again—what my daddy used to call the "sweet fever." He was a railroad man, and I grew up around trains and spent a goodly part of my early years at the roundhouse in the Sabreville yards. Once, when I was ten, he let me take the throttle of the big 2-8-0 Mogul steam locomotive on his highballing run to Eulalia, and I can't recollect no more finer experience in my whole life.

Later on I worked as a callboy, and then as a fireman on a 2-10-4, and put in some time as a yard-tender engineer, and I expect I'd have gone on in railroading if it hadn't been for the Depression and getting myself married and having Rufus. My daddy's short-line company folded up in 1931, and half a dozen others too, and wasn't no work for either of us in Sabreville or Eulalia or anywheres else on the iron.

That squeezed the will right out of my daddy, and he took to ailing, and I had to accept a job on Mr. John Barnett's truck farm to support him and the rest of my family. Was my intention to go back into railroading, but the Depression dragged on, and my daddy

died, and a year later my wife Amanda took sick and passed on, and
by the time the war come it was just too late.

But my son Rufus got him the sweet fever too, and took a switch-
man's job in the Sabreville yards, and worked there right up until the
night he died. Billy Bob was only three then; his own sweet fever
comes most purely from me and what I taught him. Ain't no doubt
trains been a major part of all our lives, good and bad, and ain't no
doubt neither they get into a man's blood and maybe change him,
too, in one way and another. I reckon they do.

The whistle come again, closer now, and I judged the St. Louis
freight was just about to enter the tunnel on the other side of the
mountain. You could hear the big wheels singing on the track, and if
you listened close you could just about hear the banging of couplings
and the hiss of air brakes as the engineer throttled down for the
curve. The tunnel don't run straight through Chigger Mountain;
she comes in from the north and angles to the east, so that a big
freight like the St. Louis got to cut back to quarter speed coming
through.

When she entered the tunnel, the tracks down below seemed to
shimmy and you could feel the vibration clear up where we was
sitting under the catalpa tree. Billy Bob stood himself up and peered
down toward the black tunnel mouth like a bird dog on a point. The
whistle come again, and once more, from inside the tunnel, sound-
ing hollow and miseried now. Every time I heard it like that, I
thought of a body trapped and hurting and crying out for help that
wouldn't come in the empty hours of the night. I shifted the cud of
blackstrap and worked up a spit to keep my mouth from drying. The
sweet fever feeling was strong in my stomach.

The blackness around the tunnel opening commenced to lighten,
and got brighter and brighter until the long white glow from the
locomotive's headlamp spilled out onto the tracks beyond. Then she
come through into my sight, her light shining like a giant's eye, and
the engineer give another tug on the whistle, and the sound of her
was a clattering rumble as loud to my ears as a mountain rockslide.
But she wasn't moving fast, just kind of easing along, pulling herself
out of that tunnel like a night crawler out of a mound of earth.

The locomotive clacked on past, and me and Billy Bob watched
her string slide along in front of us. Flats, boxcars, three tankers in a
row, more flats loaded down with pine logs big around as a privy, a
refrigerator car, five coal gondolas, another link of boxcars. Fifty in
the string already, I thought. She won't be dragging more than sixty,
sixty-five.

Billy Bob said suddenly, "Granpa, look yonder!"

He had his arm up, pointing. My eyes ain't so good no more and it took me a couple of seconds to follow his point, over on our left and down at the door of the third boxcar in the last link. It was sliding open, and clear in the moonlight I saw a man's head come out, then his shoulders.

"It's a floater, Granpa," Billy Bob said, excited. "He's gonna jump. Look at him holding there, he's gonna jump."

I spit into the grass. "Help me up, boy."

He got a hand under my arm and lifted me up and held me until I was steady on my cane. Down there at the door of the boxcar, the floater was looking both ways along the string of cars and down at the ground beside the tracks. That ground was soft loam and the train was going slow enough and there wasn't much chance he would hurt himself jumping off.

He come to that same idea, and as soon as he did he flung himself off the car with his arms spread out and his hair and coattails flying in the slipstream. I saw him land solid and go down and roll over once. Then he knelt there, shaking his head a little, looking around.

Well, he was the first floater we'd seen in seven months. The yard crews seal up the cars nowadays and they ain't many ride the rails anyhow, even down in our part of the country. But every now and then a floater wants to ride bad enough to break a seal, or hides himself in a gondola or on a loaded flat. Kids, old-time hoboes, wanted men. They's still a few.

And some of 'em get off right down where this one had, because they know the St. Louis freight stops in Sabreville and they's yardmen there that check the string, or because they see the run-down shacks of the old hobo jungle or Ferdie Johnson's melon patch. Man rides a freight long enough, no provisions, he gets mighty hungry. The sight of a melon patch like Ferdie's is plenty enough to make him jump off.

"Billy Bob," I said.

"Yes, Granpa. You wait easy now."

He went off along the slope, running. I watched the floater, and he come up on his feet and got himself into a clump of bushes alongside the tracks to wait for the caboose to pass so's he wouldn't be seen. Pretty soon the last of the cars left the tunnel, and then the caboose with a signalman holding a red-eye lantern out on the platform. When she was down the tracks and just about beyond my sight, the floater showed himself again and had him another look around. Then, sure enough, he made straight for the melon patch.

Once he got into it I couldn't see him because he was in close to the woods at the edge of the slope. I couldn't see Billy Bob neither. The whistle sounded one final time, mournful, as the lights of the caboose disappeared, and a chill come to my neck and set there like a cold dead hand. I closed my eyes and listened to the last singing of the wheels fade away.

It weren't long before I heard footfalls on the slope coming near, then the angry sound of a stranger's voice, but I kept my eyes shut until they walked up close and Billy Bob said, "Granpa." When I opened 'em the floater was standing three feet in front of me, white face shining—scared face, angry face, evil face.

"What the hell is this?" he said. "What you want with me?"

"Give me your gun, Billy Bob," I said.

He did it, and I held her tight and lifted the barrel. The ache in my stomach was so strong my knees felt weak and I could scarcely breathe. But my hand was steady.

The floater's eyes come wide open and he backed off a step. "Hey," he said, "hey, you can't—"

I shot him twice.

He fell over and rolled some and come up on his back. They wasn't no doubt he was dead, so I give the gun back to Billy Bob and he put it away in his belt. "All right, boy," I said.

Billy Bob nodded and went over and hoisted the dead floater onto his shoulder. I watched him trudge off towards the bog hollow, and in my mind I could hear the train whistle as she'd sounded from inside the tunnel. I thought again, as I had so many times, that it was the way my boy Rufus and Billy Bob's ma must have sounded that night in 1947, when the two floaters from the hobo jungle broke into their home and raped her and shot Rufus to death. She lived just long enough to tell us about the floaters, but they was never caught. So it was up to me, and then up to me and Billy Bob when he come of age.

Well, it ain't like it once was and that saddens me. But they's still a few that ride the rails, still a few take it into their heads to jump off down there when the St. Louis freight slows coming through the Chigger Mountain tunnel.

Oh my yes, they'll *always* be a few for me and Billy Bob and the sweet fever inside us both.

Some of James Holding's best recent stories have dealt with art treasures and the scheming people involved with them. Here is his latest look at the art world.

JAMES HOLDING
Rediscovery

After he had dismissed his Friday afternoon seminar in Renaissance Studies and returned to his own office in the Fine Arts Building, Professor Ferucignano put in a long-distance call to the Honeycutt Gallery of Art in Washington.

"Person to person," he told the operator. "I wish, please, to speak with Mr. Orville Carter, the director of the gallery."

"Who shall I say is calling?"

"Benozzo Ferucignano," the professor said, giving his name the proper pronunciation that eluded so many Americans. "Mr. Carter will know who I am."

Waiting for his call to go through, the professor reflected with a touch of complacency that not only Mr. Carter, but everybody who claimed to be anybody in the world of art, knew who Benozzo Ferucignano was: holder of the Rosario Chair for Art at America's most prestigious university, consultant to many of the great galleries and museums of Europe and America, and undoubtedly the world's leading expert in Italian Renaissance sculpture, a pre-eminence accorded him readily by most of the scholars familiar with the field. Unfortunately, Mr. Carter was not among them but perhaps, the professor thought wryly, he might make a believer out of even Orville Carter very soon.

Carter's voice, when he came on the phone, was cordial. "Hello!" he said. "This is a pleasant surprise, Benny. It's been a long time. What can we do for you?"

The professor said, "This time, Orville, I believe I can do something for *you*."

"Really?" Carter sounded skeptical.

"I was in Paris last week," the professor said, "and I stumbled across something that should be of considerable interest to you."

"What was it?" asked Carter. "I'm a little bit ancient now for *La Nouvelle Eve,* Benny." He laughed.

"I didn't stumble across this item in a nightclub," the professor reproved him, "but in a far more sedate milieu. The Louvre, as a matter of fact."

"The Louvre! Well, well. You going to tell me what it was, Benny?"

"Of course. But not on the telephone. Are you free tomorrow morning? I can take an early plane down."

"I'll be here. Saturday's a big day with us." Carter paused. "Is there a consulting fee involved in this thing, Benny? Because, if so—"

"This is not a matter of money, please believe me. I don't want a penny out of it. I'm merely trying to discharge what I conceive to be my duty as a responsible member of the international art community."

"Your duty to whom?"

"To a fine Renaissance artist," said the professor promptly, "and, incidentally, to the Honeycutt Gallery and the Louvre as well."

Carter said at once, "I apologize, Benny. I'm fully aware that a man of your reputation doesn't need to, ah, solicit business." He laughed self-consciously. "Won't you let us pay your expenses, at least? Shall I book you a hotel room?"

"No, thanks. I won't stay overnight. Will eleven o'clock in the morning suit you?"

"That'll be fine. See you then." Orville Carter hung up, a very puzzled man.

A hot summer sun was striking rose-tinted highlights from the sandstone walls of the Honeycutt Gallery of Art when Professor Ferucignano's taxi set him down before it next day. Orville Carter was waiting for him in his richly furnished corner office on the second floor. "Welcome to the Honeycutt," he said politely. "We see you here too infrequently, Benny."

"My university job limits my outside activities these days," replied Ferucignano with dignity. "I do not regret it. Teaching the young idea how to shoot, you know. . . "

Carter said, "I couldn't sleep last night, Benny, for wondering what you discovered in the Louvre that could possibly interest us to the degree you implied. You're killing me with curiosity!"

"You won't like what I have to say. But here goes. It concerns your Donatello bronze."

Carter's eyes grew wary. "Our Hercules," he said. "One of our greatest treasures. What about it?"

"I don't think your bronze Hercules *is* Hercules, Orville."

"No?" Carter said, trying to keep rising anger out of his voice.

"No," Ferucignano said. "And furthermore. I do not think the statuette is by Donatello."

Carter was startled. He half rose from his chair, then sank back. "You're talking nonsense, Benny! Although I can't remember the details after all these years—and I wasn't director then—I *do* remember that the Hercules was offered us as a previously unknown work by Donatello, put on the market by an English collector who needed money to pay his taxes, something like that. We weren't foolish enough to take the dealer's word for it, Benny. We called in the best man in the field to authenticate it for us before we bought it."

"I know. Demery from the Chicago Institute, wasn't it? And Gallagher from the Boston? And Helios from Stanford?"

"If *anyone* could affirm a Donatello without a complete and accurate provenance to help them, they could. Why, when we acquired our Donatello Hercules— "

"Please. Not the Hercules, Orville. And not, I repeat, by Donatello—at least in my humble opinion."

"Humble opinion! That's good!" Carter gave a bark of laughter.

The professor went doggedly on. "All the same, if you had called *me* in for my humble opinion before you acquired the piece, I could have told you then."

"You were an obscure instructor in Italian history at an obscure college thirty years ago, and well you know it! Why should we have called *you* in?"

The professor murmured, "I had already established myself with my monograph on Verrocchio. I was not entirely unknown even then, Orville."

"You were to us," Carter said sharply, "and I want to know what this odd visit of yours is all about. Are you trying to discredit our Donatello out of spite because we failed to consult you about its purchase thirty years ago? I can't believe that, Benny, even of an overweening egocentric like you!" He was trembling with rage.

The professor said austerely, "There is no need for name calling, Orville. As I told you on the telephone, my only reason for troubling you—" Abruptly he rose and turned toward the door. "But let's go down to your Hercules, Orville, shall we? I need to look at it once more before I can be absolutely sure." He grinned at Carter. "I wouldn't want to upset you unnecessarily, of course."

"Of course," Carter snapped. "Come on, then."

They descended in a silent elevator to the ground floor of the gallery and walked two hundred yards over polished hardwood floors to the Sculpture Hall in the east wing. The Donatello Hercules, a bronze statuette about fourteen inches high, stood on a plinth against the south wall of the room inside a sealed glass case.

The two men halted before it. For a moment, neither spoke. Each was deeply absorbed in contemplation of the masterpiece; each felt a lifting surge of reverence for the long-dead artist who had cast this breathing beauty into bronze.

"Donatello or not," murmured the professor at length, "it is a rare and wonderful piece, Orville." He turned impulsively to Carter. "I would rather not have had to visit you today. I would infinitely have preferred to allow this lovely thing to remain a Hercules by Donatello, just as you label it. For who, save for egocentric experts like me—" he gave Carter an apologetic smile "—would ever know the difference? But, alas, one's artistic conscience cannot be denied. So you see in me a reluctant messenger. A very reluctant messenger. Do you believe that, Orville?"

Carter's expression was puzzled. "I believe I do at that," he grudgingly admitted. "At least that you have no personal axe to grind."

"Good," said the professor with satisfaction. He took a small magnifying glass from his pocket, bent over, and peered through it at the statuette.

"Don't try to open the glass case," Carter said, watching him, "or you'll set off an alarm."

"No need," the professor said. "I can see quite well with this." He straightened and stepped back a pace. "I am right, Orville," he said. "What I suspected in Paris is confirmed beyond doubt."

Carter lost patience at last. "What the hell *did* you suspect in Paris?" he asked with some asperity. "You come all the way to Washington to tell me about it and you have yet to speak a single word of sense, as far as I can judge!"

"Patience," said the professor. "Allow me to savor for a while yet my small personal feat of detection."

"Detection?"

"Let me ask you, Orville, were your three experts agreed that this bearded, muscular, bent-shouldered giant we see before us represented Hercules?"

"No," Carter said impatiently. "As I recall it, Gallagher of the Boston thought the figure probably was meant to be Atlas, supporting the heavens on his shoulders."

"Demery and Helios plumped for Hercules?"

"Yes. Demery for Hercules preparing to strangle the Nemean lion. Helios for Hercules bending to retrieve one of the golden apples of the Hesperides. Or vice versa. I can't remember exactly."

"I see," said the professor. "Well, what I discovered in Paris proves that none of these three theories is correct. The figure is *not* that of Hercules nor of Atlas."

"Then who is it?"

"It's St. Christopher, Orville. The patron saint of travelers. And he is represented here neither preparing to strangle the Nemean lion nor yet to uphold the heavens on his shoulders. His arms, rather, are reaching up to steady upon his left shoulder a more precious burden."

Carter stared at him, then turned to stare at the statuette. He licked his lips. "You mean the Christ Child?"

"Exactly. St. Christopher carrying the Christ Child across the river."

"Nonsense!" Carter said with some heat. "In that case, where is the Christ Child?"

"In the Louvre, Orville," said the professor smugly. "In the Louvre."

"Impossible!" the curator of the Honeycutt began, then allowed his words to trail off into silence.

The professor showed his teeth. "You remember it now, don't you? That lovely smiling Christ Child seated, as is possible only for the divine, upon empty air, and bearing the globe of the world in his left hand? He was not, originally, sitting on empty air, Orville. He was seated upon the left shoulder of your St. Christopher here."

Carter had a rather wild look in his eyes, almost a look of appeal. He said, "But—the Louvre's Christ Child is by Bellano, isn't it?"

"It is. By Bartolomeo Bellano. A gifted follower of Donatello, it is true, but not to be confused with the master himself. As I could have told you if the Honeycutt had called me in . . . but never mind that now. You must face the fact boldly that your Donatello Hercules is, in reality, a Bellano St. Christopher minus the Christ Child which, unfortunately, is owned by the Louvre."

Carter made a complete circuit of the plinth, studying the statuette intently. He made a final effort. "Perhaps this is St. Christopher as you insist. And perhaps the Louvre's Christ Child does belong on his shoulder. All the same, the work could *still* be a genuine Donatello. Just because the Louvre has labeled its Christ Child a Bellano doesn't mean it *is* a Bellano, Benny."

The professor shook his head. "No good. I'm sorry. The Louvre's

Christ Child is signed, Orville; on the bottom of the globe of the world, held in the Christ Child's left hand, two tiny initials—BB—which, you will concede, identified the sculptor Bartolomeo Bellano five hundred years ago, just as they do the charming actress of our own day, Brigitte Bardot."

Carter refused to smile at this sally. "What made you link the Louvre's Christ Child with our Hercules?" he demanded.

"I made the discovery sheerly by accident," Professor Ferucignano said modestly, "guided in great measure by these new bifocal glasses—" he tapped his spectacles "—and by the newly installed brighter lights in the display rooms of the Louvre." He paused, enjoying Carter's obvious bewilderment, then went on. "I had not really seen the Louvre's Christ Child for years, Orville. Looked at it, yes, admired it, yes, on every occasion when I visited the Louvre—but with eyes grown slightly myopic with age, and in the dim unfocused lighting of the Louvre gallery. Only last week, seeing the Christ Child clearly for the first time in a long while, I detected the clues which led me to your Hercules."

"What clues?" Carter snapped.

"Two almost infinitesimal imperfections in the folds of the Christ Child's garment, imperfections which I have always assumed were caused when the bronze did not completely follow the mold during the statuette's casting."

"If not casting imperfections, what were they?"

"They were skillfully applied patches of bronze, artfully discolored and antiqued to match the rest of the figurine. But to the discerning eye *modern* patches for all that."

Carter said sarcastically, "Restoration or partial repair of masterworks is not entirely unknown."

"Wait," said the professor. "The location of these patches was what suddenly assumed new significance to me: one on the front of the Christ Child's garment below the knees, the other on the Christ Child's, ah, posterior. Do you see my point, Orville?"

Carter said nothing, only stared sourly at the professor, who continued, "Well, it instantly occurred to me, of course, that it was quite possible the patches were intended to cover scars left when some villain had brutally separated the Christ Child from another figure to which it had originally been joined."

"Our Hercules is not necessarily that figure!" Carter protested.

"Ah, but it is! Take my glass, Orville, if you please, and examine the surface of your Hercules's left shoulder and the inside of his left hand."

Carter accepted the magnifying glass and did as the professor asked, already certain of what he would find. "All right," he said ungraciously after a moment's inspection, "there are faint marks there that could be tiny patches." He gave the professor back his lens. "But you are not, I hope, trying to tell me that your artistic erudition is so nearly total that you immediately dredged up from your memory these almost undetectable marks on our Hercules to match up with the marks on the Christ Child in the Louvre? Out of thousands of sculptures?"

"No," said Professor Ferucignano, "my artistic erudition, as you call it, led me to the much simpler conclusion that since the Christ Child was an undoubted Bellano, he had probably been separated, if separated he was, from another piece of Bellano's sculpture—of which the Honeycutt Gallery owns an outstanding example, Orville, in this statuette which you persist in calling a Donatello Hercules."

A docent, closely followed by a group of students, entered the Sculpture Hall and approached them. "We now come," the lecturer was saying, "to the famous statuette of Hercules, executed in bronze by Donatello, one of the greatest masters of sculpture the Italian Renaissance produced."

"Come back to the office," Carter said to the professor. "We're in the way here."

Ferucignano assented readily. They returned to Carter's office. Carter sat down behind his desk after waving the professor to a chair. He sighed audibly. "Did you say anything to the Louvre about this, Benny?" he asked.

"Nothing. I wanted to examine your Hercules to be sure I was right. And I thought it only fair to acquaint you with the news before the Louvre, since yours would be the greater disappointment."

"That was decent of you, Benny. I appreciate it."

"I did, however, in my capacity of Renaissance scholar, evince curiosity as to the provenance of the Louvre's Christ Child, and a curator readily supplied me with the story of how they acquired it."

"How did they?" asked Carter, lighting a cigarette with nervous fingers.

"Public auction in 1935," said the professor, "in the sales rooms of a respected French firm, Garbeau Frères."

"How much did the Louvre pay for it?"

"One hundred and sixty thousand francs . . . somewhere around forty thousand dollars in those days."

Carter groaned. "We paid ten times that for our—" he hesitated "—St. Christopher."

Ferucignano nodded. "Of course. You thought you were getting a Donatello."

"Did the Louvre's records show who *owned* their Bellano Christ Child before they acquired it?"

"An antique dealer in Ferrara named Giuseppi Bruno, who brought the figurine to Garbeau Frères himself, having smuggled it out of Italy."

"Bruno," Carter said. "Then Bruno must have been your 'villain' who separated the Louvre's Christ Child from our St. Christopher? What a barbarous, uncivilized thing to do!"

"Barbarous, yes," said the professor, "and profitable as well, if Bruno *was* responsible for making two sculptures out of one and selling them separately at high prices. *If*, I say. Because the separation could have taken place any time within the last century, you know, judging from the condition of the bronze patches we've just seen."

"Where did Bruno get the Christ Child in the first place? Antique dealers in Ferrara don't carry priceless Bellanos and Donatellos in *stock*, you know that!"

"The story the Louvre gave me is this, Orville. Bruno, along with other antique dealers, was asked to bid on the contents of an old D'Este House of Grace and Favor when the last owner died without issue. He went to inspect the goods being offered and found them to consist mainly of worthless junk, as is usually the case with such houses in Italy after a long series of impecunious owners have sold off, one by one, the *good* pieces the family possessed. Worthless junk—except for the bronze Christ Child. Bruno speculated that generations of the family's girl children must have used it as a doll baby, since he found it in the cellars of the house with broken toys and a child's crib. He recognized it at once as something quite good, although he didn't realize how good until he found the artist's initials. He bought the whole collection of junk just to get the Christ Child. Bruno was very frank about all this when he asked Garbeau Frères to auction the piece off for him in Paris. He told them, too, that his business in Ferrara was on its last legs and he needed money desperately to save it. As it turned out, he got the money from the Louvre, which has not for one moment regretted its bargain."

"Didn't they check Bruno's story about having a shop in Ferrara?"

"Of course. He had one, all right."

"Well, it's a likely enough story, I guess," Carter said. "Such lucky discoveries have happened before and they'll happen again. I can't help wondering, though, if Bruno found the entire St. Christopher statuette in that house, and deliberately divided it into two figures."

"It seems probable," Ferucignano said, "although I am puzzled as to how the St. Christopher part of it turned up here in America as a Donatello. You said a few moments ago that you thought the Honeycutt had bought it from an English collector who needed money to pay his taxes. Did you buy direct from him, or was your statuette acquired at auction too?"

"I can't remember, Benny." Carter lifted his telephone receiver and asked his secretary to bring him the gallery's file on the Donatello Hercules. When he said "Hercules" he glanced the professor's way and smiled wryly.

A few minutes later, he looked up from his perusal of the documents in the Hercules file and said to the professor, "Here it is. We bought our Hercules in 1947 from Hamilton Langley, a New York art dealer."

Ferucignano nodded. "He's a personal friend of mine."

"Well, Langley was acting for a collector in England who had retained him because it was thought, quite rightly, that so soon after the war the Hercules would bring a better price in America than in England or on the Continent."

"Eleven years between the sales," the professor said. "The Christ Child in 1935, the St. Christopher in 1946. That could shoot down our theory that Bruno found the whole statuette in Ferrara. Why such a long interval between the first sale and the next? Do your records say anything about where the English owner of the St. Christopher obtained it?"

Carter read from a document in the file. "The owner claimed to have liberated the statuette just after World War II, when, as an officer in the British Army, he happened across it in the rubble of a bombed-out museum storage shed in Berlin."

"Liberated," said the professor, "means stolen, I presume?"

"Of course."

"From a museum storage shed? That's odd. I never heard of any Bellano piece, or any Donatello piece, either, being displayed in a Berlin museum, did you?"

"No. But the St. Christopher was obviously a genuine Renaissance work by a great master. Anyway, in the light of what you found out at the Louvre, I think we can discount that whole story as a fairytale."

"Really?" said the professor, raising his eyebrows. "I'm not quite—"

Carter cut him off peremptorily by holding out the document he had been consulting. "Take a look here, Benny," he said, "at the name of the English collector who 'liberated' our St. Christopher in Berlin. Second line on the page. Right there."

Professor Ferucignano leaned forward, read the name, and began to laugh. "Joseph Brown!" he chortled. "Joseph Brown. That should convince you, Orville!"

Carter capitulated gracefully. "I am convinced, Benny," he said, "and although belatedly, I congratulate you none the less heartily on your detective work. Even I can't miss that hefty coincidence: a Bellano St. Christopher sold to the Honeycutt Gallery of Art by a man named Joseph Brown!"

The Christopher Case, as it came to be known, aroused only passing interest outside art circles but caused a considerable stir within them. Professor Benozzo Ferucignano, predictably, came off as the hero of the affair, having demonstrated by his brilliant detective work that he was indeed worthy of his fame.

In October, he drove to New York for his semiannual visit with his oldest American friend, Hamilton Langley, now retired. The former art dealer, in spite of his eighty years and his failing health, retained a keen interest in the doings of his former colleagues and customers.

"How does it feel, Benny," he asked his guest as they sampled before-dinner martinis, "to be the Sherlock Holmes of the art world?"

The professor laughed. "Quite satisfying, I must admit. I received the final accolade yesterday, an engraved invitation to the private, black-tie reception at the Louvre next week, when the reunited St. Christopher and Christ Child goes on display for the first time."

"I also am invited," said Langley, chuckling, "as is only fitting for the man who sold the Donatello Hercules to the Honeycutt."

"Are you planning to go? Perhaps we can go together."

"I'm too old to fly so far now. I hope I'll see the reassembled statuette when it comes to the Honeycutt in April. The Louvre is to have it for six months each year, the Honeycutt for the other six, isn't that the agreement?"

"That's it. And a surprisingly practical solution under the circumstances."

Langley nodded. Then, looking over the edge of his martini glass at the professor, he asked curiously, "What made you do it, Benny? After all these years?"

The professor pondered. "I don't really know," he said at length, "aside from the fact that I wanted to show Orville Carter that my credentials as an authority on Renaissance sculpture are bona fide. The Honeycutt is one of the few really important museums left which has never retained me as a consultant."

"But that wasn't the only reason, I take it?"

"I suppose not. Perhaps it was partly to satisfy my artistic conscience too, as I told Carter. The thought of such a lovely piece being deliberately broken up for commercial gain seemed more and more like sacrilege to me as I thought about it. Can you understand that?"

"Of course I can understand it." Langley rang a silver bell to summon his houseman. "Another martini for Professor Ferucignano," he told him, stumbling slightly over the professor's name. When the man went out, he continued, "I can understand it only too well, Benny, because I've felt the same way upon occasion." He paused to grin at the professor. "What I *can't* understand, however," he went on, "is why a man with the simple Italian name of Giuseppi Bruno when he lived in Ferrara, and the simple English name of Joseph Brown when he lived in London, should have selected an impossible tongue twister of a name like Benozzo Ferucignano when he moved to America!"

One of the traditional themes of the classic detective story is the closed circle of suspects—neatly contained in a snowbound country house, on a speeding train, or even on a Nile steamer. But to my knowledge no closed circle has ever been quite like Charles W. Runyon's energy-saving car pool. This is truly a detective story for our times.

CHARLES W. RUNYON
Death Is My Passenger

Old Mrs. Voigt was out of the building. She's heavy in the hips and legs, so she crab-walked down the steps sideways. I fired up the engine and eased to the curb as she came off the last step. Helen Jorgensen threw open the door and Vera Thrush pulled her inside. I let out the clutch when I heard the door slam. The squall of rubber merged with Mrs. Voigt's wail.

"Breezy, you don't even let a body get comfy."

Large styrofoam dice swayed from the rear-view mirror. They showed six and six as I looped the traffic line oozing toward the expressway. Dennis Jackson, who works in the engineering section, laid twenty feet of rubber on the shoulder getting around me, then dawdled at the stoplight until it blinked amber. He shot me a bird as he pulled out, leaving me snagged on the red.

I took out my comb and ran it through my hair, counting heads in my rear-view mirror. Three in the back seat, two up front besides myself. I slid the comb back in my shirt pocket and hunched down to watch the overhead traffic light so I could get a quick jump.

Vera Thrush leaned forward from the back seat and blew her warm voice in my ear. "Relax, Breeze. We'll all live longer."

"We'll also miss the light at Forty-sixth and get caught in the five-fifteen rush at Gibbs Electronics—and that means you're all twenty minutes late getting home."

The light flashed green and my foot jumped off the clutch. I crammed the shift into second and jerked it back into third as I rocked into the high-speed lane. The needle bumped sixty.

I eased off on the gas and heard Vera's ragged sigh, "I don't know why I don't buy a bus ticket."

"You like the danger, the uncertainty," I said. "Never knowing if you'll see your family again, or the plant."

"That last part *I* can do without."

This was a soft murmur meant for my ears alone. It came from Gloria Bass, a gorgeous brunette who sat in the middle of the front seat. It had taken a couple of weeks to work it out so she "accidentally" sat there. Every time I shifted down I touched the back of my hand to her nylon-sheathed thigh. That's as far as it ever went, but she kept sitting there, and I took that as an encouraging sign for the future.

From the top of the hill I saw that the intersection at Forty-sixth had a tail on it three blocks long. We had, as I'd expected, caught the five-fifteen rush out of Gibbs.

"Two out of four this week," I muttered, braking the heap to a stop.

"You're slowing down in your old age, Breeze," said Vera.

I grunted and eyed the oncoming traffic. I saw a gap between a red Gremlin and a Ford Camper, fired myself through the slot, crossed the left-hand lane, and bounced into the alley behind the Marathon station. The old brick pavement was warped like a roller coaster and so narrow I had only six inches clearance on either side. The car went *whoomp! whoomp! whoomp!* as it bottomed out on the shocks.

A lot of yelling came from the riders, and Mrs. Voigt moaned, "Oh, my heart!"

I glanced back and saw her clutching the strap with her right hand, her powder-blue headscarf hanging across half her face, while her mouth gaped open and shut like a fish. I knew what she was trying to say, so I slowed down.

I'd hoped to find Sixth Street clear, but that's the trouble when you pioneer a new route. The word had leaked out, the intersection was jammed. I saw Dennis Jackson's electric-blue Olds immobilized in the middle of the pack and chuckled sardonically. I cut across Sixth, bounced through another alley, and came out on Fifth. I cut back to the right and wheeled out on Rogers Street about five minutes up on the rest of the idiots.

Mrs. Riggs was the first one out. She's small, plump, with gray hair and a warm smile for everyone. She spent every lunch hour shopping, so we went through the usual two-minute delay while she stood outside the car and Vera handed out her packages from behind the back seat.

Mrs. Riggs said, "Thank you, Vera," each time a package was laid in her arms. Then she said, "Goodbye, Breeze, goodbye, girls!" and started up the sidewalk. Her fat little poodle bounced off the pillared front porch and tried to climb her legs. Mrs. Riggs stooped to pick him up and dropped most of her packages.

I circled the block and came out on Rogers again, angled across two lanes of traffic, and slid into the left-turn lane just as the arrow flashed green. I did a left onto Byers, a through street marked only by a couple of yield signs. Helen Jorgensen lives in the second block from the end, in a brick house with disgusting yellow trim around the doors and windows.

She shares it with her husband, who drives a long-haul truck. She's the one who gave me my nickname. I told her the first time she rode that I'd waft her home like a breeze, and that was the night we nearly got rolled up like a paper wad between two tandem diesels. She used to tell me when her husband was away, but I never seemed to catch the hint. She's a bony-faced woman with reddish-blonde hair. Also I'd seen her old man out mowing the yard once and hadn't liked the size of his biceps.

I said, "Goodbye, Helen," and she nodded once and walked up the sidewalk. She'd been frosty ever since Gloria started riding.

I kept straight on Byers until I hit the asphalt truck route that runs alongside the railroad yards. I rolled up two miles in two minutes, then cut back up on Trowbridge Avenue to drop Vera Thrush. She wears big hats which have to be stuck on with a hatpin, which she always parks up behind the seats when she rides. Tonight she spent a minute groping around back there, then got out of the car and said, "I guess the pin fell down behind the seat. Breeze, if you'll remember to look when you stop. . . "

"Right," I said. "I'll have it for you tomorrow."

She waved goodbye and that left two—Mrs. Voigt and Gloria. The old woman had thrown her head back on the seat and covered her face with a blue headscarf. She always did it when she napped. She'd let her white leather-bound Bible slide off her lap, and that was normal too. I debated taking her home first and trying to lure Gloria to a bar for a couple of drinks and some fun later. I decided not, since it was Thursday and I was thirteen days away from my last payday. Even with the extra fifty a week from the carpool, my expenses leapfrog my income.

So I just turned on the 8-track and started off at a slow thirty-per. Gloria lit a cigarette and gave it to me, then lit one for herself. I always rack my brain for something to say at times like this, but nothing happens except that my throat gets very dry. So rather than say something stupid I say nothing.

As a matter of fact, I thought she rated something better than a mailroom clerk. I fully intend to rise in my chosen profession—as soon as I decide on one—but for the present I have a feeling she's too rich for my blood. I'd go crazy trying to beat out the competition in that rat race.

I stopped to let her out, then watched her go through the routine of tugging her wine-purple skirt down over her hips, switching her rump once left and once right.

"See you in the morning, Breeze," she said.

"Right, Gloria. See you."

I watched her walk up the green cement sidewalk and enter the glass-fronted lobby. She lived in one of those swinging singles apartments with pool and lounge and everything you're supposed to need for the good life. I'd been to parties at those places and they're just like any other kind of party. The chances of scoring with a really neat chick are about the same as outside, which is to say nil, because the neat ones are already tied up.

So . . . that left old Mrs. Voigt. I called over my shoulder, "Have you home in two minutes." She didn't answer. In the mirror I saw that she'd slumped sideways in the seat and dropped her Bible onto the floor. She didn't look like she was in danger of falling, and I was double-parked outside the condominium anyway, so I pulled out.

It was only three blocks to her rooming house, and I drove slow so she wouldn't pitch forward. She was pushing sixty, and I figured she needed all the rest she could get after a hard day on the assembly line.

Five minutes later I eased to the curb and said, "You're home, Mrs. Voigt."

Usually she struggled up with a choked snort and a bewildered look. This time—nothing. I reached back and shook her shoulder gently.

She didn't feel right. I twisted around in the seat and lifted the headscarf. Her face was an ugly, splotched gray. A trail of bloody saliva leaked out of her open mouth and down onto her lace collar. I took hold of her wrists and stared out through the windshield to avoid looking at her ghastly face.

She had no pulse. The dice on my mirror had stopped at two and one.

I must have sat there a couple of minutes staring at those dice, my brain like a dead battery. I didn't have the slightest notion what to do, because I'd never come up against a dead person before. You see a dead cat on the highway and you ignore it. A dead dog you take out in the back yard and bury it. But a dead *person*. . .

I got out my comb and ran it through my hair, which usually helps me think. I thought, *Well, she really did have a bad heart after all.* I should have believed her, I shouldn't have cannonballed through that alley, or maybe it was when I did that squealing left turn onto Rogers that her heart gave its last and final lurch. . .

I put out my cigarette and walked up the short sidewalk. My heels made a ringing echo on the wide wooden veranda. One of the porch posts held a glittery silver and black sign reading ROOMS. A smudged and faded list of names was thumbtacked under the mailslot, but I couldn't read it, so I knocked on the door. I waited a minute and knocked again. A door opened at the side of the porch, and a long narrow nose appeared in the crack. I couldn't tell if it belonged to a man or a woman because he-she-it kept the night chain in place and looked at me from eyes set deep in gray pouches.

"Who you wanta see?"

The voice was female—not that it makes much difference when you get that far up in years. I said, "The—uh—family of Mrs. Voigt, if you please, Ma'am."

"There ain't any. She lives alone, like the rest of us."

Slam went the side door. I reached out and turned the knob on the front door, aware that she was watching me through the curtain. I had a feeling she'd call the cops the minute I stepped inside—then I thought, *Well, why not?*

I walked over to her door and hollered through the glass. "Could I use your telephone, please?"

The door opened just enough to let the words out: "There's a pay phone in the hall."

"Okay if I use it?"

"If you got a dime."

I stepped into a little anteroom and saw the phone at the foot of the stairs. The carpet was threadbare, and a gray film of dust covered everything except the banister, which was worn down to the wood and shiny.

I dialed the emergency number on the front of the telephone and heard a girl answer, "Central Police Station," I pushed in a dime and noticed a door at the foot of the stairs swing open about an inch. I knew the old girl was listening, so I cupped my hand over my mouth and directed my voice into the mouthpiece:

"I'd like to report a death."

"Name and address please?"

"Well, her name is Voigt. She died in my car."

"Where is the body?"

"It's still in the car. Setting out at the curb."

"What was the cause of death?"

"Heart attack—I guess. She's all gray and blotchy."

"Street and number please?"

I stepped outside and looked at the number over the door, then went back and gave it to the girl. She said, "Don't touch the body. The patrolmen in your neighborhood will arrive shortly and take charge. Thank you."

I hung up and walked outside. Mrs. Voigt's face had darkened to the color of mud. I didn't want to sit inside with her, so I hoisted myself onto the front of the car and fired a nicotine stick.

The cops must have stopped for coffee because I burned up three cigarettes sitting there like a hood ornament. It started to get dark. Purple shadows drifted down through the naked oak branches, and I could see my breath under my nose. A prowl car came whoop-whooping down the street and cut in to the curb about twenty feet in front of my car. Two men got out and started up the sidewalk, black boots and fingertip-length coats.

I called, "Over here."

Two flashlight beams hit me in the eyes. One floated toward me and the other went around to my car. The first patrolman gave me a quick up-and-down with his beam and told me to stand up. Actually I had to get off the car and stand *down,* but I didn't bother to correct him. He wanted my name and address and I gave him that. When he flashed his light on his pad I saw he was a broad-faced kid about my age with red hair and a freckled Irish complexion.

"Who found the body?" he asked. "You?"

"I don't know if you could say I *found* her. She was one of my riders, and when I stopped to let her out she wouldn't wake up."

"I see. What was the approximate time of death? You got any idea?"

"I don't know the exact time. Somewhere between five-twenty and five-thirty. I was busy driving, and I thought she'd just dozed off—"

"Vic, c'mere a minute."

I heard the two muttering while they played the light on Mrs. Voigt's body. The old cop had bristly gray hair sticking out from under his hat. He started unbuttoning Mrs. Voigt's coat, so I turned my back. I gazed up the empty street and thought of everybody inside their homes eating supper and watching the evening news. My stomach growled, and I wondered what Mom was having. . .

The redheaded cop walked to the prowl car and the older officer came up to me. "See your chauffeur's license."

"I don't have one."

"You told my partner the old lady was a passenger."

"I meant she rides in my carpool."

"How many cars in this carpool?"

"Just mine."

"Okay, let's have your regular license."

I pulled the plastic rectangle out of my wallet and gave it to him. I had a feeling this was a routine hassle, something to do while waiting for the meat wagon. Fourteen of us hauled riders out of Hamphill Optics alone. We didn't hurt the taxis because our riders couldn't afford the fares anyway. We took most of our trade from the buses and the bus drivers couldn't care less.

Anyway, the patrolman carried my license to the prowl car. I stood until my feet got cold and wondered how soon they'd get Mrs. Voigt out of my car. If they waited until she got stiff they'd have to cut her out with a torch. She'd had enough trouble dragging herself in and out while she was alive.

Pretty soon the older cop came back and stood looking at me with his thumbs hooked in his leather belt. "Henley, you've got four moving violations against you, plus about twenty-five unpaid parking tickets."

I looked down the pike of the future and saw fifty bucks a week gurgling down the drain. Nothing to what Mrs. Voigt had lost—but then a grain of sand in your own eye hurts worse than a rock dropped on another guy's head.

"You mean you're gonna lift my license because an old lady happened to have a heart attack in my car?"

"*Heart attack?*" The cop snorted. "Come here, boy."

I didn't want to get close to the body, but the officer nudged me forward while he beamed his light into the back seat. They'd left Mrs. Voigt's green cloth coat hanging open, and I saw a dark stain the size of a speedometer dial low on her left side. Protruding from the blotch was a metal shaft capped by a lustrous gray pearl.

I knew I'd found Vera's hatpin.

I jumped back and whirled around. I couldn't help it. A pair of two-hundred-pound bodies hemmed me in. The older cop's face loomed out of the shadows like a rising moon.

"You must have thought we were pretty damn stupid, to try to pass that off as a heart attack."

I opened my mouth, but the younger cop fired a question before I could speak. "Why'd you do it?"

I gasped, "I didn't!"

"Then you better tell us who did, quick."

This was the older cop again. I managed to choke, "I—I didn't know she had a pin in her. Vera...she—"

"Vera did it?" asked the redhead.

"No. I don't know. It's her pin."

"Why would she kill the old lady?" asked the older cop.

"I didn't say she did. I said it was *her pin!*"

"You think she loaned it to somebody else so they could do it?"

"*No*! She didn't loan it. She lost it. She noticed it was missing when she got out. I said I'd find it tonight and return it tomorrow. You ask her. Ask anybody—all my passengers. I didn't take my hands off the wheel from the time we left the plant. . . "

I trailed off as a long gray limousine drifted in like smoke and stopped beside my car. A second patrol car pulled up in front of it and a black, unmarked Ford slid in behind. Both cops went to the black car and left me standing there.

I didn't know whether I was arrested or not. They hadn't hand-cuffed me or told me that everything I said would be used against me, but I decided not to tease fate by moving around.

It wasn't hard to see who was in charge. A fat character about five-five got out of the unmarked car and stood looking at Mrs. Voigt. He kept both hands in the pockets of his open topcoat while the older patrolman flashed the light on her. Finally he leaned over and did something to the body, then stepped back and wiped his hands on his handkerchief. A photographer came forward and flashbulbs lit up the overhanging trees.

I didn't watch them load her into the hearse. The gray-haired patrolman was talking to the fat plainclothesman, who looked bored. He kept putting his hand to his mouth and I thought he was yawning, but then I saw his jaws moving and I realized he was chewing something.

The gray hearse pulled out, followed by a patrol car. The plainclothesman walked over to me and said, "Okay, Henley. Let's take a ride."

My heart dropped into the bottom of my stomach. I started back to the unmarked car and he said, "Unh-uh. We'll take your car."

I opened the door and then remembered, "They took my license."

"Yates, give the kid his license. What the hell did you pull it for?"

The gray-haired patrolman handed me the plastic rectangle and mumbled: "Well, he was suspect—"

"Did you kill that old lady, kid?"

"No, sir!"

"See? You guys leave murder to the homicide squad. Let's go, Henley."

We got in and I started the engine. I felt a cold draft on my neck and glanced into the back seat. For a second I saw Mrs. Voigt sitting next to the window—then it turned into a shadow.

"My name's Dawson," said the plainclothesman. "Why are you so nervous?"

I licked my lips. "I thought I saw Mrs. Voigt sitting back there, the way she always did, with her thumb stuck in between the pages of her Bible. She never read more than a couple of verses before she dropped off to sleep. That's why I never noticed she was dead. She never acted very much alive."

"You always talk this much, Henley?"

"No, that's nervousness."

"You gotta remember that anything you say can be thrown back in your face in court. So if you got anything to hide, keep your trap shut."

"I'm not hiding anything."

"Good. What's your first name?"

"Morton. My riders call me Breeze."

"Okay, Breeze. If you're not too nervous, put the car in motion."

Having a cop in the car raised hell with my timing. Pulling it down into third I clashed gears like I haven't done since I was fifteen. To cover up my embarrassment I asked, "You wanta go anywhere special?"

"Go back over your route. Mrs. Voigt was your last stop, right?"

"Right."

"Okay. Try the one you let off before that. We'll roll it up backwards."

I pulled into a driveway, reversed and started back toward Gloria's apartment. Dawson ripped the top off a cellophane packet and threw something in his mouth. When he chewed, it sounded like a horse walking on gravel.

"I do this because I quit smoking," he said.

"Oh, yeah?"

He munched another mouthful and said, "I used to really burn up the nicotine. Three packs a day. Then I quit. Like that, I started to eat. I grew out of my clothes. I tried diets and went crazy. So I eat parched corn. You wear yourself out before you get anything in your stomach. Good for the teeth, too."

He held out the bag but I shook my head. I pulled into the traffic loop which led to Gloria's apartment and parked outside the lobby.

Dawson just sat there. "Tell me what you know about her," he said.

I told him what impressed me: long, soft wavy black hair, nice hips, nice legs, nice pair of bosoms. She smoked French cigarettes and wore a perfume that smelled like cactus blossoms. She had lavender eyes and a smooth ivory complexion.

Dawson gazed out at the deserted swimming pool, the trimmed shrubbery, the vines (plastic) that twined around the lobby.

"You know what one of these pads costs?" he asked.

"Quite a bit."

"About three bills a month. What does she do at—what's the name?"

"Hamphill Optics. She works up on four."

"That doesn't tell me a damn thing."

"It's the executive department. She's secretary to Mr. Holt. He's vice president in charge of sales."

"And what did Mrs. Voigt do?"

"She was an inspector on the line."

"Inspecting what?"

"Well..." I shrugged. "Precision instruments for laboratories, that's what we make. Microscopes and things like that."

"Pretty valuable stuff?"

"Some of our instruments sell for thirty-five thousand dollars. But very few people have a use for 'em."

He said nothing to that, just sat looking into the lobby. After a minute a tall guy came out carrying a briefcase. He looked like a salesman in his creased gray suit, but I thought I'd seen him before. As he came up to my car, I recognized him as the driver of the unmarked police car.

He crawled in the back seat and started talking. "She's home. I called and said I'd gotten her number from a friend and wanted to meet her. She wasn't interested."

"Nervous?" asked Dawson.

"No, cool as hell. Said she planned to wash her hair and read a book. I said I'd call back later in case she changed her mind and she said don't bother."

It felt good to know that Gloria had given him the icy lip. Then Dawson asked, "Who pays her rent?"

"There's two other chicks living in the same pad. I guess they split it three ways."

Dawson grunted and said, "Okay, Sergeant Dinwiddie. Who's

next, Breeze?"

"Helen Jorgensen."

"Married or single?"

"Married."

"Better not ask her for a date then, Dinwiddie. Try to sell her some insurance. Okay, let's go."

Dinwiddie got out and I put the car in gear. As I drove, I asked Dawson what he was doing.

"This is just a first run," he said. "We check out the obvious. If anybody's packing, or getting ready to leave town, or seems unduly nervous, we mark 'em down as a double prime suspect and dig a little deeper. You interested in detective work?"

"Well . . . I am now."

"Good! You might learn something on this case. On the other hand you might not. Depends on how well you listen."

I listened, but could hear nothing but the growling of my stomach. I remembered that Mom was having broiled liver and onions for supper. To a lot of people that's garbage, but it happens to be my favorite. I'm strange in other ways too.

Like when I stopped down the street from Helen's house, I started speculating which one of my riders it would turn out to be. Which one did I *expect* it to be?

I couldn't answer that, so I asked myself, *Which one did I want it to be? Certainly not Gloria, that would nip our romance before it even budded. Vera Thrush, I liked.* Even though she ripped me up with insults, she knew how to take a joke in return.

But not Helen Jorgensen. She had a prickly, snarling quality, even when she tried to be nice. She carried trouble—and that was confirmed when Dinwiddie lunged out of her house. The hulking shadow of Helen's old man filled the doorway behind him.

He threw himself in the car, panting. "Wouldn't believe I sold insurance. Holy Christ, talk about suspicion!"

Dawson interrupted. "Did *she* believe you were an insurance man?"

"I don't know *what* she believed. She was busy trying to convince her husband she didn't know me from Julius Caesar. I don't think she even noticed me."

"What do you say? Cross her off?"

"Yeah—tentatively."

"Right," said Dawson. "Drive on, Breeze."

Vera Thrush wasn't home. The baby-sitter came to the door and told Dinwiddie she'd be at the corner bar. Dinwiddie found her holding down the end stool as if she'd taken a ninety-nine-year lease on it.

"Juice is an expensive habit," observed Dawson later in the car. "Does she do it much, Breezy?"

I bit my lip, but couldn't see any way out of telling the truth. "She carries a jug in her purse. She passed it around when we got hung up in a two-hour jam at the cloverleaf. We had a helluva time in the car."

"Mrs. Voigt too?"

"She had a rosy glow. That was before she got religion."

"How about—who's the next one?"

"Mrs. Riggs. She wasn't with us then. She only started riding three months ago."

"Let's go see her, shall we?"

Five minutes later, I pulled up across the street from a white-pillared house set back on a broad sloping lawn. An incandescent porch light made black cutouts of the shrubs and evergreens.

Dawson grunted softly and asked, "She live there alone?"

"She has a housekeeper who stays during the day. I don't know about nights."

"What does she do that she can afford a housekeeper?"

"You mean at the plant?"

"Okay—back at the plant," he said.

"She works in the employee's lounge. Or I should say out of it. She's the coffee-cart lady. Serves coffee, milk, rolls, doughnuts, stuff like that through the plant."

Dawson said nothing. He sat there eating parched corn while I fiddled with the dice and tried not to think about food. I kept thinking about diced carrots, cube steak, boxcars full of french fries. . .

After about ten minutes, Dinwiddie slid into the car and reported that Mrs. Riggs was not only in, but calm and collected and in no hurry to go anyplace. She had insisted that Dinwiddie drink a cup of coffee, and had even asked to see his insurance policies, until Dinwiddie confessed that he'd left them in his other briefcase and would come back tomorrow night.

At that point Dawson interrupted to ask if he was sure Mrs. Riggs wasn't onto him.

"I don't think she was onto me," said Dinwiddie. "It's just a case of a friendly woman living alone who doesn't get many visitors."

"You agree with that, Breeze? She's a friendly lady?"

I nodded. "She's very popular at the plant. Dudes in the mailroom borrow money from her. Some don't pay it back. She never hassles them."

"That so?" He crumpled a cellophane bag and shoved it into the trash bag under the dash. "Okay, Breeze, let's go get some food. A drive-in would be nice."

I drove to Freddie's, a seafood place with carry-out service. While we waited for our orders I realized that he hadn't let me out of his sight since he'd saved me from arrest. I decided to find out where the boundaries were, so I asked him if I could call Mom.

He said, "Sure, only don't tell her what happened."

I walked to the phone booth at the corner of the lot and was about to drop in my dime when his words sank in. I walked back to the car and asked:

"How can I say what I'm doing if I can't tell her what happened?"

"Tell her you're having dinner with a friend."

"I don't know if she'd believe a lieutenant from Homicide."

"You think I don't have friends, kid?"

"I don't mean that. What if she asks how we happened to run into each other?"

Dawson looked up at me and sighed. "Does your mother *ever* ask how you happen to run into people?"

"Hardly ever."

"Well then, go—take the risk, lie if you must. Just don't spill the beans."

So I called Mom and no problem, she'd put some liver back for me and I was supposed to drive carefully and be home early and not forget I had to work tomorrow. I could have played a tape of my own side because it rarely varied from Thanks—I will—I won't.

I got back to the car as the food arrived. I put away a dish of fish and chips while Dawson shoveled in deep sea scallops, a bowl of oyster dressing, a basket of fried shrimp, a slab of apple pie and two scoops of ice cream. While he had coffee he told me he'd built his theory of crime detection on the techniques newspapermen use in getting a story.

"They look for the who-what-when-where-why-and-how. They gotta have all those to round off a story. I look for the same things, but I'm only after the 'who.' "

" 'Who' is the murderer?" I asked.

"That's right."

"Which is the what?"

"Somebody stuck a hatpin in the old lady's heart. That's 'what'. The why, when, where, and how, we ain't got."

"We've got the 'how'. The hatpin."

"No, no. That's only the murder weapon. *How* did it get stuck in there without anybody seeing it done? That's the question."

He took a big bite of pie and swigged it down with coffee. "I like to start with motive. Once I find out why a person was killed, I'm usually not far from finding the killer. Say the motive is jealousy. I automatically rule out strangers and most professional hoods. If the motive is theft, I rule out the well-to-do. I mean petty theft. Rich people steal too, but they won't risk it unless there's a pretty big pile and not much risk of getting caught.

"Say the motive here was hate. This wasn't what you'd call a passion killing, like you get between married folks and close relatives. This was planned down to the split second. Whoever did it was prepared to be one of five obvious suspects—to hang tough and brazen it out."

I started counting in my head—Gloria, Vera, Helen J., and Mrs. Riggs. That made four. It wasn't hard to figure out who was number five.

"You've ruled me out now?" I asked.

"I did that at the beginning."

"Why? Not that I'm complaining—"

"When I heard your knees knocking together, I knew nobody that scared could pull off a caper like this. Whoever did it *had* to be cool."

My face prickled with embarrassment. "Because I found the *body,* man. What would you get if you put my other passengers up against a corpse in the back seat?"

"Screams, yells, fainting spells, tears—and one of them would be faking it all the way." He tossed his paper cup in the littered tray. "Get rid of that stuff while I make a phone call."

When he came back to the car, he told me to drive back to the point of origin—Mrs. Voigt's rooming house. While I drove, he said he'd called the lab and gotten a report on the weapon.

"So now we've definitely got a murder-one," he said.

"What's that?" I asked.

"First-degree—premeditated. That wasn't a regular hatpin. That was a surgical probe made out of high-tensile steel alloy. Somebody stuck on a phony pearl."

I gasped. "Oh, Lord! Vera Thrush?"

"Not necessarily. There could have been a switch."

"So we rule out Vera?"

"We don't rule out anybody yet. Think about your other passengers a minute. How'd Mrs. Voigt get along with them?"

"Well—pretty good most of the time. After she got religion she didn't have much to say. She'd get in the car, open up the Bible, and drift off to sleep."

"Was she tight with any one particular passenger?"

"I don't think so."

"Who'd she sit beside?"

"She sat on the right, in the back. Vera sat in the middle. Mrs. Riggs sat on the left."

"Was it always that way?"

I frowned. "No. When Mrs. Riggs first started riding, three months ago, *she* sat in the middle. But Vera's cigarettes bothered her on certain mornings, so she moved next to the window so she could get fresh air."

"What does Vera Thrush do for a living?"

"She's in accounting. She hands out the paychecks."

"Helen Jorgensen?"

"I think she's in shipping. Yeah, that's it. Sometimes when we had a big shipment she'd have to work overtime and couldn't catch her ride."

"And Gloria—you said she worked for a vice-president?"

"Yeah. She couldn't have been involved."

"You got any idea how many times I've heard that?"

"No—a thousand?"

"Anytime anybody says that—then I bear down. I bear down really hard. So why couldn't Gloria have done it?"

"She was sitting beside me in the front seat."

"Couldn't have reached back and *zonk* with the hatpin?"

"No."

"Not even when you were bouncing through that alley? Or charging through a line of oncoming traffic? I heard about your citations. Left turn on red. Jumping the light at Thirty-eighth. Jumping the light at Forty-sixth. Passing twelve cars in a no-pass zone. You have any money left out of your paycheck after you pay your fines?"

"Sometimes enough for cigarettes."

"And you're trying to tell me you know what goes on behind you?"

"It's like I know, when I think about it. I'm not listening, but I'm taking it in. I'd know if Mrs. Voigt was quarreling with the other passengers. And she wasn't. Anyway, I can't imagine a quarrel that would cause somebody to stick a hatpin in somebody else."

"Would you believe somebody killing his wife because she burned the toast? Or a guy plugging his neighbor with a forty-four magnum because the dog dug up his roses? Those things happened. When murder comes in, logic flies out the window. Because murder ain't logical."

I pulled up outside the rooming house and switched off the engine. The porchlight spread a daylight brilliance over the postage-stamp yard, but the house was dark except for a dim flickering glow against a downstairs curtain. I asked Dawson what he planned to do here.

"There's a connection," he said, "between Mrs. Voigt and one of your other passengers. So far we've missed it. Now we'll go see if we can find it among her effects."

Funny how little you know about somebody you've seen every working day for over a year. Mrs. Voigt lived in a corner apartment with windows facing south and east. She'd covered the walls of her living room with photos of people dressed in the style of the Forties. Looking at the long dresses, the piled-up hair, and the tight collars, I got the feeling she'd kept on living in those bygone years, and was just marking time in the present.

A uniformed policeman was guarding the apartment. Dawson told him he could take off, then started going through her little half-desk, taking out letters and reading a few paragraphs, then putting them back in the drawers.

Finally he slumped down in a chintz-covered easy chair and said, "She's got one relative—a father living in a retirement home in Arizona." He picked up a sheaf of receipts and riffled them like playing cards. "Cost her six bills a month to keep him at Desert View Ranch. That's heavy bread for a production worker."

"Maybe she owned stocks."

He shook his head. "No evidence of that. She didn't pay by check either. Postal money orders, which she bought every month with cash. She also paid a hundred-and-a-half for this apartment. According to her rent receipts she paid in cash. Now. . . " He held up a little green booklet. "She drew two-fifty an hour at the plant. What did she do with her check? She put it in a savings account without cashing it. Can you put it together?"

"Sure. She had a cash income."

"Right. But from what?"

I shrugged, and Dawson stretched out his hand and picked up the phone. He dialed information, got the number of the Desert View Ranch, and asked for Theodore Voigt. From Dawson's end of the conversation, I knew they'd refused to call him to the telephone:

"You *can't*? Not even in case of emergency?"

After about ten seconds, Dawson said, "This *is* an emergency, Miss . . . or is it Missus? His daughter was found dead in suspicious circumstances."

Dawson listened a minute, then shook his head. "No, I don't wanna go into the circumstances right now. I'm Lieutenant Dawson, Homicide. Regulations say we gotta notify the next of kin. . . . No, I'm not trying to pressure you, dear. I'm sitting in the middle of all her personal possessions and I found her father's name. Yes. . . . Well, I appreciate your position, but I'd like to ask *him* a few questions. . . "

He listened a minute longer, shook his head in disgust, and held the receiver out to me. I put it to my ear and heard a clipped feminine voice.

"You have your responsibility and I have mine, and mine is to my patients and yours is of course to find the murderer. In this case you'll have to do it without her father's help. He cannot walk or talk and has to be fed through a tube, so obviously. . . "

Dawson took the phone and said, "Thank you, dear, we'll be hearing from you, I'm sure." He put the phone on the hook and glared at me. "Those hypocrites. All that sweet talk about responsibility to the patient ends about one minute after the money stops." He ripped the top off a fresh packet of parched corn. Chewing seemed to calm his nerves, because he spoke in a musing tone.

"So, we deal with the evidence we got. The way it worked out, with you letting those people off one by one, if we can find out where it was done, we'll know when. I want you to think about that. Try to remember the last time you heard any sign of life from her. We'll cross off everybody who got out before that."

He went to the couch and lay down, pulled his hat over his eyes, and muttered, "Let's both meditate for a spell."

Five minutes later I heard him snoring. I guess that's what he meant by meditation. Meditation for me was going over the whole trip in my mind and remembering every squeak, grunt, and giggle.

After a half hour I shook him awake and asked, "Would she make any noise when she got stuck?"

He blinked, rubbed his eyes and yawned. "Probably, she'd gasp and moan and maybe even kick her legs a little bit. Why?"

"Just wondered."

He groaned and pulled his hat over his eyes again. I got busy with pencil and paper and drew a map of my route. Then I went through and marked every spot where I'd noticed Mrs. Voigt. The last thing I remembered her doing was hanging onto the strap as we bounced through the alley. And in that place I'd had all the passengers aboard.

I woke up the lieutenant and gave him this information. He growled without opening his eyes and turned his face to the back of the sofa. I went to the chair and tried to imitate his technique. Twice I nearly broke my neck but finally I got my head pillowed to where I slept more or less comfortably.

When I woke up, I thought I was having nightmares. There stood Mrs. Voigt in her blue silk dress and white dickey and a flop-brimmed gray hat with a thick veil pulled down over her face. I watched a hand lift the veil, I glimpsed a hairy wrist. . .

Dawson's face divided into a shark's grin. "Took you in, didn't I?"

"You sure did. What's the idea?"

"I thought I'd ride along on your morning run."

A light started to glow inside my head. "You mean . . . fool the murderer with that disguise?"

"Not the murderer. Everybody else." He lifted off the hat and set it on the arm of the sofa. "Whoever stuck that pin in her *knows* they did it. So what'll they do when they see her sitting there?"

"*Wow!*" I shook my head in admiration. "You figure they'll start screaming, thinking you're a ghost?"

"Boy, people don't react like that anymore." He hoisted the hem of the dress and tucked it under his belt. "They'll have listened to the news, and when they don't hear the announcement of Mrs. Voigt's death, they'll know there's a trick. So what'll they do?"

"Turn and run?"

"If they do that, we got 'em. But I doubt if it's that simple." He sat down in the chair and started rolling down his trouser legs. "No, they'll figure they have to cover up their surprise and act natural. But they won't be able to."

"Why not?"

He hung one of my cigarettes in the corner of his mouth. "*This* is why not."

"You've lost me," I said, tossing him my lighter.

"Don't worry about it." He flicked the lighter and puffed out a cloud of smoke. "Just study everybody's reaction. Tell me what isn't normal."

It was six A.M. when we left the apartment. We ate steak and eggs in an all-night diner and I could feel the pressure building up inside me. When Dawson lit another cigarette I asked him if the case was beginning to wear down his nerves.

"It's a game of nerves all right. But it won't be mine that crack."

Back in the car, Dawson pulled on Mrs. Voigt's coat and settled himself by the window. He rolled up his pants legs and pulled the dress down over his knees. His hairy legs were a giveaway, so I got an army blanket out of the trunk and tucked it around his feet. He opened the Bible in his lap, pulled down the veil, and tipped his head forward on his chest. "How do I look?"

"Keep the wrists covered and you'll pass."

He pulled the coat over his arms so that only his thumbs protruded. Then he lit another cigarette and said, "Let's go."

A cold bluish light was beginning to drift along the deserted streets. I could have believed that Mrs. Voigt was sitting back there in her usual place, dozing beside the window—if it hadn't been for the cigarette smoke boiling out from under the veil.

"Did it ever occur to you," I asked over my shoulder, "that the murderer's reaction might be—like, violent?"

"That's a risk. Any of those women you can't handle?"

"I dunno. If they start coming at me with hatpins—"

"Don't worry about it. Dinwiddie is backing us up."

I glanced in the rear view mirror and saw the unmarked Ford nose out onto Byers a half-block behind me. "When did you arrange that? Last night?"

"I did a lot of things while you were crapped out in that chair. Don't sweat it. Get your riders talking if you can."

"About what?"

"Murder...you know, nothing specific. Just a general rap."

I pulled up outside Gloria's apartment house at six fifty-five. She threw a kiss at the doorman and ran to the car like a high school girl and I thought, *That's unusual.* I watched her carefully as she opened the door.

She glanced in back and said, "Hi, Mrs. Voigt," then without waiting for an answer slid in beside me. She had seven minutes before Helen crowded up the front seat, and she always used it to stretch her legs and smooth out her hose. I usually enjoyed watching the operation out of the corner of my eye but this morning I was thinking, *What's unnatural?* Gloria seemed unusually cheerful—but then everybody's a little bit brighter on Friday. Thursday's a dead day because we're facing two more days on the rock pile, but Friday we get paid and everybody's thinking about the money. . .

Money. What if Mrs. Voigt was one of those solitary misers who one day carries fifteen thousand dollars to the bank in a paper bag? And what if somebody found out?

I wanted to ask Dawson about it but couldn't see any way to communicate.

Gloria asked, "What's the matter with you today, Breeze? You seem kind of morose."

"Morose. *Ha-ha*! What's to be morose about? Friday—payday. I was thinking about all that bread, and how I was gonna spend it all on myself."

She moved closer, until all that separated us was the gear-shift. "We're having a party in my apartment tonight. Could you come?"

"Well, I. . . " My mouth went dry. "I dunno."

"You don't have to tell me now. This evening, okay?"

"Yeah, okay." Another time I'd have bounced my head on the roof with joy, but now I wondered, *Why is she doing this? Is it part of her scheme? Is she trying to distract me?*

Suspicion was a dye which colored everything you looked at. I made a mental note to ask Dawson how detectives managed to live with their wives.

There was a two-minute delay at Helen J's. I saw her in a clinch with her old man in the doorway and I thought, *What can this mean?* When she got to the car I saw a bruise on her cheekbone, but her eyes were shiny and sort of calm and inward-looking, and I decided that things must have gotten interesting in the yellow-trimmed brick house after Dinwiddie's visit.

But what did it have to do with the murder?

Then I thought, *Well if I don't act normal how can the passengers act normal?* So I gave Helen a big smile and said, "Hi there, Mrs. J. and a fine good morning to you."

She slid into the seat and slammed the door. "You act pretty breezy today, Breeze."

She didn't even glance into the back seat; an indication of *something* but I didn't know what.

"Well why shouldn't I be?" I said. "It's payday and we'll all be filthy rich by evening."

"Sure we will—until we do our grocery shopping."

She and Gloria drifted into a woman's type conversation about the price of groceries which lasted until I reached Vera's. Vera had big gray splotches around her eyes and squeezed into the back seat without even looking at Mrs. Voigt. She didn't ask about her hatpin and I thought, *Is that significant?*

As I turned onto Rogers I said, "I didn't find your hatpin, Vera. Sure you didn't walk out with it stuck in you somewhere?"

"Ha-ha," she said in a dull dead voice.

I saw Dawson's head come up behind the veil and make a slight up-and-down movement, and I thought, *Now what does that mean? Is he encouraging me, telling me I'm doing fine? Or does he mean that Vera's the one?*

Talk about a lot of nerves. . .

I was supposed to talk about murder. How did one bring up the subject? "Heard about any good murders lately?"

I heard the words and realized I'd spoken out loud. Gloria asked, "What's a good murder and what's a bad one?"

"Well, I guess if you happened to get killed yourself, it's a bad murder."

"Then what's a good one?" asked Helen.

"From your own point of view, that would be when you get away with it."

Gloria asked, "You thinking about killing somebody, Breeze?"

"Well, it's a thought—if riders don't pay up on time."

In the rear-view mirror I saw Vera turn and say something to Dawson, alias Mrs. Voigt. I said, "She got a sore throat this morning, Vera."

"Oh!" Vera was nervous, I could see that. She laid her hand on the back of the seat and I saw that her fingernails were gnawed off to the quick. She lit a cigarette with trembling hands and I thought, *She's the one.*

Then I stopped to pick up Mrs. Riggs. She stood for a second on the grassy strip between the curb and the sidewalk, squinting into the car with her bright, birdy eyes, and for a second I thought she was going to turn and run. Then she got in chattering about the weather and how she'd have to get her storm windows up this evening, and it struck me that she was an utter and complete phony. Everything she said was like a tinkling bell, all noise and no meaning.

Somewhere around Forty-sixth Street, everybody seemed to run out of words. A curious silence fell in the car. It swelled, billowed, and pulsated until I wanted to scream. By the time I pulled into Hamphill's parking lot I felt like my stomach wouldn't hold food for a week. I sat numb and silent while everybody got out—Helen J. with a friendly see-you-later, Gloria with a warm just-between-the-two-of-us smile, Mrs. Riggs with a bright, birdlike chirrup.

That left only Vera and Dawson (alias the late Mrs. Voigt). I glanced back to see if he might have slipped the cuffs on her while I wasn't looking. But no, she had her handbag on her lap and was nervously rolling a cigarette between nicotine-stained fingers.

"I won't be riding this evening, Breeze."

"Oh, and why not?"

"Quitting. I'm sick of this eight-to-five. I smoke too much, drink too much—the hell with it. I'm heading out...somewhere. Goodbye, Breezy."

She put both hands behind my head and covered my mouth with a soft, warm kiss which might have led to something beautiful if she hadn't been a murderess.

That's what I thought as I watched her walking toward the building. I glanced back as Dawson lifted off his hat and veil. His face wore a sad-whimsical smile.

"When you gonna make the arrest?"

"In about—two minutes." He pulled up the blue dress and started throwing himself around in the seat while he yanked it up over his hips. "Soon as my other car gets here."

I slumped down in the seat, looking at the dice. They showed one and one. Bad luck for Vera.

"*Everybody* acted abnormal. How'd you get onto her?"

"It was Mrs. Voigt's financial affairs that started me in the right direction. She spent a lot of bread to keep her father in that home. So I knew she had another deal going. I run into that a lot. If a girl is young and not bad-looking, I figure she's hooking. But an old bird like Mrs. Voigt—well, it had to be blackmail or theft.

"I called the security man at the plant while you were asleep. He said yes, there'd been a lot of pilfering from the assembly line. Instruments worth three, five thousand dollars disappeared every week. They'd search the production workers and catch one now and then, but it would always start again. Never seemed to fall below a minimum of, say, five thousand a week. That's about five hundred at fence prices.

"This had been going on for eight years—about the same period of time that Mrs. Voigt's dad was in that rest home. She was in a good position, being an inspector—but she had to pass the items to someone who visited the department regularly and wasn't searched. Got it so far?"

I nodded, remembering how Vera used to show up in the mail-room on payday with a sheaf of yellow checks, saying, "Merry Christmas, men." Nobody ever searched her.

I watched the black car pull up in front of the building. Four men got out. Two wore police uniforms. I saw Dinwiddie come out with a plant security guard and signal the car.

Dawson got out and said, "This is it, Breeze. Wanta see us make the collar?"

My stomach felt like a lump of lead as we walked up the steps. It was going to be a memorable day for Hamphill Optics, but I couldn't get with the happy scene because I felt sorry for Vera.

We crowded into the self-service elevator—myself feeling like a midget among giants—and I saw Dawson press the button for the second floor.

"The accounting department's on three," I said.

"So?"

"Vera Thrush works in accounting."

"So?"

"But I thought—"

I broke off as the elevator stopped. I trailed the group down a long, shiny hallway toward a doorway with a sign above it. EMPLOYEES LOUNGE

My head was spinning as we walked into the room. I saw Mrs. Riggs at the counter loading up her cart, doughnut boxes on the bottom, coffee urn on top, wastebasket on the side where she threw the used cups.

She looked up, and I saw the color drain out of her face. "Breezy, who are these men?"

Dawson moved in with his flasher held up in his open hand. "Mrs. Riggs, I'm arresting you for the murder of Edna Voigt."

Her eyes flew wide and her pupils darted from right to left. Her lips trembled as she said, "I don't understand. Mrs. Voigt was in the car this morning." She looked at me. "Tell him, Breeze."

I shook my head.

Dawson said, "That wasn't Mrs. Voigt and you knew it. Because you killed her. You took Vera's hatpin and substituted a lethal weapon. You thought Vera would get the blame. You studied anatomy so you'd know where to stick the needle for the quickest effect. You'd ridden Breezy's route, so you knew exactly where the noise would cover the job. There's only one thing I don't know, and that's why you did it. You wanta tell us that?"

Mrs. Riggs whirled and took a half-step, bumped into Dinwiddie, then just seemed to give up. She dropped into a chair, buried her face in her hands and said, "She wanted out. She said her father's stroke was God's way of telling her to quit stealing."

"But that's no reason to kill her," said Dawson. "Just because she was quitting."

Mrs. Riggs lifted her tear-stained face. "She was going to *tell,* don't you understand? I tried to tell her it wasn't necessary, that she'd be sending me to jail for no reason at all. She said we both needed it for the good of our souls. We'd get our reward in the hereafter. The old fool. That's why I killed her. The . . . *old* . . . *fool*!"

She buried her face in her hands and sobbed.

The cops stood around shuffling their feet and looking embarrassed. I could tell they were sympathetic but it wasn't going to help Mrs. Riggs. Dawson walked over and gave me a light tap on the shoulder.

"Call you later, Breeze. You better go, or you'll be late for work."

I took the stairs to the basement, walked into the mailroom, slipped on my fingerguards and started metering packages. A half-hour later the supervisor called me to the phone and I heard Dawson's voice.

"Well, Breeze, did you have it figured?"

"She did it while we were bouncing through the alley, right?"

"Right, Breeze. Slipped her hand behind Vera and—*zap*!"

My stomach lurched, as I remembered Mrs. Voigt clutching the strap and trying to speak. She'd been dying then—and I'd thought she was trying to complain about my driving.

"It's hard to believe, you know, that she could have done it with so many people around."

"Well, she had a lot of things working for her. Mrs. Voigt was probably asleep, which gave her plenty of time to put the needle exactly where she wanted it. There was Vera Thrush—who I noticed usually rode with her nose practically stuck in your ear. That gave her room to work.

"The fact that Mrs. Voigt usually took a nap caused nobody to be alarmed when she didn't move any more. She was dead when you cut across Sixth Street—and her face would have showed it if Mrs. Riggs hadn't pulled down the headscarf. Like I said, she had it planned.

"Leaving the pin in the hole kept the blood from leaking out onto Mrs. Voigt's clothes. It simply backed up into her veins when the heart muscle stopped, so that her appearance was exactly like that of a heart attack victim. She used the hatpin to direct suspicion toward Vera Thrush—the worst thing she could have done, since the first suspect is always the first one cleared."

"Okay. But I'm missing something. You disguised yourself so that only the murderer would know you weren't Mrs. Voigt. You figured she'd give some sign—"

"That's right."

"But nobody did!"

"Correction—Mrs. Riggs did. Mrs. Voigt didn't smoke—and I had the smell all over my clothes."

He was right. My mom doesn't smoke. I light up in the basement and she's in the upstairs bathroom, she knows it.

"So what'd Mrs. Riggs do?"

"Nothing. That was the tipoff."

"But—she was the only one who didn't smoke. You did the cigarette scene before you ever got in the car—so you must have already known."

"Well, I admit I had strong suspicions. She lived in a better house than she should have. She had the ideal setup, going through the plant twice a day with her coffee cart. She gave Mrs. Voigt a supply of doughnut boxes, see? So Mrs. Voigt would lift one of these expensive instruments off the assembly line, shove it into a doughnut box, and slip it under the cart."

"Mrs. Riggs would go out and buy something, get her package stamped by the security men when she came in, then shift the loot into the stamped package. Probably she bought something every day, so there'd be a couple of dummy packages to cover up the real one. I'm surprised you never wondered why a mild-mannered old doll like Mrs. Riggs would ride with a notorious kamikaze like you."

"Now wait a minute—"

"Traffic records don't lie, boy. She started riding with you when Mrs. Voigt first told her she was going to quit. She didn't plan to kill her then. She just wanted to let her know she was being watched."

I could hardly believe what I was hearing. Two of the sweetest ladies I ever knew.

"Mrs. Riggs always tipped me a dollar when she paid for her rides," I said.

"That should have made you suspicious right there."

"I'll pin that motto on my wall, Lieutenant."

"You do that, Breeze. And if you ever learn to control your driving, we could use you on the force."

He hung up, and I walked back to my postage meter. I couldn't help thinking that only Helen, Gloria, and myself were left. The carpool was, in a word, *fini*.

My mind drifted to the scheme Mrs. Riggs had worked for eight years. The inspector-to-coffee-cart play was out now. But we shipped a lot of instruments through the mailroom, and secretaries were always coming down to pick up packages for their bosses. The security men never touched the cupbearers to the mighty.

I shook my head and started piling packages on the belt. Gloria would never go for it.

Here is a very fine story of family life–but Jane Speed's family is quite different from the one portrayed by Etta Revesz in our opening tale.

JANE SPEED
View from the Inside

I never could see the point to going around with a long face. I like to kid back and forth with people, crack a few jokes, you know—keep things cheerful. Of course, it comes a little harder now—since I lost my family.

There were just the three of them, the mister and the two young ones, Susan and Jamie. That Jamie! He was just a little fella, not quite two years old, when I first come there. Curly hair, big brown eyes, sweetest child you ever want to see.

I never met the missus. She passed away before they moved to Lakeside. I think that's why there was always a touch of sadness in the mister's eyes, even when he laughed. Logan was his name— Charles Logan.

He'd hired an older woman first off, but she had kids of her own and didn't like to live in.

Well, that was sure no problem in my case. I remember my dad, just the year before he went, he come right out and told me—he was always a blunt-spoken man—"Blanche," he says, "God didn't give you the looks to get a husband, so you better hustle around and make yourself useful if you want to get along in the world." And that's what I did—started in working when I was sixteen. I was big for my age, though, and good and strong, so I always did all right. Day work it was, mostly for the summer people. Lakeside was kind of a vacation town and summer was our busy time.

Anyways, like I said, with nobody but myself to worry about, why, I was just tickled pink to get a steady place. I pitched right in and kept that house spick-and-span and, while I never learned to cook fancy, I always put three good square meals on the table. And there was never a day those children didn't have fresh-washed clothes to wear.

I still have a picture the mister took of Susan the day she started school, in a red-and-white pinafore and red bows on her pigtails, looking proud and excited and just a little bit scared. And then a couple of years later there's Jamie all scrubbed and clean and hanging onto his big sister's hand for dear life. Oh, they were full of mischief, those two, but they were good kids. Good as gold. And no wonder, with a daddy like they had.

He was an educated man, the mister was. Had more books than I'd ever seen before in one house. Hardly anything he didn't know—all kinds of funny little stuff. Like when he first heard my name, he just smiles that nice smile of his and says, "Well, how do you do, Miss White White." My last name's White, you see, and he right away explained how Blanche means white, too. I got the biggest kick out of that. Made my old name seem something special.

I often wondered how he happened to settle in Lakeside. Oh, it was a nice enough town, 'specially in summer. But I don't think there's many people ever heard of it outside the ones that come back year after year. It wasn't like one of those famous resorts, you know. Anyways, I asked him about it once and he said he'd come there a few times years ago, when he was a boy. Come up on vacation with his folks. Then, after his missus went, he was trying to think of somewhere to get the young ones away to and he remembered Lakeside. And it suited him so well he just stayed on.

He'd been some kind of a writer. Still was, more or less. Many's the time during the off-season I'd hear him pecking away at his typewriter till all hours. Now and then he sold something, and when he got the check he'd bring home a treat for supper and I'd bake a cake and we'd have a real celebration.

He made his living mainly in the summer, though, like most people around there. He'd got himself a launch and he took parties out on tours of the little islands on our lake. Did real well at it, too. He kept his boat trim and he was a nice-looking man and had a pleasant way with him. And he'd read up on the local history so he could tell folks a lot of interesting things—how it was in Indian times and all.

And, of course, it didn't hurt a bit that the ladies took a particular shine to him. Seems there was always a lot more women than men around there in the summer. Even the married ones, a good part of the season their husbands only come out on weekends. Anyways, the mister would always joke back and forth with them, young and old alike, and they just ate it up.

Mel Jarvis used to kid him about that. Mel owned the hardware store in town. "Charlie Logan here," he used to say, "is one of our great natural attractions."

The summer people would start to come in around June, and we were always mighty glad to see them. Well, for one thing, they were our bread and butter. But most of them were pretty good folks, you know. That Mrs. Corbett now, a widow lady, she owned the place just next up the way from ours, and she was always nice and friendly as could be.

Still, when the last of them left after Labor Day, that was kind of nice, too. Like when you have your house to yourself again after company goes. And there was plenty else to do. You had to get the kids ready to start school and pretty soon there was Thanksgiving to think about and then Christmas and, well, before you knew it, it was time to get things spruced up again for the summer crowd.

So that's the way the years went. There was a pleasant sort of pattern to them, if you know what I mean. You could just about count on certain things happening at certain times. Until that last summer.

There was no sign it was going to be any different. Oh, Susan was going on seventeen by then—had just one more year of high school—and pretty as a picture, too. So, of course, Jamie was forever teasing her about her boyfriends. But outside of that things seemed pretty much as usual.

You remember I mentioned that nice Mrs. Corbett who owned the house next over? You could see her place, with the little wood pier out back, right from our kitchen window. Well, come June I'd always keep an eye out, and as soon as I saw the house was open I'd fix a basket of vegetables from our garden and take it over to her.

Anyways, when I saw the windows up one morning I figured she must have come in the night before, and I took my basket right out to the garden. Just shows what habit can do to a person. I had that basket half filled before I remembered she'd said she probably wouldn't be coming up this year. Her nephew and his family had moved out west and she thought she'd spend the summer with them and maybe just rent out her place in Lakeside. So I went back indoors feeling kind of let down.

I kept glancing across the way from time to time, though, because I'd got to thinking maybe she'd changed her mind and it was her over there after all. So it was a real surprise when suddenly this other woman come out back. Believe me, she was about as different from Mrs. Corbett as could be.

Mrs. Corbett was a lady of middle years, you see, and a bit on the portly side. This one looked about half her age. She sure wasn't much more than half her size. Slim and elegant, like one of those models you see in the magazines, big sunglasses and all. She was wearing tight-fitting pants and a skimpy top—looked real good in them, too—and those funny shoes with soles about four inches thick. They always put me in mind of a person with two clubfeet, but they were the big fashion then and all the girls wanted them. Susan had been pestering the mister for a pair, but so far he'd held out—said she was too likely to break an ankle or even her neck trying to walk in them.

Well, this young lady stood there for a while looking around. Looked over towards our place so long I wondered what she was staring at. Then I saw Susan out back taking her bathing suit off the line. She must've come around by the side of the house.

"Hey," I called out to her, "I thought you'd already left."

"Oh, boy, so did I!" She laughed and come inside all breathless. "But there's been a change of plans. Betsy Jarvis' dad said we could take their outboard over to one of the islands for a picnic. So I had to come back and get my suit."

"You'll be home for supper, though, won't you?"

"Oh, sure. You know her dad—he'd have a fit if we kept that boat out a minute past five-thirty. I've got to run, Richie and Bob are waiting for me. But, oh Blanche, guess *what*? Richie's getting his own *sailboat* next week!" She gave me a little squeeze and then she was off like a shot.

By that time, of course, the lady next door had gone back inside, and I had so much to do I forgot all about her. Jamie'd gone out on the launch with his dad that day, and I wanted to give the house a good cleaning while I had them all out from underfoot.

It must've been after three o'clock—I'd finished the cleaning and just put a pot roast on for supper—when I heard this clop-clop-clop sound out front. Well, you can believe it or not, but the first thing I thought of was that lady and her cloppy shoes. And, sure enough, when I peeked through the curtains there she was coming along the brick walk. What's more, she turned right into our place. So I quick run a comb through my hair and went to the door.

"Good afternoon," she said, all smiles. "I'm Claire Chalmers. I've taken the house next door for the summer."

"I know. I saw you over there on the pier this morning. Nice to meet you."

And she just laughed like I'd said something comical. "I guess I'd better watch my step with you on the lookout. Tell me, this *is* where the Logan family lives, isn't it?"

"Why, yes, it is." Her knowing the name kind of took me by surprise. "But there's none of them here right now."

"I see. Well, may I come in then and wait?"

"If you like," I said, which was about all I could say since she was already inside. "Of course, if it's the kids you want to see, you'll have quite a wait. Susan's gone on a picnic and Jamie, once he gets off the launch, usually plays baseball till suppertime. The mister should be back around four, though."

"That will do very well for now," she said, taking off her dark glasses and looking around. " 'The mister' and I have a lot of reminiscing to do."

That slim figure of hers had fooled me. Made her look taller at a distance, for one thing. And up close now I could see she wasn't as young as I'd thought either. Oh, she was good-looking all right, and her makeup was put on real nice. But underneath it I bet she wasn't all that far from Mrs. Corbett's age.

And it was the funniest thing. Small as she was, she had a way about her that didn't allow for any back talk. She was a lady used to being in charge, you could see that. Walked right into the living room and sat herself down in the best chair like it had been put there special for her.

"And you," she said, "must be Blanche."

Well, now, that *really* surprised me. She might know the mister and the kids from somewhere else, but she'd never laid eyes on me before.

It must've showed in my face because she laughed again and said, "Mrs. Corbett told me a lot about this household."

"Oh, so you're a friend of Mrs. Corbett's."

"Well, I don't think I can quite claim that. Mrs. Corbett and I met for the first time only recently. And, frankly, I doubt that our paths ever would have crossed if we hadn't both happened to contribute rather generously to the same charity. There was a party, you see, in honor of the major contributors. I think it was meant to be our reward, but it turned out to be more like a punishment—too many people, too few chairs, execrable food.

"At any rate, Mrs. Corbett and I found ourselves pinned into a corner at this dreary affair, so we really hadn't much choice but to introduce ourselves and try to make conversation. It wasn't easy, because we didn't seem to have much in common. But I must say Mrs. Corbett did her best, dear soul. She rattled away about all sorts of things—her relatives, some little out-of-the-way place she spent her summers, the nice neighbors she had there, and so on. I'm afraid I wasn't really paying very strict attention, until suddenly I caught the name of Charlie Logan. And when she told me that he did indeed have a daughter named Susan and a son named Jamie, I was certain it was the same Charlie Logan I knew. Well, to make a long story short, I discovered that Mrs. Corbett wasn't planning to use her house this summer and she had been thinking of renting it, so we made a deal right on the spot—and here I am."

All I could think of to say was, "Well! I guess it was a lucky thing you went to that party after all."

"Oh, my dear girl! It was the greatest piece of luck I've had in years. Worth every dull moment, believe me."

I just didn't know what to make of her. She talked so much and smiled so much—with her mouth, anyways, I wasn't so sure about her eyes. And as far as I knew, she'd never set foot in that house before, yet there she sat looking right at home while I perched on the edge of a chair feeling like I was the stranger.

I guess I'd been staring at her because she said, "Is something wrong?"

"Oh, no, I—I was just admiring your earrings." Which wasn't altogether a fib. They really caught your eye—little silvery dangles that moved in a pretty way when she talked.

"They are rather nice, aren't they? They're handcrafted—no two pairs alike, you know. In fact"—she pulled them off and passed them over to me—"even these two are not quite identical."

It was true. Oh, they were meant to be a pair, all right. But up close you could see little differences in them, and they looked expensive. I handed them back to her and she clipped them on again.

"Could I get you a glass of lemonade?" I asked her. "Or maybe some iced tea?"

"No, no, don't bother. But if I could have an ashtray—"

"Oh, sure thing." And I quick fetched her one, just glad of something to do.

She lit up a cigarette and settled back in her chair. "How long have you been with the Logans, Blanche?"

"Well, let me see . . . it was early spring when I come to them, so it's going on twelve years now."

"Twelve years!" For a minute there even her mouth stopped smiling. "That's a long time. You must know them very well."

"Oh, yes, ma'am. Why, I guess there's hardly anything I don't know about the family."

She puffed away at her cigarette a couple of seconds more, then she stubbed it out. "Well, there's evidently one thing you don't know about them." Then she looked straight at me and said, "I am Susan's and Jamie's grandmother."

Well, it hit me like a ton of bricks. I just couldn't take it in. The mister had said his own folks passed away some years back and I'd always figured it was the same on the missus' side. It was funny he'd never mentioned a word about this one. But I knew he must've had a good reason.

Then, before I could get my thoughts collected, I heard his laugh outside. I remember to this day just how it sounded—I guess because I never heard him laugh much after that. He was talking to Joe Thompson from the grocery. They sometimes walked up this way together. Anyways, I heard them say goodbye and I just got up and made a beeline for the front door. I had it in mind that I ought to try to warn him somehow.

But I wasn't quick enough. He come up the porch steps and right in the screen door and I'd no more than opened my mouth when she beat me to it.

"You have company, Charles," she called out behind me.

The mister stopped dead still. Then he looked over my shoulder and saw her sitting there, and a little muscle in his jaw kind of jumped. He took a deep breath and said, "Hello, Claire," and then went on into the living room and sat down.

"You're looking very well," she said, lighting another cigarette.

"And you."

It was funny. They spoke so polite and careful and all, yet they put me in mind of a couple of dogs circling each other for a fight.

I was still standing there beyond the archway, afraid to stay and afraid to go, if you know what I mean. Then she settled it. She turned to me and said, "I'm sure you must have something to do in the kitchen, Blanche."

So I went into the kitchen and closed the door. But that catch never did work right and the door come back open an inch or so. And I'll be honest with you, I didn't bother to ease it shut. I never before or since listened at a door, I swear. But I did that day and I did it on purpose. There was something in the air in that room made me uneasy, and I wanted to know what it was. I just took a quick look at my pot roast and then I tiptoed back to the door.

"Well, Charles," she started right in. "So this is where you've been hiding away. A perfect spot. Lakeside. Even the name is a dime a dozen. And from what I've seen of it, it's hardly the sort of place anyone I know would ever hear of, much less visit. That, of course, is what you counted on, isn't it?"

"Yes." His voice was so much quieter than hers, kind of tired-sounding, that I had to listen sharp to catch his words. "And it worked—for quite a while. May I ask how you did happen to find us?"

"By a fluke, pure and simple. After all these years fate sat me down next to a plump little party named Corbett who went on at great length about her nice summer neighbor, Charlie Logan. I've taken her house for the season."

"I see. Well, I suppose something like that was bound to happen sooner or later."

"It's so ironic, really. When I think of all the time and effort I spent trying to find you. . . . I wanted to go right to the police, you know, but my lawyer talked me out of that. He said it just wasn't a police matter. Technically, you had committed no crime. You couldn't be charged with kidnapping. They were your own children, and those grubby little neighbors of yours saw you as quite the devoted father. And you hardly qualified as a missing person since you'd obviously left of your own volition—settled your affairs and just moved out bag and baggage. So, instead, I hired a private investigator."

"I rather thought you would."

"For all the good it did. Oh, he tried, I'll say that for him. Put several men on it. Questioned all your friends and associates, everyone who'd ever spoken two words with you and Ann. But he couldn't shake a single one of them. They all loyally maintained they had no idea where you'd gone."

"They hadn't. They still don't."

"My God, how could you cut all ties like that?"

He took almost a minute before he answered her. "I hated to do it. But I felt I couldn't take that chance, put that burden on them. None of them would have given me away intentionally, but all it would take was one slip of the tongue. And if we'd kept in touch—well, I wouldn't have put it past you to find a way to check their mail. Maybe you even had some of them followed."

"I did, for many months. Oh, I ran up quite a bill."

"Well, there you are then."

"It's incredible. Just when you were beginning to establish yourself. Don't you write at all any more?"

"A little. But not under my own name. I knew you'd watch for that."

"Why, then you had to start all over again!"

"That's true."

"You fool! You unmitigated, stubborn, wicked fool! After the fuss you made about your precious little 'career,' after what Ann had to put up with so you could pursue it, you simply walked away from it.

And all that just to spite me. It wasn't enough that you tried to turn my daughter against me. Once she was gone, you had to rob me of my grandchildren. Do you realize I haven't had even a glimpse of them for twelve years? *Twelve years,* Charles! How could you do such a thing to me?"

"Claire, believe me, I didn't do what I did *to* you or anyone. For better or worse, I did it *for* the children. It was the only way I could see to give them a chance to be themselves, to grow up without being hounded and managed and *owned*—the way poor Ann was."

" 'Poor Ann,' is it? Well, let me tell you something, Charles Logan. There was nothing poor about my daughter's life while *I* was in charge. I saw to it that she always had the best of everything."

"So you did, Claire, whether she wanted it or not. And you never let up, even after we were married."

"Well, what was wrong with that? I had plenty and she was my only child. Why shouldn't I see that she had decent clothes and a proper vacation once in a while? And I could have done much more—for both of you—if only you hadn't been so mired in foolish pride. You know the trouble with you, Charles? You just never learned to accept gifts gracefully. Quite a few people have that failing."

"Possibly. But the trouble with your largess, Claire, was that it always had strings attached. It was like an investment that gave you the controlling shares in the life of whoever received it."

She laughed a short, nasty little laugh. "What a convenient theory to justify your stubbornness. And, oh, how stubborn you were. If only you could at least have let me get you and Ann out of that squalid little apartment—"

He cut right in. "It wasn't 'squalid.' It wasn't even all that little. And Ann didn't want to leave it any more than I did. As a matter of fact, she told me once that she'd been happier there than anywhere else she'd ever lived."

"Indeed." She said it in a very ladylike way, but you could tell he'd really got to her. "Well. If she was so happy there—with you—then why did she kill herself?"

I could hardly believe I'd heard her right. And it was so deathly still in there for so long I was almost afraid to breathe.

"Well, Charles? Have you got a 'theory' about that?"

"I think, Claire, you and I"—he spoke so slow and heavy, like every word come hard—"between the two of us we had Ann on a rack. She was pulled in opposite directions so—mercilessly—that she was finally torn apart. I just, I just couldn't let that happen to Susan and Jamie, too."

"I see. And so you solved the problem by pulling them entirely in *your* direction. Really, Charles! How you can delude yourself that you did such a selfish thing 'for the children.' It was all very well for you. You made a conscious decision, however foolish, to hole up in this godforsaken little backwater. But what right did you have to impose such limitations on Susan and Jamie, to deny them all the advantages I could have provided?"

"They've been happy here. I don't think they've wanted for anything important."

"Oh, well—children. They can be happy anywhere, especially if they don't know any better. But did you *really* think this little summer kind of existence you have here could go on forever? I saw Susan out in your back yard this morning and, believe me, Charles, she is no longer a child."

"I know that. She'll be ready for college next year."

"Well, thank heaven I found you in time to see that she goes to a decent college at least."

Right about then I went over to the stove to turn off the fire under the pot roast, and it was just a lucky thing I did. I'd have hated to have the kids catch me listening at the door.

They came tiptoeing in the back way and Susan kind of whispered, "Who *is* that in there with daddy?"

"I better leave that for him to tell you," I said.

"Aw, Blanche, come on," Jamie coaxed. "Who is it?"

"Never you mind now. You just help your sister get the table set. I'm running a little late here. And put on an extra place, will you? I think she may be staying to supper."

Well, they got out the plates and silverware and took them into the dining room. But they got to teasing each other and making such a clatter I was afraid they'd wind up breaking something, so I went in to put a stop to it. And right at that moment *she* come around by the hall with the mister following behind.

"Well," she said, earrings twinkling and that smile going full blaze, "Susan and Jamie. How wonderful to see you at last."

The kids just looked kind of blank—you could hardly blame them—and she turned to the mister and said, "I think you'd better introduce us, Charles."

So he come right out with it—wasn't much else he could do. "This is your grandmother," he said. "We lost touch with each other for a long time, but now she's come to visit us."

"You just call me Claire," she chimed in real quick. "It's so much shorter." And maybe it was better, too. She sure didn't look like anyone you'd call Grandma.

Anyways, I'd been right about supper. She stayed. As a matter of fact, she had supper with us just about every night for the next month or so. Never ate much, though. You could see why she stayed so thin.

It took Jamie a while to warm up to her, but Susan was just bowled over right from the start. Spent most of the time next door and all she could talk about was Claire this and Claire that. Her friend Richie got his sailboat, but Susan hardly took any notice. I guess it didn't seem like much after all those yachts her grandmother kept telling us about.

And every few days the two of them would drive off in that long shiny car of hers—go to some town nearby that had bigger stores and come back with all kinds of new clothes and stuff. You can bet it wasn't long before Susan had a pair of those cloppy shoes she'd been wanting. And, "Oh, guess *what?*" she says one day, "Claire's going to take me to *Europe* next summer. It'll be my graduation present."

It was like seeing Susan get sucked into a whirlwind, and just about as easy to stop. Oh, the mister did try once. One night at supper near the end of July this Claire announced she's going back to the city for a week.

"You see, Charles," she said, "it just occurred to me what an advantage it would be for Susan if she could have at least one year at Ann's old preparatory school. Of course, the registration for the fall semester closed long ago. But after all, her mother was a graduate and I've been *very generous* to that school over the years. I'm quite sure I can persuade them to make room for Susan."

"No." The mister laid down his knife and fork. "I won't let you do that, Claire. Susan should finish at Lakeside High. She's done well there and that's where her friends are."

"But, Charles, she'll soon be making a whole new set of friends at college. And she'll feel so much more—comfortable—with them if she goes from a good private school. Believe me, I know what I'm talking about. Some things may change, but that never does."

The mister got that grim set to his jaw and said, "What do *you* want, Susan?"

Susan looked from one to the other, and you could see she hated to take sides. I couldn't help thinking of what the mister had said about her mother being caught between the two of them. I guess he remembered that, too, because he tried to give her a little smile and said, "It's all right, honey. Whatever you want to do will be fine with me."

"Well"—she hesitated a minute—"it would be sort of nice to go to the same school my mother did."

So that was that. The next morning the grandmother come out all dressed for the city. "I don't think this will take me more than a week," she said. "I plan to be back sometime after noon next Saturday." And off she drove in her long shiny car.

Well, sir, once she was gone it was like we'd all woke up from some kind of spell. In no time at all there was Susan hanging around again with Betsy and Richie and Bob, and Jamie was down at the sandlot playing baseball again, and suppertime was so nice and easy with just the four of us. That whole week, I swear, you could almost believe she'd never been there at all.

But she had, of course, and she was coming back. And before you know it, there it was Friday already. Well, I just wanted to make the most of that last day without her—cook something special, you know. I'd got a nice ham because they were all so fond of it. And as soon as everybody'd left—Susan was spending the day sailing with Richie and the others, and Jamie was going out on the launch with his dad—I got busy and baked a cake. Took me a while with icing and all, so I just gave the house a lick and a promise.

Then about a quarter to three I put my ham in the oven and hiked on down to Thompson's to get some fresh sweet corn. I kidded around there with Joe for a couple of minutes and then I stopped in at the hardware store and bought myself a new squeeze mop. The metal clamp on my old one hadn't been working right for some time.

I don't think I was gone more than half an hour. But when I turned in the walk at our place I looked over next door and there was that long shiny car parked at Mrs. Corbett's. The sight of it just took the heart right out of me. Why did she have to come back early and cheat us out of this last day?

Well, I sure didn't want to see her any sooner than I had to, so I ducked inside. From the frying pan into the fire, you might say. Because when I went out to the kitchen there she was, still in her city clothes, those earrings jiggling away, fussing around over by the sink.

I can't tell you what a shock that was, seeing her making herself right at home in my kitchen. I just stood there like a dummy, my groceries in one hand and my mop in the other. Must've looked a fool.

"Oh, *there* you are, Blanche. I finished up all my business a day early, so surprise! Here I am back." She gave me the big smile and went right on with whatever she was doing while she talked. "Really,

I had such wonderful luck. There was no trouble at all about Susan. *And*—I have good news for Jamie, too. A friend of mine introduced me to the headmaster of an excellent prep school and—well, you'll hear all about it later."

I set the groceries down on the table. "May I ask what you're doing over there?" I finally managed to say.

"Well, some of these things were packed in dry ice, so I thought I'd better get them into the refrigerator before I changed my clothes. They're some goodies I brought for our dinner. You see? We can make a lovely salad with this cold lobster. And I brought a box of those heavenly pastries I was telling Susan about, and some—"

"I already got supper started," I told her.

"Oh, you mean in the oven. Well, I turned that off. Really, Blanche, it's much too warm a day to have the oven going. You just save whatever you have in there for another time." And she turned back to unwrapping her stuff, still chattering away, but I wasn't even listening any more.

I thought of all the trouble she'd caused, and more to come, and—I don't know—something just all of a sudden come over me. I gripped the handle of that new mop with both hands and I walked right over and whacked her—so hard one of those darned earrings flew off.

It really caught her unawares. She gave a little gasp and grabbed hold of the sink to steady herself. Oh, I was done for, I knew that. The minute she got her wind back she was going to turn around and order me out of that house forever. So I don't know why I should've felt like laughing, but I did. I couldn't help it, she looked so funny standing there.

Only, then, instead of turning around, she sagged sideways against the drainboard and just sort of slipped on down to the floor. I could see then there was blood on the side of her head and, well, I sure wasn't laughing any more. The metal clamp on that mop had mean corners and I'd hit her a pretty good wallop.

I knew I ought to try to do something for her, but I just couldn't seem to move. I couldn't take my eyes off her face. She had such a peculiar look—she was staring at me and yet she wasn't. Then after a while it come to me that she'd never once blinked. I guess that's when I knew she was gone.

Well, the mister was so nice, he did everything he could—hired me a lawyer and all. But I couldn't deny I'd done a terrible thing and I knew I had to pay for it.

And it's not so bad here, you know. I never was afraid of hard work and, like I said, I'm always cracking little jokes with everybody, so I get along fine.

Now and then, though, at night, I lie awake a long time and I get to thinking back. And I wish—oh, I just wish in the worst way that it was summer again.

Lawrence Block is turning up more frequently in the mystery magazines these days. Often his short, sharp tales remind one of Roald Dahl or John Collier.

LAWRENCE BLOCK
A Pair of Recycled Jeans

On what a less resourceful writer might safely describe as a fateful day, young Robert Tillinghast approached the proprietor of a shop called The Last Resort. "Actually," he confided, "I don't think I can buy anything today, but there's a question I'd like to ask. It's been on my mind for the longest time. I was looking at those recycled jeans over by the far wall."

"I'll be getting another hundred pair in Monday afternoon," the proprietor said.

"A hundred pair," Robert marveled. "That's certainly quite a lot."

"It's the minimum order."

"Is that a fact? And they'll all be the same quality and condition as these you have now?"

"Absolutely. Of course, I won't know what sizes I'll be getting."

"I guess that's just a matter of chance."

"It is. But they'll all be first-quality name brands, and they'll all be in good condition, broken in but not broken to bits. That's a sort of an expression I made up to describe them."

"I like it," said Robert, not too sincerely. "You know, there's a question that's been nagging at my mind for the longest time. You get six dollars a pair for the recycled jeans, and it probably wouldn't be out of line to guess that they cost you about half that amount." The proprietor agreed that it wouldn't be far out of line to make that estimate. "Well, that's the whole thing," Robert said. "You notice the jeans I'm wearing?"

The proprietor glanced at them. They were nothing remarkable, a pair of oft-washed Lee Riders that were just beginning to go thin at the knees. "Very nice," the man said. "I'd get six dollars for them without a whole lot of trouble."

"But I wouldn't want to sell them."

"Of course not. Why should you? They're just getting to the comfortable stage."

"Exactly!" Robert grew intense, and his eyes bulged slightly. "Exactly," he repeated. "The recycled jeans I see in all the shops are just at the point where they're breaking in right. They're never really worn out. Unless you only put the better pairs on display?"

"No, they're all like that."

"That's what everybody says." Robert had had much the same conversation before in the course of his travels. "All top quality, all in excellent condition, and all in the same stage of wear."

"So?"

"So," Robert said in triumph, "who throws them out?"

"Oh."

"The company that sells them. Where do they get them from?"

"You know," the proprietor said, "it's funny you should ask. The same question's occurred to me. People buy these jeans because this is the way they want 'em. But who in the world *sells* them?"

"That's what I'd like to know. Not that it would do me any good to have the answer, but the question preys on my mind."

"Right," the proprietor said. "I could understand about children's jeans, that kids would outgrow them, but what about the adult sizes?"

"I'll be wearing jeans as long as I live," Robert said recklessly. "I'll never get too old for jeans."

The proprietor seemed not to have heard. "Maybe it's different out in the farm country," he said. "I buy these jeans from a firm in Rockford, Illinois—"

"I've heard of the firm," Robert said. "They seem to be the only people supplying recycled jeans."

"Only one I know of too. Maybe things are different in their area. Maybe out there people like brand-new jeans and once they break them in they think of them as worn out."

"I guess that's possible."

"It's the only explanation I can think of." He shook his head. "Funny you should ask a question that I've asked myself so many times and never put into words."

"That Rockford firm," Robert said. "That's another thing I don't understand. Why would they develop a sideline business like recycled jeans?"

"Well, you never know about that," the man said. "Diversification is the keynote of American business these days. Take me. I started out selling flowerpots, and now I sell flowerpots and guitar strings and recapped tires and recycled jeans. There are people who would call that an unusual combination."

"I suppose there are," said Robert.

An obsession of the sort that gripped Robert is a curious thing. After a certain amount of time either it is metamorphosed into neurosis or it is tamed, surfacing periodically as a vehicle for casual conversation. Young Robert Tillinghast, neurotic enough in other respects, suppressed his curiosity on the subject of recycled jeans and only raised the question at times when it seemed particularly apropos.

And it did seem apropos often enough. Robert was touring the country, depending for his locomotion upon the kindness of passing motorists. As charitable as his hosts were, they were apt to insist upon a quid pro quo of conversation, and Robert had learned to converse extemporaneously upon a variety of subjects. One of these, of course, was that of recycled blue jeans, the subject close at once to his heart and his skin. His own jeans often served as the lead-in to this line of conversation, being either funky and mellow or altogether disreputable, depending upon one's point of view, which in turn largely depended upon one's age.

One day in West Virginia, on that stretch of Interstate 79 leading from Morgantown to Charleston, Robert thumbed a ride with a man who, though not many years older than himself, drove a late-model Cadillac. Robert, his backpack in the back seat and his body in the front, could not have been more pleased. He had come to feel that hitching a ride in an expensive car endowed one with all the privileges of ownership without the nuisance of making the payments.

But as the car cruised southward, he noticed that the driver was glancing repeatedly at Robert's legs. Covert glances at that, sidelong and meaningful. Robert sighed inwardly. This, too, was part of the game, and had ceased to shock him. But he had been looking forward to riding in this car and now he would have to get out.

The driver said, "Just admiring your jeans."

"I guess they're just beginning to break in," Robert said, relaxing now. "I've had them a while."

"Well, they look just right now. Got a lot of wear left in them."

"I guess they'll last for years," Robert said. "With the proper treatment. You know, that brings up something I've been wondering about for a long time." And he went into his routine, which had become rather a set piece by this time, ending with the question that had plagued him from the start. "So where on earth does that

Rockford company get all these jeans? Who provides them?"

"Funny you should ask," the young man said. "I don't suppose you noticed my license plates before you got in?" Robert admitted he hadn't. "Few people do," the young man said. "*Land of Lincoln* is the slogan on them, and they're from Illinois. And I'm from Rockford. As a matter of fact, I'm with that very company."

"But that's incredible! For the longest time I've wanted to know the answers to my questions, and now at long last—" He broke off. "Why are we leaving the Interstate?"

"By-pass some traffic approaching Charleston. There's construction ahead and it can be a real bottleneck. Yes, I'm with the company."

"In Sales, I suppose? Servicing accounts? You certainly have enough accounts. It seems every store in the country buys recycled jeans from you people."

"Our distribution *is* rather good," the young man said, "and our sales force does a good job. But I'm in Aquisitions myself. I go out and round up the jeans. Then back in Rockford they're washed to clean and sterilize them, patched if they need it, and—"

"You're actually in Acquisitions?"

"That's a fact."

"Well, this *is* my lucky day!" Robert exclaimed. "You're just the man to give me all the answers. Where do you get the jeans? Who sells them to you? What do you pay for them? What sort of person sells perfectly good jeans?"

"That's a whole lot of questions at once."

Robert laughed, happy with himself, his host, and the world. "I just don't know where to start. Say, this by-pass is a small road, isn't it? I guess not many people know about it and that's why there's no other traffic on it. Poor saps'll all get tangled in traffic going into Charleston."

"We'll miss all that."

"That's good luck. Let's see, where can I begin? All right, here's the big question and I've always been puzzled by this one. What's a company like yours doing in the recycled jeans business?"

"Well," said the young man, "diversification is the keynote of American business these days."

"But a company like yours," Robert said. "Rockford Dog Food, Inc. How did you ever think to get into the business in the first place?"

"Funny you should ask," said the young man, braking the car smoothly to a stop.

We welcome Joyce Porter's wonderfully irritating Inspector Dover to these pages. Here's a clever tale of pure detection that might be compared to Harry Kemelman's "The Nine Mile Walk"–but there's a decided difference!

JOYCE PORTER
Dover Does Some Spadework

"You're supposed to be a detective, aren't you?"

Chief Inspector Dover—unwashed, unshaved, still in his dressing gown, and more than half asleep—stared sullenly across the kitchen table at his wife. The great man was not feeling at his best. "I'm on leave," he pointed out resentfully as he spooned a half pound of sugar into his tea. "Supposed to be having a rest."

"All right for some," muttered Mrs. Dover crossly. She slapped down a plate of bacon, eggs, tomatoes, mushrooms, sausages, and fried bread in front of her husband.

Dover had been sitting with his knife and fork at the ready but now he poked disconsolately among the goodies. "No kidney?"

"You want it with jam on, you do!"

Dover responded to this disappointment with a grunt. "Besides," he said a few minutes later when he was wiping the egg yolk off his chin with the back of his hand, "I'm Murder Squad. You can't expect me to go messing around with piddling things like somebody nicking your garden tools. Ring up the local coppers if something's gone missing."

"And a fine fool I'd look, wouldn't I?" Mrs. Dover sat down and poured out her own cup of tea. "My husband a Chief Inspector at Scotland Yard and me phoning the local police station for help! And I told you, Wilf—nobody stole anything. They just broke in."

Dover considerately remembered his wife's oft-reiterated injunctions and licked the knife clean of marmalade before sticking it in the butter. Well, it didn't do to push the old girl too far. "It's like asking Picasso to decorate the back bedroom for you, you see," he explained amid a spray of toast crumbs. "And if there's nothing actually missing. . . "

"Two can play at that game, you know." Mrs. Dover sounded ominously like a woman who had got all four aces up her sleeve.

A frown of sudden anxiety creased Dover's hitherto untroubled brow. "Wadderyemean?" he asked nervously.

Mrs. Dover ignored the question. "Have another piece of toast," she invited with grim humor. "Help yourself. Enjoy your breakfast. Make the most of it while it's here!"

"Oh, 'strewth!" groaned Dover, knowing only too well what was coming.

Mrs. Dover patted her hair into place. "If you can't do a bit of something for me, Wilf," she said with feigned reasonableness, "you may wake up one of these fine days and find that I can't do something for you. Like standing over a hot stove all the live-long day!"

"But that's your job," protested Dover. "Wives are supposed to look after their husbands' comfort. It's the law!"

But Mrs. Dover wasn't listening. "I wasn't brought up just to be your head cook and bottle washer," she claimed dreamily. "My parents had better things in mind for me than finishing up as your unpaid skivvy. Why"—she soared off misty-eyed into the realms of pure fantasy—"I might have been a concert pianist or a lady judge or a TV personality, if I hadn't met you."

"And pigs might fly," snickered Dover, being careful to restrict his comment to the range of his own ears. "Well," he said aloud and making the promise, perhaps a mite too glibly, "I'll have a look at the shed for you. Later on. When the sun's had a chance to take the chill off things a bit."

Mrs. Dover was too battle-scarred a veteran of matrimony to be caught like that. "Suit yourself, Wilf," she said equably. "Your lunch will be ready and waiting for you . . . just as soon as you come up with the answer." She began to gather up the dirty crockery. "And not before," she added thoughtfully.

"So that," snarled Dover, "is what I'm doing here! Since you were so gracious as to ask!"

Detective Sergeant MacGregor could only stand and stare. Almost any comment, he felt, was going to be open to misinterpretation.

But even a tactful silence gave no guarantee of immunity from Dover's quivering indignation. "Cat got your tongue now, laddie?"

MacGregor suppressed a sigh. He didn't usually come calling when his boss was on leave, having more than enough of the old fool when they were at work in the normal way; but he needed a counter-signature for his Expenses Claim Form and, since most of the money had been dispensed on Dover's behalf, it was only fitting that his uncouth signature should grace the document.

So when, at eleven o'clock, the sergeant had called at the Dovers' semi-detached suburban residence, he had been quite prepared to find that His Nibs was still, on a cold and foggy December morning, abed. What he had not expected was Mrs. Dover's tight-lipped announcement that her better half was to be found in the tool shed at the bottom of the garden. It had seemed a highly improbable state of affairs but, as MacGregor was now seeing for himself, it was true.

Dover, arrayed as for a funeral in his shabby black overcoat and his even shabbier bowler hat, was sunk dejectedly in a deck chair. He glared up at his sergeant. "Well, don't just stand there like a stick of Blackpool rock, you moron! Come inside and shut that damn door!"

Even with the door closed the tool shed was hardly a cozy spot, and MacGregor was gratified to notice that Dover's nose was already turning quite a pronounced blue. "Er—what exactly is the trouble, sir? Mrs. Dover wasn't actually very clear about why you were out here."

Dover cut the cackle with the ruthlessness of desperation. "She's got this idea in her stupid head that somebody bust their way into this shed during the past week and borrowed a spade. Silly cow!"

"I see," said MacGregor politely.

"I doubt it," sniffed Dover. "Seeing as how you're not married."

"A stolen spade, eh, sir?" For the first time MacGregor turned his attention to his surroundings and discovered to his amazement that he was standing in the middle of a vast collection of implements which, if hygiene and perfect order were anything to go by, wouldn't have looked out of place in a hospital operating theater. As MacGregor's gaze ran along the serried ranks of apparently brand-new tools he wondered what on earth they were used for. Surely not for the care and maintenance of that miserable strip of barren, cat-infested clay which lay outside between the shed and the house? Good heavens, they must have bought the things wholesale!

The walls were covered with hoes and rakes and forks and spades and trowels, all hung on special hooks and racks. A couple of shelves groaned under a load of secateurs, garden shears, seed trays, and a set of flower pots arranged in descending order of size, while the floor was almost totally occupied by wheelbarrows, watering cans, and a well-oiled cylinder lawn mower. MacGregor only tore his mind away from his inventory of sacks of peat and fertilizer when he realized that the oracle had said something. "I beg your pardon, sir?"

"I said it wasn't stolen," snapped Dover. "It was only borrowed."

The lack of comprehension on MacGregor's face appeared to infuriate the Chief Inspector. "That one, you idiot!"

MacGregor followed the direction of Dover's thumb which was indicating the larger of two stainless steel spades. He leaned forward to examine the mirrorlike blade more closely. "Er—how does Mrs. Dover know it was—er—borrowed, sir?"

Dover blew wearily down his nose. "Why don't you use your bloomin' eyes?" he asked. "Look at it all!" He flapped a cold-looking hand at the tools on the wall. "They're all hanging on their own hooks, aren't they? Right! Well, every bloody Tuesday morning without fail Mrs. Dover comes down here and turns 'em all round. Get it? Regular as ruddy clockwork. One week all these spades and trowels and things have got their backs facing the wall and then, the next week, they've got the backs of their blades facing out to the middle of the shed. Follow me?"

"I understand perfectly, thank you, sir," said MacGregor stiffly.

Dover scowled. "Then you're lucky," he growled, "because it's more than I do. She reckons it evens out the wear, you know. Silly cow! Anyhow!"—he heaved himself up in his deck chair again and jerked his thumb at the spade—"that thing is hanging the wrong way round. Savvy? So that means somebody moved it and that means, since this shed is kept locked up tighter than the Bank of England, that somebody must have broken in to do it."

He sank back and the deck chair groaned and creaked in understandable protest. "Mrs. Dover's developed into a very nervous sort of woman over the years."

MacGregor's agile mind had already solved the problem. "But, if you'll forgive me saying so, sir, the spade *isn't* the wrong way round." He moved across to the appropriate wall so as to be able to demonstrate his thesis in a way that even a muttonhead like Dover could understand. "All the tools are currently hanging with their backs turned toward the shed wall, aren't they? With the prongs and the—er—sharp edges pointing outward toward us. Right? Well, the spade in question is hanging on the wall in just the same way as all the other tools, isn't it? So, it's *not* hanging the wrong way round, unless of course"—he ventured on a rather patronizing little chuckle—"Mrs. Dover has got a special routine for that particular spade."

Dover didn't bother opening his eyes. It would be a bad day, he reflected, when he couldn't outsmart young MacGregor with both hands tied behind his back. "She killed a spider with it last week," he explained sleepily. "When she was in doing a security check. God knows what a spider was doing in this place, apart from starving to death, but there it was. On the floor. Mrs. Dover's allergic to spiders, so she grabbed that spade and flattened the brute."

"I see, sir," said MacGregor who had not, hitherto, suspected that Mrs. Dover was a woman of violence.

"Then," said Dover, pulling his overcoat collar up closer round his ears, "the spade had to be washed, didn't it? And disinfected, too, I shouldn't wonder." He tried to rub some warmth back into his frozen fingers. "Well, nobody in their right senses, it seems, would dream of hanging a newly washed spade with its back up against a shed wall. In case of rust. So Mrs. Dover broke the habit of a lifetime and replaced the spade the wrong way round so that the air could circulate freely about it."

"I see," said MacGregor for the second time in as many minutes. "Our mysterious borrower, when he returned the spade, then understandably hung it back on its hook in the same way that all the other implements were hung—with their backs to the wall. Yes"—he nodded his head—"a perfectly natural mistake to make."

" 'Strewth, don't you start!"

"Sir?"

Dover wriggled impatiently in his deck chair. "Talking as though this joker really exists. He damn well doesn't!"

"Then how do you explain the fact that the spade is hanging the wrong way round, sir?"

"I don't!" howled Dover. "I wouldn't be sitting here freezing to death if I could, would I, dumbbell?"

There was a moment's pause after this outburst. By rights Mac-Gregor should have emulated Mrs. Dover's way of dealing with pests by seizing hold of the nearest sufficiently heavy instrument and laying Dover's skull open with it; but the Metropolitan Police do too good a job on their young recruits. MacGregor swallowed all his finer impulses and concentrated hard on trying to be a detective. "Are there any signs of breaking in, sir?"

There was a surly grunt from the deck chair. "Search me!"

MacGregor crossed the shed and opened the door to examine the large padlock which had been left hooked carelessly in the staple. It looked as though it had recently been ravaged by some sharp-toothed carnivore.

Dover had got up to stretch his legs. He squinted over Mac-Gregor's shoulder. "I had a job getting the damn thing open."

Oh, well, it wasn't the first time that Dover had ridden roughshod over what might have been a vital clue, and it wouldn't be the last. Just for the hell of it, MacGregor gave Dame Fortune's wheel a half-hearted whirl. "I suppose you didn't happen to notice when you unlocked the padlock, sir, if—"

Dover was not the man to waste time nurturing slender hopes. "No," he said, "I didn't."

MacGregor closed the door. "Well, presumably our chappie knows how to pick a lock. That's some sort of lead."

"Garn," scoffed Dover, "they learn that with their mother's milk these days." He began to waddle back to his deck chair. "Got any smokes on you, laddie?" he asked. "I'm dying for a puff."

MacGregor often used to bewail the fact that he couldn't include all the cigarettes he provided for Dover on his swindle sheet but, as usual, he handed his packet over with a fairly good grace. He waited patiently until Dover's clumsy fingers had extracted a crumpled coffin nail and then gave him a light.

"Fetch us one of those plant pots," ordered Dover. "A little one."

A look of horror flashed across MacGregor's face. A plant pot? Surely Dover wasn't actually going to. . .

"For an ashtray, you bloody fool!" snarled Dover. "Mrs. Dover'll do her nut if she finds we've made a mess all over her floor."

MacGregor felt quite weak with the relief. "I've been thinking, sir," he said.

"The age of miracles is not yet past," snickered Dover.

MacGregor turned the other cheek with a practiced hand. "We can deduce quite a bit about our Mr. Borrower."

"Such as what?" Dover leered up suspiciously at his sergeant.

MacGregor ticked the points off on well-manicured fingers. "The spade must have been purloined for some illicit purpose." He saw from the vacant look on Dover's face that he'd better watch his language. "If the fellow just wanted a spade for digging potatoes or what-have-you, sir, he'd have just asked for it, wouldn't he? Taking a spade without permission and picking a padlock to get at it must add up to some criminal activity being concerned, don't you agree, sir?"

Dover nodded cautiously, unwilling to commit himself too far at this stage. "You reckon he nicked the spade to dig something up?" he asked, eyes bulging greedily. "Like buried treasure?"

"I was thinking more along the lines of him wanting to hide something, actually, sir. By concealing it in the ground. He returned the spade to the shed, you see. Surely, if he was merely digging up buried treasure, he wouldn't have gone to the trouble of putting the spade back carefully in its place?"

"*Burying* buried treasure?" Dover, dribbling ash down the front of his overcoat, tried this idea on for size.

"Or a dead body, sir," said MacGregor. "That strikes me as a more likely explanation."

Dover's heavy jowls settled sullenly over where his shirt collar would have been if he'd been wearing one. For a member (however unwanted) of Scotland Yard's Murder Squad, dead bodies were in his mind inextricably connected with work, and work always tended to bring Dover out in a cold sweat. He tried to concentrate on an occupation more to his taste: nitpicking. "How do you know it's a 'he?' " he demanded truculently. "It could just as well be a woman."

MacGregor was so anxious to display his superior powers of reasoning and deduction that he, perhaps, showed insufficient regard for Dover's slower wits. "Oh, I doubt that, sir! I don't know whether you've noticed, but Mrs. Dover had two spades hanging on the wall. The one that was 'borrowed' and a smaller one which is called, I believe, a border spade. You see? Now, surely if our intruder were a woman, she would have taken the lighter, more manageable border spade?"

Dover's initial scowl of fury was gradually replaced by a rather constipated expression, a sure indication that his thought processes were beginning to swing into action.

MacGregor waited anxiously.

"A *young* man!" said Dover at last.

"Sir?"

"You'd hardly find an old-age pensioner nipping over garden fences and picking locks and digging bloomin' great holes big enough to take a dead body, would you? 'Strewth, what you know about the real world, laddie, wouldn't cover a pinhead. We've had a frost out here for weeks! The ground's as hard as iron."

MacGregor's unabashed astonishment at this feat of unsolicited reasoning was not exactly flattering, but Dover, the bit now firmly between his National Health teeth, didn't appear to notice.

"And I'll tell you something else, laddie," he went on, "if our joker borrowed my missus's spade to bury a dead body with, I'll lay you a pound to a penny that it's his wife!"

MacGregor perched himself gingerly on the edge of a wheelbarrow, having first inspected and then passed it for cleanliness. Mrs. Dover certainly ran a tight garden shed. There was another deck chair stacked tidily in a corner but, since it was still in its plastic wrapper, MacGregor didn't feel he could really make use of it.

Having settled himself as comfortably as he could, MacGregor gave his full attention to putting the damper on Dover's enthusiasm. "Oh, steady on, sir," he advised.

"Steady on—nothing!" Dover had his fixations and he wasn't going to have any pipsqueak of a sergeant talking him out of them. In Dover's book, wives were always killed by their husbands. This was a simple rule of thumb which had more than a little basis in fact and saved a great deal of trouble all round—except for the odd innocent husband, of course, but no system is perfect. "A strapping young man with a dead body to get rid of, nicking a neighbor's spade. Use your brains, laddie, who else could it be except his wife?"

MacGregor retaliated by taking a leaf out of Dover's book and, instead of dealing with the main issue, quibbled over a minor detail. "A *neighbor's* spade, sir? I don't think we can go quite as far as—"

Dover went over his sergeant's objection like a steamroller over a cream puff. "Well, he didn't bloomin' well come over by tube from Balham, did he, you nitwit? Twice? Once to get the bloody spade and once to put it back? Of course he comes from somewhere round here. He wouldn't have known about our tool shed otherwise, would he?"

Without really thinking about it, MacGregor had pulled his notebook out. He looked up from an invitingly blank page that was just aching to be written on. "Actually, sir, I have been wondering why anybody would pick on this particular tool shed to break into in the first place."

Dover had no doubts. "Spite!" he said.

"There must be dozens of garden sheds round here, sir. Why choose this one?"

Dover belched with touching lack of inhibition. His exile was playing havoc with his insides. "Could be pure ruddy chance," he grunted.

"He had to prize open a good-quality padlock to get in here, sir. There must be plenty of sheds that aren't even locked."

Dover turned a lackluster eye on his sergeant. "All right, Mr. Clever Boots, so what's the answer?"

"It's because Mrs. Dover's tools are all kept so spotlessly clean, sir, and in such immaculate order. I'm sure our unwelcome visitor thought he'd be able to take the spade and return it without it ever being noticed that it had so much as been touched. You see, if the shed were dirty and dusty and untidy and covered, say, with cobwebs, it would be virtually impossible to borrow a tool and put it back without disturbing something. Do you follow me, sir? He'd be bound to leave a trail of clues behind him. But here"—MacGregor swept an admiring hand round the shed—"our chap had every reason to believe that, as long as he cleaned the spade and replaced it neatly on the wall with all the others, no suspicions would ever be aroused."

"He was reckoning without my old woman," said Dover with a kind of gloomy pride. "Like a bloodhound. More so, if anything." He shook off his reminiscent mood. "Anyhow, what you're saying just goes to show for sure that this joker is living somewhere round here. That's how he knows this is the cleanest garden shed in the country."

He broke off to stare disgustedly around him. "She got all this lot with trading stamps, you know. It's taken her years and years. Never asks me if there's anything *I* want, mind you," he mused resentfully, "though they've definitely got long woolly underpants because I've seen 'em in the damn catalogue."

"I agree our chap probably does live near here, sir," said Mac-Gregor, who'd only been debating the point just to keep his end up. "It's hard to see how he could have known about the tool shed or the tools otherwise. On the other hand, he must be something of a newcomer."

Dover snapped his fat fingers for another cigarette and used the time it took to furnish him with one in trying to puzzle out what MacGregor was getting at. He was forced to concede defeat. "Regular little Sherlock Holmes, aren't you?" he sneered.

Privately, MacGregor thought he was a jolly sight smarter than this supposed paragon, but he wasn't fool enough to confide such an opinion to Dover. "Our Mr. Borrower would hardly have come breaking into this particular tool shed, sir, if he'd known that you were a policeman. A Chief Inspector from New Scotland Yard, in fact."

Dover, almost invisible in a cloud of tobacco smoke, mulled this over. He was rather taken with the idea that all the barons of the underworld might be going in fear and trepidation of him. "He might be potty," he observed generously. "Otherwise he'd know he couldn't hope to pull the wool over the eyes of a highly trained observer like me."

Another thought struck him and he flopped back in his deck chair, suffering from shock. " 'Strewth," he gasped, "it's only a couple of hours since I first heard about this crime, and look at me now! I've solved it, near as damn it! All we've got to do is find a young, newly married villain who's recently moved into the district. And I'll lay odds he's living in that new block of flats they've built just across the way. They've got the dregs of society in that place.

"So, all we've got to do now is get onto the local cop shop and tell 'em to send a posse of coppers round to make a few inquiries. Soon as they find somebody who fits the bill, all they've got to do is ask him to produce his wife. If he can't—well, Bob's your uncle, eh? And that," added Dover, seeing that MacGregor was dying to interrupt and being determined to thwart him, "is why he had to borrow a spade in the first place! Because people who live in flats don't have gardens, and if they don't have gardens they don't have gardening tools, either!"

MacGregor put his notebook away and stood up. "Oh, I don't think our man is living in a flat, do you sir?"

Dover's eye immediately became glassy with suspicion, resentment, and chronic dyspepsia. "Why not?"

"He'd have nowhere to bury the body, sir."

Dover's scowl grew muddier. "He could have shoved it in somebody else's garden, couldn't he?" he asked, reasonably enough.

MacGregor shook his head. "Far too risky, sir. Digging a hole big enough to inter a body would take an hour or more, I should think. Now, it would be bad enough undertaking a job like that in one's own garden, but in somebody else's—" MacGregor pursed his lips in a silent whistle and shook his head again. "No, I doubt it, sir, I really do. I think we must take it, as a working hypothesis, that—"

"He could have planted her in the garden of an empty house," said Dover doggedly and, as a gesture of defiance against society, dropped his cigarette end into the empty watering can.

"Well, I suppose it's a possibility, sir," said MacGregor with a sigh, "and I agree that we ought to bear it in mind. The thing is, though, that you're hardly in the depths of the country out here, are you? I mean—well, everywhere round here does tend to be a bit visible, doesn't it?"

There are plenty of suburban mortgage holders who would have taken deep umbrage at such a damaging assessment of their property, but Dover was not cursed with that kind of pride. He simply reacted by nodding his head in sincere agreement. "Too right, laddie!" he rumbled.

"There's another point that's been puzzling me, sir," MacGregor said. "Why did our chap go to all this trouble to *borrow* a spade? The way he broke into this shed may carry all the hallmarks of a professional job, but he was still running a terrible risk. Anybody might have seen him and blown the whistle on him."

"He'd do it after dark," said Dover, "and, besides, you don't go in for murder if you aren't prepared to chance your arm a bit. And what choice did he have? With a dead body on his hands and no spade? He could hardly start digging his hole with a knife and fork."

"He could have bought a spade, sir."

"Eh?"

"He could have bought a spade," repeated MacGregor, quite prepared for the look of horror that flashed across Dover's pasty face. The Chief Inspector regarded the actual purchasing of anything as a desperate step, only to be contemplated when all the avenues of begging, borrowing, and stealing had been exhaustively explored. "It wouldn't have cost all that much, sir, and it would have been a much less hazardous operation."

Dover wrinkled up his nose. "The shops were shut?" he suggested. "Or he didn't have any money?"

"A professional villain, sir? That doesn't sound very likely, does it? And if he's going to nick something, why not nick the money? A handful of cash wouldn't be as compromising, if something went wrong, as Mrs. Dover's stainless steel spade would be."

Dover shivered and shoved his hands as deep as they would go in his overcoat pockets. The shed wasn't built for sitting in and there was a howling gale blowing under the door. The sooner he got out of this dump and back into the warmth and comfort of his own home, the better. "That's why he didn't buy a spade!"

"Sir?"

"Put yourself in the murderer's shoes, laddie. You've just knocked your missus off and you're proposing to get rid of the body by burying it in a hole. Sooner or later people are going to come around asking questions. Well, I'd have said the last thing you wanted was a bloomin' spade standing there and shouting the odds. No, borrowing the spade and putting it back again shows our chap has a bit of class about him. He's somebody who can see further than the end of his nose. An opponent," added Dover with a smirk, "worthy of my steel. Well"—he raised a pair of moth-eaten eyebrows at his sergeant—"what are you waiting for? Christmas?"

"Sir?"

Dover sighed heavily and dramatically. "It's no wonder you've never made Inspector," he sneered. "You're as thick as two planks. Look, laddie, what's a detective got to do if he wants to be everybody's little white-haired boy, eh?"

MacGregor wondered what on earth they were supposed to be talking about now. "Well, I don't quite know, sir," he said uncertainly. "Er—solve his cases?"

" 'Strewth!" snarled Dover, giving vent to his opinion with unwonted energy. "Look, you know what they're like, all these Commissioners and Commanders and what-have-you. They're forever yakking about a good detective being the one who goes out and finds his own cases, aren't they?"

"Oh, I see what you mean, sir."

"Well, look at me!"

"Sir?"

"I'm on leave, aren't I?" asked Dover, warming gleefully to the task of blowing his own trumpet. "But I don't go around sitting with my ruddy feet up! On the contrary, from the very faintest of hints—the sort any other jack would have brushed aside as not worth his attention—I've uncovered a dastardly murder that nobody else even knows has been committed."

Too late MacGregor saw the danger signals. "But, sir—"

"But, nothing!" snapped Dover. "With the information I'm giving 'em, the local police'll have our laddie under lock and key before you can say Sir Robert Peel!"

"But we can't go to the local police, sir," said MacGregor, breaking out in a sweat at the mere idea. "After all, we've only been theorizing."

Dover's face split into an evil grin. "Of course *we* are not going to the local police, laddie," he promised soothingly. "Just you!" There was a brief interval while the old fool laughed himself nearly sick. "Ask for Detective Superintendent Andy Andrews and mention my name—clearly! Tell him what we've come up with so far—that we're after a young, agile, newlywed villain who's just moved into a house in this area: a specialist in picking locks."

"Oh, sir!" wailed MacGregor.

"There can't be all that many jokers knocking around who'd fit that bill," Dover went on. "And, if there are, Andrews will soon spot our chap because he'll be the one with a newly turned patch of soil in his garden and no wife. Or girlfriend. You never know these days."

MacGregor tried to believe that he was just having a nightmare. "You're not serious, sir?"

"Never been more serious in my life," growled Dover. "And I've just thought of something else. If they're newcomers to the district, that's why nobody's reported the wife missing. She won't have had time to establish a routine yet or have made any close friends. Her husband will be able to give any rubbishy explanation for her absence." He realized that MacGregor was still standing there. "What's got into you, laddie? You're usually so damn keen they could use you for mustard!"

"It's just that I don't feel we're quite ready, sir."

But Dover wasn't having any argument about it. He cut ruthlessly through his sergeant's feeble protests. "And stick to old Andrews like a limpet, see? Don't move from his side till you've got the handcuffs on our chummie—I don't want Andrews stealing my thunder. I've solved this case and I'm going to get the glory for it. Well"—he glared up at a very shrinking violet—"what are you waiting for now? A Number Nine bus?"

MacGregor answered out of a bone-dry throat. "No, sir."

"Leave us your cigarettes," said Dover, not the man to get his priorities mixed. "You'll not be having time to smoke."

Reluctantly MacGregor handed over his pack of cigarettes and even found a spare packet of matches. When, however, he'd got his hand on the door handle he paused again. "Er—you're staying here, are you, sir?"

In all the excitement Dover had not overlooked his own personal predicament. "Call in at the house on your way out and tell Mrs. Dover that I've solved the problem of her bloody spade and that you're off to arrest the bloke for murder. I'll give you five minutes' start, so she's got time to digest the good news, and then I'll follow you. And I don't mind telling you, laddie"—he surveyed the scene of his exile with a marked lack of enthusiasm—"I'll be glad to get back to my own armchair by the fire." He waggled his head in mild bewilderment. "Do you know, she's never let me come in here on my own before. Funny, isn't it?"

Long before the allotted five minutes was up, however, Dover was infuriated to discover that Sergeant MacGregor was coming back down the garden path at the double. Extricating himself from his deck chair, he dragged the door open and voiced his feelings in a penetrating bellow of rage. "That damn woman! Is she never satisfied?"

MacGregor glanced around nervously, although the silent, unseen watchers weren't his neighbors and he really didn't care what they thought about the Dovers. "It's not that, actually, sir."

"Then what is it, *actually*?" roared Dover, mimicking his sergeant's minor public-school accent.

"It's a message from Mrs. Dover, sir."

Dover knew when he was being softened up for the breaking of bad news. "Spit it out, laddie," he said bleakly.

MacGregor grinned foolishly out of sheer embarrassment. "It's just that she's remembered she turned the spade round herself, sir. Mrs. Dover, I mean. It had quite slipped her mind, she says, but she popped down to the shed before she went to church on Sunday morning to count how many tie-on labels she'd got and the spade being hung the wrong way round on the wall got on her nerves, she says. And since she reckoned it must have dried off after having been washed, she—"

"You can spare me the details," said Dover as all his dreams of fame and glory crumbled to dust and ashes in his mouth.

"Mrs. Dover was going to come down and tell you herself, sir, when she'd finished washing the leaves of the aspidistras."

Dover seemed indifferent to such graciousness. "You didn't get in touch with Superintendent Andrews, did you?"

MacGregor shook his head. "There didn't seem much point, sir. As it was Mrs. Dover who changed the spade back to its proper position, well"—he shrugged—"that did rather seem to be that. Nobody broke into the shed to borrow the spade and, if nobody borrowed the spade, that means there was no dead body to be buried. And if there's no dead body to be buried, that means that we haven't got a wife murderer and—"

But Dover had switched off. He had many faults, but crying over spilt milk wasn't one of them. He was already lumbering out through the shed door, his thoughts turning to the future. He tossed a final question back over his shoulder.

"Did she say what she was giving me for my dinner?"

Robert Bloch was famous as a short-story writer long before the movie "Psycho." I still remember the thrill of reading "Yours Truly, Jack the Ripper" for the first time, and it's hard to believe that this modern classic appeared in Weird Tales *way back in 1943. Here is Bloch in an unusually whimsical mood.*

ROBERT BLOCH
Crook of the Month

Edison was right.

Genius is one percent inspiration and ninety-nine percent perspiration.

Jerry Cribbs started sweating long before the plane touched down in the Rio dawn and continued all through Customs inspection. But the black bag preserved its secret, and he hugged it in his lap during the long taxi ride to his Copacabana hotel. Anyone who survives a cab trip through Rio de Janeiro traffic is entitled to feel relieved, but by the time Jerry checked into his room he was still perspiring. And a shower didn't help even though he took the bag into the stall with him.

Jerry dried off, only to find himself wringing wet again in the few moments it took him to dress and shave. Then he sat soaking and waiting for the phone to ring. He held the black bag on his lap, hugging his secret—and his genius—to him for reassurance.

Why didn't the call come?

A knock on the door answered his question. Of course they'd never risk using the telephone; they'd rely on personal contact.

Or would they?

Jerry shoved the bag under the bed and moved to the door.

A soft voice from the hall outside murmured, "Mr. Cribbs?"

Jerry flinched. He'd registered downstairs as Mr. Brown, figuring that any alias good enough for the late Al Capone should be good enough for him. And yet the stranger beyond the door knew his name. In a way it was reassuring, but he had to make certain.

"Who sent you?" he whispered.

"The Big Bird."

With a sigh of relief, Jerry opened the door.

A baldheaded black giant entered, nodding curtly. He was dressed in the ornate uniform of a Brazilian general or chauffeur—it
didn't matter which, because the Big Bird could have sent either if he
chose.

"Come with me, please," said the giant.

Jerry turned and started out, but a hand gripped his shoulder.

"Aren't you forgetting something?" the giant asked.

"Sorry." Jerry stopped and retrieved the black bag from its hiding
place beneath the bed. The giant reached for it but Jerry shook his
head.

"I'll carry it," he said.

The giant shrugged. "As you wish." He followed Jerry through
the doorway and down the hall. He didn't speak in the elevator or in
the lobby below, and his silence continued as he led Jerry to the huge
limousine parked insolently on the sidewalk outside the entrance.

Jerry slid into the back seat and his escort got behind the wheel.

If Jerry had any doubts about the black giant being a chauffeur,
they were quickly dispelled as the car weaved through Rio's noonday
traffic—from the way he drove, he was obviously a general.

Once aboard the waiting launch at the wharf the man proved
himself to be an admiral too. The boat raced off across the harbor
and out into the open sea while Jerry crouched in the bow with the
black bag between his trembling knees.

The long sleek lines of the yacht loomed ahead, bobbing in the
swell. As they pulled astern Jerry looked up at the gold-leaf lettering
which identified the vessel as *The Water Closet.*

The black giant killed the engine and rose, cupping his hands.
"Ahoy there!" he called.

A bearded seaman peered down from the deck above.

"Let down the ladder," the black man muttered.

Climbing a rope ladder while holding the handle of the black bag
in his teeth wasn't easy, but Jerry managed it. Once on deck he
followed the giant along the deck, past an elegant array of
staterooms, a sauna, a private projection room, a bowling alley. They
stopped just beyond an outdoor bar, at an Olympic size swimming
pool.

"He's expecting you," said the black man.

Jerry squinted at the pool. Over the stereophonic screech of
raucous rock, shrill shrieks rose from the pool, where a half-dozen
figures splashed and sported, stark naked in the sunlight.

Jerry had no trouble recognizing his host; he was the only male.

"Mr. Buzzard?" he murmured.

The scrawny balding little man climbed out of the water, scowling against the sun as a waiting attendant instantly draped a gold lamé robe over his shoulders.

The Big Bird nodded. "I'm Al Buzzard," he said. "You've met my wife." He gestured vaguely toward the naiads in the pool.

"Oh—sure."

"Come on then." Buzzard held out both hands. The alert attendant placed a frosted full triple martini glass in one of the hands and a lighted Upmann in the other, then Buzzard turned and led Jerry aft.

From the appearance of the stateroom they entered, with its mirrored walls and ceiling and king-size circular bed covered with leopardskin, Jerry decided he was in the Captain's cabin.

The scrawny man closed the door. With a lightning-fast gesture he swallowed his drink, then set the empty glass on the mink carpet. He sprawled back on the bed, puffing his cigar and staring moodily at his visitor.

"Did you ever have one of those days when nothing goes right?" he sighed. "Just look at that!" He gestured toward the empty glass. "A triple martini with only two olives in it! As soon as we get out into international waters, remind me to have the bartender keelhauled."

"Really, Mr. Buzzard, it isn't all that bad—"

"Hah!" Buzzard snorted and sat up. "You sound just like Barabass."

"Barabass?"

"My publisher. He was out here last week. We got into a conversation during the orgy and he said to me, 'Why don't you look on the bright side of things for a change? After all, you're the world's most popular author, next to Conway Mann, that is. Ten all-time best sellers, eight blockbuster movies, a hit television series that lasted almost an entire season—what more do you want? Why, your name is a household word—like Drāno and Sani-Flush.' That's what he told me."

"Well, it's true, isn't it?"

"No—it's a damnable lie! I'm much more popular than Con Mann. Him and his sexy romances—"

"But you're rich and famous." Jerry gestured at the mirrored walls. "You live on this big yacht, you have a lovely wife—"

Buzzard shrugged. "Boats make me seasick. I have to stay on board because the minute I set foot on land the I.R.S. will lay a suit on me for thirty-three million dollars in back taxes. And my wife isn't all that lovely—the first nine were much more attractive. Trouble is, none of them could understand me. This one doesn't understand me, nor do any of my mistresses. The shrinks all tell me we don't have the right chemistry. So what am I supposed to do about that?"

Sighing wearily, Buzzard rose and threw his cigar out of a porthole. When he turned back he was a different man; his shoulders straightened beneath the gold robe and his beady eyes matched its glitter. "Now, to business," he said. "Have you got it?"

"It's in the bag."

Jerry held out the black bag and Buzzard's twitching fingers closed around the handle. He carried it to the bed and scrabbled at the lock.

"The key!" he panted. "Where's the key?"

Jerry rolled up his trouser leg and ripped the adhesive tape from his right ankle. He handed the key to Buzzard, who inserted it in the lock with a vicious twisting motion. The bag sprang open and its contents tumbled out onto the leopardskin coverlet.

Buzzard stared down at the bed, rubbing his hands together.

"How many pages?" he whispered.

"Three hundred."

"It's all there then?"

"All but the last chapter. I expected to finish by the end of next week, but then your wire came—"

"You can knock off the ending when you get back," Buzzard said. "Just so's I get the whole thing to the publisher by the end of the month. We gotta hit the fall list before Conway Mann beats us to it. I hear he's got a big one coming up, but we'll show him." He paused, eyeing Jerry suspiciously. "It *is* a goodie, isn't it?"

"I think so."

"Think? I'm not paying you to think—I'm paying you to write." Buzzard made a face. "It better be good. After all, I've got a reputation to live down to."

"Don't worry, Mr. Buzzard. Just read it and you'll see for yourself."

"Yeah, yeah—later sometime." Al Buzzard gathered up the pages, hefting them. "Feels nice and thick, anyhow. Barabass likes them that way." He frowned. "Where's the carbon?"

"Home, in the safe."

"Good." Buzzard nodded. "Speaking of home, we better get you on the next flight out of here. I'd invite you to stay for lunch, but seeing as how you still have a chapter to go there's no sense wasting time. Besides, you can grab a sannich or something on the plane, right?"

"Uh—aren't you forgetting something, Mr. Buzzard?"

Buzzard scowled. "I know. That's the difference between guys like you and a creative artist like I am. All you writers ever think about is money."

Sighing, he reached under the bed and pulled out a locked metal box. "OK, if that's the way you want it."

He fiddled with the combination until the box flew open, cascading a heap of glittering objects over the bed.

"Damn!" he muttered. "I told you this wasn't my day. Wrong box—I got the diamonds by mistake!"

Buzzard stooped and fumbled until he found a second metal container identical with the first. When its tumblers clicked and the lid rose, Jerry stared down at the stacks of currency.

"Petty cash," Buzzard explained. "Only fifties and hundreds." He extracted a wad of bills and began to count. "Let's see now. Three hundred pages at ten dollars a page—"

"You promised me fifteen this time, Mr. Buzzard."

"Oh, yeah—fifteen times three hundred—"

"Forty-five hundred," said Jerry.

"What's the matter, don't you think I know how to count?" Scowling, Buzzard thrust a sheaf of currency into Jerry's hands. "That's a lot of loot, fella. If you ask me, you're being overpaid."

"But it took me almost six months to write the book, Mr. Buzzard. Nowadays a plumber can make that much in three weeks."

"So take the money and study plumbing," Buzzard told him. "Just so you finish up that last chapter first. If you got a pencil and paper, maybe you can write it on the plane."

But Jerry Cribbs did no writing on the return flight. He brooded.

The plane slipped between the crowded peaks, plunged into a few air pockets above Latin America, then sped like a thief up the Atlantic Coast. When it landed at Kennedy, Jerry was still brooding.

"Darling—what's the matter?"

Jerry halted at the terminal exit and stared at Ann Remington's troubled face. Then he kissed it. "I'll tell you later," he said.

Thanks to the marvels of modern technology Jerry got through Customs, into Ann's car, out of the airport, and through the city traffic in less time than it had taken him to fly from South America.

In the car he unburdened himself. "Don't you see?" he sighed. "It's the same old story."

"But it's a *good* story," Ann said. "I was reading one of your carbons just last night. I like that hero of yours, Lance Pustule. And having him murder his parents at the age of eight—it's going to win a lot of reader sympathy. Everybody has a kindly feeling for orphans."

"Ann, please—"

"That scene where he's raped by his grandmother is terrific! And all those killings and tortures he uses to get control of the television network—you really tell it like it is! The drugs and violence and kinky sex are dynamite. By the way, what's the title of the book?"

"The Aristocrats."

"Perfect!"

Jerry shook his head. "Al Buzzard pays me forty-five hundred dollars for ghostwriting a book that will make him millions. What's so perfect about that? All he does is sit on his big fat yacht, divorcing wives and having affairs with movie stars and throwing fashion models overboard—"

"But that's why he gets all that money," Ann said. "Doing those things makes him a celebrity. His life-style is front-page news, so when he writes a book that's news too."

"Only he doesn't write books. *I* do, and I can't even earn enough for us to get married." Jerry sighed. "If I could just write my own book, under my own name—"

"Why don't you?"

"Because I can't find the time, or the money."

Ann smiled. "We could manage. There's my secretarial job at the travel agency."

"I'm not going to live off your salary."

Ann's smile faded as she gripped the steering wheel and swung the car toward the curb in front of the dingy run down apartment building where Jerry spent his dingy run down life.

"I don't understand you," she murmured. "How can a man who writes such trendy modern porn have such old-fashioned ideas?"

"Because I *am* old-fashioned." Jerry lugged his bags out of the car. "And when I do write my book, it isn't going to be trendy either. A good novel doesn't need all that cheap sensationalism." Ann started to get out of the car, but he checked her with a gesture. "Sorry, you'd better not come up with me. I have to get to work on the last chapter right away. The big identity-crisis scene when Lance finally discovers where his head is at—he gets rid of his wife and girlfriend and becomes a child molester."

"When will I see you?"

"I should have everything wrapped up by tomorrow night. Suppose you come around and we'll have dinner together then. Make it about seven."

They clung together for a moment, then Ann drove away and

Jerry hastened upstairs to commit a statutory offense on paper.

Neither of them noticed the little man crouching behind the pillars before the apartment house entryway. "Seven o'clock," the little man whispered. "Tomorrow night."

It had been a good day's work, Jerry decided. Three thousand words, many of which were four-letter; twelve pages of solid hardcore sex and violence. Al Buzzard and his readers would be happy, and Jerry was satisfied with a dishonest job, well done.

He showered, shaved, and dressed, and when the doorbell rang shortly before seven he was ready.

He lifted the latch and the door swung open.

"Ann—" he said.

"Wrong." The little man stood in the doorway, staring him up and down.

Jerry frowned, perplexed. "Who are you?"

"Sorry, no time for introductions." The little man moved past him into the apartment. "You're coming with me."

"Now wait a minute—"

"I don't have a minute." The intruder crooked a commanding finger. "Let's go."

"No way," said Jerry, eyeing the stranger. Whoever he was and whatever he wanted, Jerry had no intention of being pushed around by this little character.

He turned, and that was his mistake.

Because a big man loomed up in the doorway behind him, raising a rubber truncheon.

As the weapon descended on Jerry's skull, the little man looked at his wristwatch and nodded approvingly.

"Six forty-nine," he said. "Right on schedule."

"Yah," said the big man, who was preoccupied by the task of stuffing Jerry into a large gunnysack. Grunting, he swung the sack over his shoulder and carried it down the hall to the backstairs exit of the building.

The little man followed and they descended the steps together.

The big man scowled at him apprehensively. *"Mach schnell,"* he panted. "Maybe somebody sees us."

"Don't worry." The little man nodded. "It's in the bag."

In the bag was no place to be, and when Jerry recovered consciousness he wanted out.

Voicing these sentiments through a mouthful of burlap he was conscious of a shuddering drone and a sound like far-off thunder, gradually fading.

Then a knife slashed through the cloth above his head, the gunnysack shredded and fell in folds about his shoulders, and Jerry emerged. He wobbled to his feet, blinking at his surroundings.

He stood in the capacious cabin of a private plane—a Lear jet, from the looks of it. Only a man wealthy enough to own such an aircraft could afford to decorate its interior with the original artwork exhibited on the walls.

Jerry recognized a Renoir, a Picasso, a Modigliani. And then, turning toward the far end of the cabin, he recognized the owner of the paintings.

There was no mistaking the identity of the bearded figure seated behind the ornate Chippendale desk, wearing an incongruously crumpled hat and peering at him through tinted glasses. The face would be instantly familiar to anyone who had ever watched a television interview program or Bowling for Dollars.

"Conway Mann!" gasped Jerry.

The bearded author nodded. He smiled and beckoned Jerry to the Heppelwhite chair before the desk.

"Welcome to my humble digs," he said. "I trust you'll excuse the crudity of my invitation, but I had to see you, Mr. Gibbs."

"Cribbs."

"Exactly." The pudgy hand investigated the contents of a desk drawer, emerging with a fistful of yellow pills which disappeared between his bearded lips. He gulped and nodded. "I suppose you're wondering what brought you here."

"I already know," said Jerry. "Two goons and a gunnysack."

"My dear Hibbs—"

"Cribbs."

"Ah, yes." The hand fumbled in the drawer once more, then rose to extend a crumpled sheet of paper. "Please be good enough to read this proof of an advertisement scheduled to appear in *Publishers Weekly*. I think it may interest you."

Jerry stared down at the bold lettering of the full-page ad.

SHOCKING! SCANDALOUS!
SENSATIONAL!

Searing sex . . . vicious violence . . . raw and raunchy . . . a novel that rips aside the last shreds of convention to reveal the hidden world of secret passions and unbridled lusts behind the locked

doors of America's power-mad masters...as they move from
boardroom to bedroom in their savage search for forbidden
pleasures! Don't miss

The Taste-Makers
by
CONWAY MANN
The best-selling blockbuster of the year from
SCRIBBLER'S & SONS

Jerry put the ad down on the desktop. "Your new novel?"

"Precisely so."

"Is it good?"

Conway Mann shrugged. "That's up to you. You're going to write
it."

"Now hold on—"

"I am holding on, Mr. Dribbs. But I can't hold on much longer.
The manuscript is due at the publisher's office by the end of the
month."

"Let me get this straight. You mean to say you don't write your
own books?"

"Why should that surprise you? That wretched Al Buzzard
doesn't write his novels either."

"Then you know?"

"Of course. Why else would I bring you here?" Conway Mann
shook his head. "Don't get me wrong. I'm perfectly capable of doing
the job myself, but lately I've suffered from writer's block."

"When did it start?"

"In 1959." The pudgy hand popped red capsules into its owner's
mouth. "I have a full schedule of commitments ahead of me—
Johnny Carson, Merv Griffin, Hollywood Squares—best-selling authors must live up to their responsibilities, even at the sacrifice of the
creative impulse. And that's where you come in."

"That's where I get out," Jerry told him.

"At forty thousand feet in the air?" Conway Mann shrugged
again. "Very well, suit yourself."

"Now see here," Jerry cried, "you kidnapped me! That's a federal
offense. I can push charges."

"You'll push up daisies if you refuse."

"But why me?" Jerry said. "Surely you must have a regular
ghostwriter. What happened to him?"

"He refused," Conway Mann murmured. "Would you like to see
where he's buried?"

Conway Mann, with his royalties and reputation at stake, wasn't conning. When his hand again descended to the desk drawer, Jerry expected it to reappear holding a revolver.

Instead it clutched a bundle of bills.

"Six thousand," said the bearded man. "In advance."

"Six thousand?"

"That's more than you get from that chintzy Buzzard, if my spies are correct." The pudgy hand extended. "Now take it and get out—you've got a deadline to meet."

"But I couldn't possibly write an entire novel by the end of the month," Jerry said.

"You can and you will," Conway Mann told him. "Unless you're awfully fond of daisies."

Jerry pocketed the bills, not an easy task for trembling hands. "I'll try," he said. "Only you haven't told me what the book will be about."

"Ninety thousand words, that's what it's about." Conway Mann gestured at the proof sheet on the desktop. "This ad doesn't mention much about a plot, so you can suit yourself. You know what readers expect. Behind the scenes in politics and big business, and the further behind the better. Maybe a touch of necrophilia in San Francisco, a Black Mass at the U.N., orgies in the White House—I leave it to your discretion."

Jerry took a deep breath. "I'll do my best."

"Your best isn't good enough," Conway Mann said. "I want your worst."

He rose and came around the desk, glancing at his watch. "I'll tell the pilot to take us down, and the boys will see to it that you get home safely."

"That's not necessary."

"I think it is." Conway Mann's eyes narrowed behind the tinted lenses. "They're going to be keeping tabs on you until the book is finished."

"And if it isn't?"

"Then they'll finish you."

"I'm not afraid of your threats," Jerry said. "I can call the police—"

"That's already been taken care of. Your phone is dead. And unless you want to follow its example, you'll stay in your apartment from tonight until the manuscript is in the hands of my publishers." Conway Mann put his hand on Jerry's shoulder and smiled. "If you want to stay healthy, learn a lesson from the flowers. Daisies don't tell."

It was good advice, but Jerry couldn't take it. Not when he found

Ann waiting for him outside the apartment door.

"It's after nine o'clock!" she told him. "I've been waiting here for two hours. Where on earth have you been?"

"I wasn't exactly on earth," Jerry said, looking toward the car from which he'd emerged. The headlights glared, the motor growled, and its sleek black length crouched at the curb like a panther waiting to spring.

Ann followed his gaze, noting the big man behind the wheel and his small companion beside him.

"Please, darling, come inside." Jerry gripped her arm and drew her through the doorway. "I can explain everything."

"It better be good."

But once inside the apartment, it wasn't good.

"Not good at all," Ann said, after she'd listened to Jerry's account of the evening. "It took you months to knock out the novel for Buzzard, and now Mann expects you to do one in a couple of weeks!"

"It's impossible." Jerry nodded. "But there's no way out."

"Not for *you*," Ann said. "But *I'm* free to come and go."

"Meaning?"

"It's simple." Ann smiled. "I'm going to leave now. The minute I get home I'll put through a call to the police. They'll get over here, you tell them what happened, and you're home free."

"Dynamite!"

Ann smiled reassuringly as she moved to the door and opened it. Then her smile faded. The little man stood in the doorway, his eyes bulging. There was another ominous bulge where his hand rested in his pocket.

"I heard what you just said, lady. Nobody's calling the fuzz."

Ann stared at him. "You mean you intend to keep me locked up here with Jerry?"

The man shook his head. "I didn't say that. Somebody's got to go for groceries and it might as well be you. But whenever you cut out, I go with you. And my buddy downstairs keeps an eye on your boy friend. Boss's orders."

Jerry faced him, frowning. "He thinks of everything, doesn't he?"

"You better believe it." The little man gave him a crooked smile. "Time for you to start thinking too, fella. You got a book to write."

The days that followed moved in a blinding blur. Ann spent most of her time in the living room, while Jerry's typewriter pounded away behind the bedroom door. Sometimes she read, sometimes she watched television, sometimes she just stood at the window and

stared down at the black limousine. On occasion she took brief walks
or shopped at the supermarket, but always under escort. She didn't
talk to the little man and he didn't talk to her. She scarcely talked to
Jerry when he came out of the bedroom for meals.

One look at his haggard face told the story. He was racing the
deadline, racing for his life, and she resolved not to nag him with
questions.

But as the end of the month inched closer there came a moment
when she could keep silent no longer.

They were seated at the kitchen table over coffee, and the sight of
Jerry's gaunt features and glassy stare was too much for her to bear.
From her lips burst the age-old question, the question every writer
dreads.

"How's it going?" she asked.

Jerry shook his head. "It isn't," he muttered.

"You mean you won't finish in time?"

"I haven't started."

"Haven't started?" Ann frowned. "But you've been in there typing
night and day."

"I type at night because I can't sleep. And I can't sleep because of
what I type during the day. Page after page of new beginnings—
none of them making sense, all of them going into the wastebasket.
I'm afraid it's finally happened, just the way it did to Al Buzzard and
Conway Mann."

"What are you talking about?"

"When they started, they wrote their own stuff. Then gradually it
got to them. No man can stand such a pace forever—a daily diet of
corruption, brutality, mayhem, incest, voyeurism, sado-masochistic
satyriasis, all of it so hard to spell. So they hired ghostwriters, people
like myself. The trouble is, now the same thing is happening to me."
Jerry raised his anguished face. "All those rapes and murders—it's
too much! Even Jack the Ripper had to quit in the end."

Ann rose and moved to the stricken man. "Listen to me," she said
softly. "It's not that bad. All you have to do is get Buzzard's last
chapter to the publisher. If you can only go on a little longer, until
you do Conway Mann's novel—"

"Don't you understand?" Jerry slammed a clenched fist on the
table. "It's too late now. Even if I stay at the typewriter twenty-four
hours a day, I'll never beat the deadline. There isn't time."

Ann sighed, and walked to the living room. Jerry followed. Together they stared out of the window, down at the black car crouched
and waiting. Neither of them said a word. Words wouldn't help

now—unless Jerry could put ninety thousand of them onto paper within the next three days.

It was Ann who broke the silence, her face and voice thoughtful.

"Maybe it's all for the best," she said.

"What do you mean?"

"Even if you could have finished on time, it wouldn't help. At first I hoped this would be a blessing in disguise. Forty-five hundred from Al Buzzard and six thousand from Conway Mann—that's ten thousand five hundred dollars in cash, enough to live on until you realized your ambition. With that much money you could finally write a novel of your own. But it doesn't matter now, does it? If you say you can't write any more—"

"I never said that!" Jerry gripped her hands tightly with his own. "I said I couldn't turn out any more sex and violence. The novel I want to write is different. No sensationalism, no cheap anti-heroes, no ripoff of celebrities disguised under other names. My book would be about ordinary people, coping with everyday problems that all of us have to face."

"But would such a book sell?"

There was doubt in Ann's voice, but none in Jerry's. "Why not? At least I'd give the readers some reality, something to think about and remember. Those porno fairytales Buzzard and Mann are credited with are just the same thing repeated over and over again—you can't tell one from another in the long run. I'm talking about real literature."

Ann eyed him dubiously. "How would you promote it?"

"An honest book doesn't need promotion," Jerry told her. "A good writer doesn't need notoriety. Think about it—did Thackery have a yacht? Did Henry James wear a funny hat and fly around in a Lear jet? Did Jane Austen sleep around? Did Shakespeare ever appear on a late-night talk show?"

"I am thinking about it," Ann told him. An odd note crept into her voice. "Jerry, do me a favor. Come into the bedroom with me for a minute. I want you to show me where you keep your files."

Together they went to the bedroom. "Right here in this cabinet," Jerry said.

"I see." But Ann's glance strayed from the filing cabinet to Jerry's desk—the typewriter, the paper, the carbons resting under a heavy paperweight. Her eyes narrowed. "Jerry—about this book of yours. Do you really want to write it?"

"More than anything in the world."

"And you're sure it could sell?"

Jerry nodded, then turned away. "If I'm wrong, may I be struck dead on the spot."

It was then that Ann hit him with the paperweight.

"Dead," Jerry mumbled. "Well, I asked for it—"

"Wake up." Ann was shaking him by the shoulders. "You're not dead."

Jerry opened his eyes. The room was dark and he could just make out Ann's shadowy face peering anxiously over him.

"Why did you do it?" he said, sitting up and rubbing the lump on the side of his left temple.

"I'll explain later. Right now there isn't time. We've got to get out of here."

"What about the goon squad?"

"See for yourself."

Legs shaking, Jerry allowed her to lead him back into the living room and over to the window. He stared down.

The black limousine was gone. Ann's car stood in its place.

"Come on," Ann said. "We've got to get to the airport. Your bags are packed and in the car."

"Where are we going?"

"Costa Rica."

Jerry frowned. "I don't get it."

"You will."

And once the plane took off, he did.

"What you said about writing your own novel convinced me," Ann told him. "That's when I got the idea. I'm sorry about knocking you out, but I knew you'd never agree to go through with it on your own."

"Agree to what?"

"Delivering Conway Mann's new novel to his publisher."

"But there is no new novel!"

"There is now. I took one of the carbons of Al Buzzard's manuscript. All I did was go through it and change the names of the characters."

"You mean you gave both publishers the same book?"

"Including the last chapter." Ann nodded. "You said yourself that these things are all alike."

"So that's why Conway Mann's goons let us go."

"Right. Once the manuscript got to the office of Scribbler's & Sons, they took off. And so have we."

"But why Costa Rica?"

"They don't have an extradition law. Even if Mann and Buzzard find out, you can't be touched. You've got the cash, enough to keep us going for a year. And you can write your book." Ann smiled. "Besides, darling, if what you say is true, nobody will find out. Not Buzzard, or Mann, or the publishers, and certainly not the readers."

Jerry groaned. "I hope you're right," he whispered.

Ann patted his hand. "I know I am," she said.

And she was.

In the months that followed, *The Aristocrats* hit the best-seller lists with such force that Al Buzzard bought a new yacht, with two swimming pools, one of which he kept filled with champagne. If anything, *The Taste-Makers* was an even bigger success. Conway Mann was able to purchase a Jackson Pollock, a Van Gogh, a Rembrandt, and another hat.

Best of all, Jerry Cribbs finally wrote his own novel, which was duly published under his own name. You may have read it.

Then again, you may not. It sold 148 copies.

Because 1976 was the nation's bicentennial, it's not surprising that mystery writers, along with writers in other fields, found plots in America's past. The most ambitious bicentennial tribute in the mystery field was S. S. Rafferty's series about colonial sleuth Captain Cork, with one story set in each of the thirteen colonies. Here's his Georgia story, a "social puzzle" about slavery and superstition.

S. S. RAFFERTY
The Georgia Resurrection

"To be sure, Captain Cork, I agree," Tolliver Smyth said, readjusting himself in the high-back cane chair after refilling our drinks. "Superstition is a weakness in the chain of reality, but even a weak link is better than none, especially here in the Georgia plantations."

Out in the darkness, through the heavy muslin screens that gave entry to a slight breeze and yet protected us from the fierce insects that churned out of the swamps, came the rhythms of drums. They had been beating since supper, and although a bit unnerving, the crude timpani was oddly hypnotic. Suddenly Smyth chuckled to himself.

"Was that meant to be a pun, Captain?" he asked. "Calling it *black* magic? Very clever when you come to think of it. The slaves call it *vodo*."

"Yes," Cork said. "I have run into it in the Indies, especially on Hispaniola. It is outlawed there, I believe."

"And frowned on here, sorry to say. What harm can a few drumbeats and a chant or two do, yet it scares the locals hereabout out of their skins. I say, if it keeps the slaves happy and productive, let them conjure away."

"You are most progressive, sir," Cork remarked, hiding his pejorative intent in mild observation. I, of course, could interpret his true feelings, for I know my employer better than any other man in the American colonies. Cork detests the concept of slavery; in fact, it was this abhorrence that had brought us to the Georgia colony in the summer of 1761.

When he first devised a machine for the harvesting of rice, I thought he had finally decided to put his mind to industry rather than the solution of what he calls "social puzzles." But the fervor with which he approached the task and the speed with which he implemented it soon told me his real mission. If he could successfully prove the economy of his intention, he would render slavery unnecessary in these terribly hot and dank deltas, where no white man could toil more than an hour or two at a time.

Tolliver Smyth's plantation was near the Brunswick settlement several miles up one of the many small rivers that finger this remote and sparsely populated area. The Tolliver lands were called a "spread" by its master, in contrast to the smaller farms scattered about the back country. Smyth himself was an amiable young man of thirty who had recently come out from England to try his hand at a frontier fortune. And he had the strong hands for it, despite all his gentlemanly ways.

During supper, before the drums from the slave quarters had started, our main topic of conversation had centered on the harvesting scheme itself, and there was much chiding at my expense because I was the only one of the trio who was beardless. Before we left Charleston, Cork had begun to allow his usually trim barba to spread into a full beard. I found the suggestion that I too grow a beard ludicrous, since the excessive heat of this semi-tropical place would roast a man to the bone.

Cork hadn't prepared me for the mosquitoes and gnats that had been eating me alive since we arrived. However, the bugs did not seem to bother Tunxis, the tamed Quinnipiac Indian who serves as the Captain's shadow. His method is to smear himself with a foul mixture of skunk oil and berry juice. It not only helps keep the insects away, but all humankind as well. As usual, he was out of doors somewhere—he refuses to enter under a roof.

We had arrived at Finderlay, as the plantation was called, earlier that day, and were now relaxing as best we could in the incessant heat. Overhead, from the veranda ceiling, swung a broad woven reed plank that served as a fan, its locomotion provided by some unseen black hand. We were sipping dark rum, Smyth and I having refused to join Cork in his own ritual of eating raw clams liberally laced with vinegar.

"Well, I can see where a Christian community would be upset by occult arts being practiced in their midst," I put in.

Cork looked up from a clamshell. "The only thing that doesn't upset a Christian is another Christian, Oaks," he said, devouring the clam meat, "and then only if he totally agrees with him. It seems you are the only white man on the place, Smyth."

"I plan to marry one of these days, but I have to get Finderlay in shape for womankind, I'm afraid. What is it, Neela? You look like a startled fidget."

The tall black woman who had just come out onto the veranda was indeed astir. When we arrived earlier, I had noticed that her button-brown eyes were bright and minikin gay; they were now horse-wide with fear. She didn't speak, and merely cocked her head toward the front of the house.

"What the deuce has gotten into you, girl?" Smyth said impatiently. "Are there callers?"

She merely nodded.

"Then show them out here," Smyth told her. "Must be the devil himself," he said as we waited. "She's usually a calm woman."

Seconds later we had evidence of her consternation. I felt my own throat tighten as they loomed into view through the candle haze, presenting us with a bizarre duo of ominous dimensions.

Though the temperature had to be well over ninety degrees, and the humidity thickly oppressive, both men were dressed in winter greatcoats of immense bulk and mourning blackness. Despite their out-of-season bundlement, they showed no sign of discomfort; their alabaster faces glistened like hoarfrost on chipped stone. They could have been citizens of the netherworld, and instinctively I was repelled by them.

The taller of the two was heavyset, with a leonine head and a cavernous mouth that echoed his speech in deep drum tones. The other man was snipelike in stature, with pathetically thin legs supporting an immense upper torso; when he spoke, he had a habit of turning his oblong head from side to side as if he were unable to see over his sharply pointed nose.

The latter announced himself as Zachary Gooms, and the black scarf trailing from the rim of his tricorne had already told us his profession of gravesman. The taller one announced that he was Simon Cratch, who made his living as a hangman. This was certainly strange postprandial companionship, and Smyth seemed annoyed at the intrusion by men of such low station.

"We bury our own here at Finderlay, Gooms, and slaves are too expensive to hang, Cratch, no matter what the crime."

"Well, sir," Cratch said uneasily, "we thought we could save you some trouble, since we understand you let your nigras practice heathen religion."

"What my people do on Finderlay is my affair," Smyth said

sternly. "What *trouble* are you talking about?"

"Well, sir, Gooms is the local man, so I'll let him tell it," Cratch acceded to his companion.

Smyth raised a hand in tacit approval. "Go on, Gooms, I thought you looked familiar. You have a coffin shop in Brunswick."

"Correct, sir, coffins and burials and fine furniture, if you wish. But even as the official county gravesman, it's a poor living. Now the coffins are gaining favor with the townsfolk, although you people out in the back country still make your own. But the furniture's another matter, with people sending to England for it."

"At least you can make a living," Cratch lamented. "I purposely came to Georgia thinking there would be a great need for my services."

"Why is that?" Cork queried.

Cratch looked at Smyth, who said, "This is Captain Jeremy Cork and his yeoman, Wellman Oaks."

"Well, Captain Cork," Cratch went on, "it seemed to me that since many of the felons were being transported from our gaols at home to Georgia, and felons never changing their ways, as you know, there would be a brisk business for me.

"But it turned out not to be the case, and I near starved for lack of commissions. To add to my misfortune and a stroke of bad timing, I requested transfer back to England and was granted it. Of course now the Escape Commission is a-comin' over and there'll be lots of work for the new man at the derrick."

"Escape Commission? Sounds royal and self-contradictory," I said.

"Its mission has received quite a broadcast in these parts, gentlemen," Smyth explained. "Not only are the colonists perturbed by the legally transported convicts, but terror is slowly building up over the escaped cutthroats who somehow make it to these shores and seek refuge among old criminal friends."

"Yes," Cork said, "several newspapers in the north have come out quite strongly for an end to transportation."

"Aye, and woe to my timing of transfer," Cratch consoled himself.

"The Commission will bring with them a warder from each of the main prisons who know these escaped scoundrels on sight. They'll be full gibbets from here to Canada, they will. Now as luck would have it I missed my ship at Brunswick and happened by Mr. Gooms's shop. I wouldn't want the foul deed on my record."

"Foul deed? What are you talking about, man?" Smyth was irritated and abrupt. Cork seemed interested, however, and tried to calm our host.

"Perhaps these fellows have a tale to tell, Smyth. It will pass the evening. Why don't you two sit down?"

Smyth nodded agreement and they took seats.

"Well, gentlemen, the problem seems to be Arthur Briddleton here." As Gooms said it, he took a white plaster sculpture from under his greatcoat and laid it on the table. The object was a man's face in repose. The nose was aquiline, the skin smooth and unlined. It was the death mask of a man in his late twenties.

"You are quite expert in the art of death masks, Gooms. Is that one of your services to clients?" Cork asked.

"No, sir, it's more trouble than it's worth to me, but the Governor has ordered that one be made of every executed criminal."

I shot a quick glance in Cork's direction, but he ignored me. Just six months ago he had suggested this method of verifying the deaths of criminals to Major Philip Tell, a special King's agent at large. I could see that Tell had wasted no time in turning Cork's advice to his own advantage. However, I could not fault the Major, for I could see little profit in the business. Cork was speaking again. "And this, you say, is Arthur Briddleton's face?"

"Well, sir," Simon Cratch's voice boomed over us like cannon fire, "that's the heart of the matter, so to speak. I say that's *not* the face of the man called Briddleton who I hanged on Monday last, and Mr. Gooms insists that it is."

"Nay, Mr. Cratch, that's not correct. I claim that is the death mask of the body I picked up at the gibbet at Landsdown crossing at sundown on Monday last. I never knew Arthur Briddleton and could not swear what he looked like. I say the man hanging there bore the face you see in the mask."

"Gentlemen," Cork said, raising an open palm, "if you will let me ask a few questions to put the problem in its traces, I think we can be of help. Would you care for a drink?"

Gooms said no, but Cratch eyed the bottle near Cork's plate of clams. "Would that be vinegar I smell, sir?"

Cork nodded. "Yes, I believe a red wine gone sour, and quite tart."

"Then I'll happily take a cup. Helps with the heat."

My own mouth felt like cotton as I watched him drink down the acetose liquid and wondered if indeed it did keep one cool. Cork proceeded with a methodical interrogation, from which I have summarized the following.

On the previous Sunday (this being a Thursday evening), a stranger to the locality, who gave his name as Arthur Briddleton, was

seized while stealing a horse in an inland village known as Landsdown. He was immediately brought to the local Justice of the Peace,
who tried and convicted him. The punishment, as usual, was hanging. There was some argument about executing a man on the Sabbath, and it was decided to hold it on the following day.

"And most fortunate for Briddleton at that," Cratch said. "I was
on my way up from Waverly to take ship at Brunswick for England
when I heard there was supposed to be a hanging at Landsdown.
Believe me, I'm not one to miss a fee. Lucky lad, Briddleton."

"Lucky?" I echoed unconsciously.

"Certainly, Mr. Oaks," Cratch said with a wink. "A man con-
demned to death can suffer on the string, for if the noose is applied
by some amateur, the hanging can be most unpleasant. But old
Simon Cratch was handy, and he went swiftly and sweetly. But that
mask isn't Arthur Briddleton."

"And just what did your Briddleton look like?" Cork asked.

"Well, the first thing I noticed when I happened to stop by
Gooms's shop and saw the mask was that the scar along the left cheek
was missing. Then the nose was different. This one is quite pointed,
whereas the nose of the man on the gallows was flatlike."

"Of course this was a public execution," Cork said.

"Out in the open, but with no witnesses except the J.P., Bill Tooks.
Folks want justice, gentlemen, but they don't like to see it dispatched.
I put him on the string about two in the afternoon and went my way,
for I had the ship to catch. As luck would have it, I missed her. Now,
by the look you're aiming at me, Captain, I know you're asking
yourself, was the man dead, and I can assure you he was. I've put
fifty men on the derrick in my day, and not a manjack of them ever
walked away." He sat back with a self-satisfied, smug, "I'll take some
more of that vinegar, if you please, sir. It's got a fine bite."

Cork refilled the cup and turned to Zachary Gooms. "Now will you
tell your part in all this?"

"Glad to," the gravesman said, clearing his throat. "When I heard
the nine tolls plus one for a dead man on the Landsdown bell, I knew
I was needed for a felon burial. It's part of my contract to care for
public graves, and when the bell is rung nine times and one, it's to tell
me to come at sundown. The body is left on the gibbet till that time as
an example, although most people avoid the Crossing when a body
has swung.

"Well, sir, I took my cart out there to that deserted gibbet and
brought the corpse back to Brunswick. As I was passing through the
delta road by your bottom acreage, Mr. Smyth, I came upon a group

of your nigras dancing and cavorting in a grove just off the road. It was like a witch's sabbath, it was, with drums and rattles and the like. Most hellish.

"I can't tell you how uneasy I was, and I gave the horse a crack to get out of the neighborhood, for I wanted no truck with black devils. Then, damnation, my old Ned rears up and pushes the cart into a gulley. The noises attracted the nigras, and they came running to see. I'll say this for your boys, Mr. Smyth, they were most helpful. They got the cart back on the road and I was off like cannonshot. I got back to Brunswick, made the mask, and buried the body outside town to the west, in the poor-field, in an unmarked grave. The face you see in that mask is the face of the man I buried. I swear to it, sir!"

Tolliver Smyth, who had been sitting with his booted feet spread in front of him during the narration, now stood up menacingly. "Are you implying that my slaves had something to do with this?"

"Now, Mr. Smyth, sir," Gooms said hesitantly, "I just state the facts."

"Despite the heat," Cork put in, "let's keep cool heads. Did you look at the corpse when you took it down at the gibbet, Gooms?"

"It was hard to see in lanternlight, Captain. The first good look I got of him was when I reached my shop."

"Then the bodies could have been switched on the gibbet," Cork suggested.

"Switched!" Gooms said in confusion, "I never thought of that. I thought those black devils put a spell on the body. You know, used magic."

"Gooms," Cork said, "it is best to look to reality for an answer before bringing in the occult. Consider your own precarious position, sir. You bury a body that does not resemble the hanged man. That, my lad, is suspicious."

Gooms was visibly disturbed. "Why would I do anything like that? I made the mask, didn't I?"

"Of course, but you assumed that Cratch would be off to England and the J.P. at Landsdown would never see the mask, since it would be sent to the officials in Savannah."

"I beg you, sir," the gravesman pleaded, "I am an honest man."

"And you shall have a chance to prove it."

"Thank God for that," Gooms said fervently, "but how can I?"

"With the greatest ease—by resurrection." As Cork said the word, a sudden silence fell over the company. Gooms looked horrified, and Cratch—yes, even that grim hangman seemed uneasy. Tolliver Smyth was shocked. For myself, I was appalled.

"Dig up the body?" I said. "Why, that's sacrilegious!"

"Well, my fellows, you can't have it both ways," the Captain admonished us all. "We have a dispute over identity, so we must let the corpse speak for itself."

"Begging the Captain's pardon," Cratch said, "I'm as hard a man as any—but resurrection! I'd as soon forget the whole affair. In fact, the more I look at this mask, the only thing different is the scar and the nose."

"But I can't forget it; nor can you, Smyth," Cork said. "These fellows have made a serious accusation against your slaves, and it's bound to start disquieting rumors. No, the body *must* be resurrected at once. Let's see, buried just four days ago. Hmmm, should be still in fine condition for identification."

"Well, an official will have to pass on it," Gooms said humbly. "I'm all for it, but I'll not take it on my own head."

"To be sure. Let us keep it legal," Cork advised. "And who better to order Briddleton resurrected than the man who sentenced him to the grave? Now get you both to this J.P. and resolve the issue."

Both men got up to leave when Cork stopped them. "Oh, yes, you lads had better leave the death mask here, for safekeeping."

After our eerie visitors had left, Smyth suggested we turn in, for we had a long day ahead of us in the rice fields. I was all for it and, despite the heat, dropped off to sleep in minutes. It was still dark of night when I sat bolt upright in bed, a hand covering my mouth.

"By Jerusalem, Oaks, be quiet," Cork's voice whispered. "Come, get dressed, we have work to do."

Minutes later we were out of the main house, prowling about the outbuildings. We came upon a small shed, and Cork slipped inside, returned in a trice, and tapped my shoulder. "Come in, I've found it," he said.

Once inside he shut the door and relit a candle. It was nothing more than a workshed, quite like any that one would expect to find on a self-sustaining plantation which makes everything from shoes to shingles for itself. I watched the Captain as he uncovered a barrel of chalky white powder and scooped some into a bowl. To this he added water from a bucket in a corner and proceeded to beat the mixture into a paste.

"It is fortunate that the Smyth main house has plaster walls, and that the materials are at hand," Cork said.

He dumped the paste onto a worktable, and then, to my surprise, took the Briddleton mask from inside his shirt. He laid the mask next to the heap of white paste and began to shape the stuff into a facsimile, smoothing the features of a face on it. I watched him work in silence, and after half an hour he stepped back and cupped his bearded chin with his hand, as if admiring a masterpiece.

"If your creation is supposed to match the original, I can assure you that you are no sculptor, Captain."

"It will do. Same general shape, similar nose, eyes. Yes, it will do fine. Now this will have to dry before we can move it." He picked up the original and tucked it back into his shirt. "Now we shall take a little stroll, old son," he said, going out into the moonlit, drum-beating night.

We were only ten yards from the workshed when he stopped and put both hands to his mouth, one cupped over the other, and delivered the most perfect imitation of a lake loon I have ever heard. I have tried it myself several times and failed, to Tunxis's amusement, for this is how the savage and Cork sometimes communicate. At the edge of a clearing I could hear the return call and knew that Tunxis was nearby. Cork walked off to meet him. When he returned to me, I said, "This is all so befuddling."

"That is because your mind is on other things. Come, our stroll is not over."

I followed him across the clearing into the underbrush, and ten minutes later found myself in a deep swamp, gingerly trodding along a hummock that snaked its way across the dark black water, hiding God knows what in its depths. Ahead of us the drums grew louder. I was amazed at the way Cork so assuredly picked his way along, till I realized that Tunxis must have marked the trail for him. We stopped for a moment while he got his bearings, and I asked him where we were headed.

"One of the sad thoughts in my life, Oaks, is that my adventures have kept you from romance. Tonight we shall rectify the oversight. Ah, there are lights ahead, and our destination."

The hummock suddenly broadened into a small island that rose slowly out of the swamps. Giant mangroves tentacled out of the water to make it a fortress, an evil bastion.

When we came into the clearing, the drums suddenly stopped. A group of black men and women were sitting by a fire, looking at us in wonderment. A huge muscular fellow rose slowly to his feet and came toward us.

"Why, it's the Cappin' who's visitin' the mastah," he said with a smile of relief. "You musta lost your way. Load a danger in the swamp at night, sirs. Come, I take you back so's you don't get ate by a 'gator."

"You are called Big Blue, I believe. I saw you this afternoon in the fields. You're a good worker."

The man smiled at the flattery. "Big Blue worth ten men, the mastah say. Make's Big Blue head man. Come, I take you back, sirs."

"No. First I must see the *mambo*."

Big Blue's amiable face froze in terror. "No *mambo* here at Finderlay, sir. No *vodo*. No priest woman, no sir."

"A *zohop* then, one who knows the plants and leaves. My friend here is in need of *vervain*." As he said it, he placed his hands over his heart and feigned a swoon, which brought hearty laughter from the campfire. Although it broke the tension, I didn't like having it done at my expense. I assumed *vervain* had something to do with the romance he had alluded to.

Amid all the laughter an ancient black woman emerged from the shack and sat herself on a tree stump. She was old and wizened; a bright red bandanna covered her head, while a gingham shawl hid her shrunken body. She let out a cackle and motioned us forward.

When we reached her, Cork bowed slightly and handed her two coins. "This is Mamabin," Big Blue said. "Very old, very much head for dreams."

The crone looked up at Cork and told him, "You are as high as a tree, which means your head always clear. How do you come by the tongue of the swamps?"

"I have put time in the Indies, old mother."

"Pirate?" she shouted.

"No, mother, a traveler. Please, a *vervain* for my friend."

She cocked an eye at me and looked me over from head to toe. "Hard to do, hard to do, but we try." She put her hand into a grass-woven satchel at her feet and took out a handful of leaves. She scrutinized her palm and then selected five leaves of equal size and handed them to me. They were nothing more than oleander leaves.

"Pin one each to the corner of your pillow and one in the center. Then you sleep and dream of lady you will marry." It was all nonsense, but I took them and thanked her.

"Tell me, old mother," Cork said, "what is the way to make a zombi walk?"

She immediately cringed, and he was quick to calm her.

"I know you don't make zombi, but I have great interest, and it may help your master."

"Mastah Tolliver good man," she said. "No whips here at Finderlay. Make Blue head man. Good mastah. Someone has spell on him?"

"Not yet, but in case it happens."

"They say make zombi drink salt water and he speak."

"You are very wise, old mother. I am told you can make zombi if you hang a dead man from his heels and take three drops from his nose."

She tossed her head back and cackled. "That would be a *pizen,* child."

"Or is it a pin stuck into a lime while still on the tree from sunup to sunup and then squeezing the juice?"

She cackled again. "More *pizen.*"

"Or is it the black-leaf tea, old mother?"

At this remark she went silent. "*Houngan.* You *houngan.*"

"I know more of magic than these people should hear old mother. Come, let us go inside where we can talk."

He was in with her for almost half an hour, while I stood in the campfire-lit grove a bit uneasily. He finally came out, and we left the place hurriedly. Once back at the main plantation, we picked up the now dry, rude copy of the death mask, and crept up to our rooms.

"I take it she is a witch of some kind," I said to him before going into my own bedchamber.

"More an herbal magician, or a *docteur feuilles*, as the French colonists call them. These old tribal rites and beliefs brought over from Africa have been diluted and fragmented by time and locale, but the basics are still there. That's what I was after tonight."

"And did you get it?"

"Sweet dreams, old son," he said, shutting his door.

All this confusion had muddled my mind, and only sleep could clear it. I fell asleep for the second time that night with a bit of difficulty, for the oleander leaves on my pillow kept scratching my ear.

For the next two days we heard nothing from Cratch or Gooms and had little time to think of their problem. We were up with the sun and into the rice fields, where Cork made elaborate calculations and closely observed the method of harvesting. I spent most of my time swatting bugs. Each night Cork spent long hours at his drawings, leaving me to bide my time with Tolliver Smyth, who proved to be a well-read fellow.

Even Saturday night could not drag the Captain from his work, and Smyth and I repaired to drink once again on the veranda.

"One of my men, Big Blue, tells me that you paid a visit to the old woman in the swamps," he said, lighting a seegar. "Best be careful back in there. Hundred of quicksand places that could swallow a man forever."

I shuddered inwardly and thanked the Lord for Tunxis's trailblazing ability. I hadn't seen the savage since that night, and wondered where he was off to. But he does that now and again, so I paid it no heed.

"I'm afraid your visit has spoiled me, for I shall miss our talks and fellowship when you are gone," Smyth said.

"Not many neighbors?"

"These plantations are so vast that there is little sociality, and then in the small villages they don't take to strangers, at least not to me."

"They think you are too easy on the slaves?"

"Yes. Always talk of keeping them down for fear of an uprising. If the poor devils do a day's work, let them be. But then maybe it's me personally they don't like. After all, Bill Tooks is as new out here as I am, and the locals took to him like a duck to water. Elected him J.P. and all that."

"Never confuse competence with popularity." We looked up to see Cork coming out onto the veranda from the house. "It is one of the flaws of the human race. We seem to have visitors, gentlemen."

Out in the darkness was the sound of horses' hooves, and one of the house slaves ran into the yard with a torch illuminating the arriving party. Three men were a-horse—Gooms, Cratch, and an unknown man. The fourth person, on foot, was known well to me.

"Take a care, sirs!" Cork shouted. "That's a war chief of the Quinnipiac you have bound by rope and lead on a halter."

"Runaway slave from the West Indies, if I have it right," growled the stranger. He was a fierce man with a black beard and wore rough back-country clothes. Smyth got to his feet and was seemingly about to corroborate Cork, when the Captain stopped him.

"Never shout a truth when you can exhibit it," he said to our host. "Very well, sir, you operate at your own peril."

Then, to Tunxis he said something in Indian jabber, and in a second the redskin's hands were not only free, but whipping the tether and the stranger from his horse.

"Help the gentleman up, Tunxis, and dust him off a bit. I suggest you let him do it, sir, for he could have your scalp in a trice if he cared to."

"It's all right, Bill, the Indian is with Captain Cork!" Smyth shouted.

There was much swearing from Justice of the Peace Tooks as the three men climbed to the veranda. Cork went into the yard and talked with Tunxis, who handed him a piece of paper he had concealed in his moccasin.

Tooks was saying, "How was I to know he was a bloody prince or something?" when Cork returned.

"No harm done, Mr. Tooks. An Indian in unfamiliar country walking alone is, of course, suspicious, since the red man is used as a slave in the Indies. I can see that you were only doing your duty as a J.P."

This seemed to placate the man for a few moments, and then he became irritable again. "And I'm here to do my duty, I can assure you. These are strange doings indeed. Never saw the like of it. Gooms and Cratch arguing over who's hung and who's buried. I've been off in the wilderness for two days or I'd have been on this sooner. I'm not opening a man's grave, felon or not, until I find out which one's lying. I'm told you have the death mask, Cork, and I want it produced now."

"Of course, Justice Tooks, I'll fetch it and along the way I'll make you some of my own Apple Knock. Would you rather have more vinegar, Mr. Cratch?"

The hangman smiled. "I'm not against a bit of liquor, sir."

Cork asked me to assist him, and, as we left the veranda, Tooks was growling at Smyth, "If any of your damned darkies had anything to do with this, they'll all hang."

Once inside, Cork sent me to his room to get the mask. He was mixing the Knock when I returned below stairs. How he expected to pass off this childish copy as a death mask, I had no idea. I was preceding him out the door when he tripped me and sent me sprawling forward. The mask flew from my hands and smashed to pieces.

"Oaks, you jackanapes!" he shouted at me. "Now look what you've done. You'll be flogged for this!"

"Is that the mask?" Tooks cried.

"*Was* the mask, I'm afraid, Mr. Justice," Cork apologized. "You must forgive this menial of mine."

I was stunned at such treatment from the man I considered my friend. Seeing my anger, Cork admonished me, "Hold your tongue, man, that's an order!"

"Now that's done it." Tooks was red with anger. "Now I'll have to open the grave."

"I think not, sir," Cork said, handing the drinks around. "The explanation to this is quite simple. Tell me, Mr. Cratch, when did you arrive at Landsdown?"

"Why, Sunday in the forenoon, right after the trial."

"And how did you spend your time, sir? The hanging wasn't until

Monday afternoon, which in itself is strange, since executions are normally at dawn."

"I'll tell you what he did, he got himself drunk as a lord." Tooks pointed a finger at Cratch. "Couldn't get the sot awake till almost one on Monday. I wouldn't have paid him a fee in advance if I knew he was a drunkard."

"So we have a bleary-eyed rumpot who says the man hanged is not the man buried. Your proclivity for vinegar is not uncommon among men who drink too much, Cratch. It is the fool's notion that acid thins the blood and makes one sober. In the Pennsylvania colony sauerkraut juice is the common remedy."

"You mean all this trouble was caused by a drunken hangman?" Tooks was now livid. "By thunderation I'll put *him* on the gibbet, I will!"

"Have a care, Mr. Justice, you may not be so lucky next time."

"Lucky? What do you mean, lucky?"

"Well, Mr. Tooks—" Cork took a piece of paper from his pocket "—two days ago I dispatched my Indian friend to Savannah by coaster with an accurate description of the death mask. Now in my report to the Governor, I failed to mention that you tried Arthur Briddleton on a Sunday, which is illegal, and thus so was his sentence. I did not mention that you might have committed judicial murder, for it was not my purpose to bring the Royal Governor down on your head. I have an interest in this death-mask system, sir, because I am its inventor. Well, lo and behold, you are a bit of a hero, for Tunxis brings me word that you have successfully tried, convicted, and hung none other than Black Jack Herleigh."

"The escaped highwayman? My word!" Tooks beamed. "He was one of the blackguards mentioned in the Escape Commission's proclamation. Think of it, gentlemen—me, Bill Tooks, captured and hung a notorious robber that all the King's men couldn't keep or find!"

He took a long draught to his success from his Knock and smiled anew. Suddenly, in the instant of a swallow, his face went white and he fell forward on the floor.

"Quick, you two! To the well for cool water!"

"It's no use, Captain Cork," the gravesman said, looking down at Tooks's face. "I knows a corpse when I sees one."

"I said water and fast!" Cork said with a roar that sent both men scurrying outside.

Smyth bent over the body, rolled back the eyelids, then put his head to Tooks's chest.

"Too much excitement, I would guess," Cork said.

Smyth got to his feet and rushed indoors, mumbling, "Damn fool." He returned seconds later and poured liquid from a small blue philtre into Tooks's mouth. The man's eyes began to flutter and his breath came heavy at first and then steadied.

"You're all right, Mr. Tooks," Cork said, kneeling down. "You've had a bit of a fright, that's all. You should take things easier in the future, for I think you may have some trouble with your heart."

Within the hour the Justice of the Peace was on his feet again and as feisty as ever. "You, Cratch, had better be on the next boat out of Brunswick, if you know what's good for you. And you, Zachary Gooms, help me to home. I'm sorry to have caused you trouble, Tolliver. Drop over soon to meet the folks at Landsdown. There's a young widow I'd like you to meet."

When the hoofbeats were out of earshot, we all sat down again to our drinks and relaxed.

"Well, I must say all's well that ends well," I chuckled. "But this affair must have had little zest for you, Captain, since it proved to be no puzzle at all."

He gave me that smirk-a-mouth. "More of a puzzle than you think, old son." He turned to Smyth. "Why don't you take off the false beard, Black Jack? Your own must be grown in fairly well by now."

"Black Jack? Black Jack Herleigh? Come now, Captain."

Then, before my eyes, the planter removed his thick beard and revealed a good seven-days' growth.

"When did you get on to me?" he asked.

"I was sure when you went for the antidote to the datura and gave it to Tooks. If you hadn't, I would have administered my own concoction."

I was astounded. "I don't understand this at all. Isn't Herleigh supposed to be in his grave?"

"Hold fast, Oaks. Let us start from the beginning. You will recall when Cratch and Gooms first brought us the problem, I offered the simplest of solutions. One body, probably Briddleton's, was replaced by another. But whose, and, more pointedly, why? The who, of course, would have required clairvoyance; the why, however, although a puzzling question, was not beyond *all* conjecture."

"Well, I've thought about that," I said, "and fell upon the idea that someone had been murdered and that his corpse had somehow gotten into Gooms's hands for a legal burial."

"Then you didn't think hard enough, Oaks. A murdered corpse could be hidden eternally in the quicksand of the swamps. No, the

purpose of the replacement was one of *identity*. Either to hide Briddleton's or to expose the face on the mask. And the answer leans to
the latter in light of the Escape Commission's imminent arrival.
Briddleton was a complete stranger hereabouts with no friends to
identify him. And even if he were an escaped felon, what could be
gained by hiding his identity after death?"

"And that's why you sent the original mask to Savannah?" I asked.

Smyth-Herleigh looked agitated. "I thought you said you sent a
description, and that those smashed bits of plaster are the remains of
the mask."

"A mere diversion, Jack Herleigh, or should I say Tolliver Smyth,
for you are forever safe in your new identity. The Commission has
now written you off as dead, and will not look for a man who has
been officially buried. Hanged and buried. You can be assured that
Tooks is so inflated by his capturing and hanging a notorious highwayman that nothing could convince him to the contrary. Black Jack
Herleigh is 'dead.' "

"But that's what I don't understand," I said. "If Herleigh—that is
Smyth—posed as a corpse to have his freshly shaved face cast in a
mask, how could he fool a gravesman?"

"Because to all intents and purposes he *was* dead, Oaks. He was a
zombi until his slaves could dig him out of the grave and put Briddleton's body in his place."

"A zombi? Why, zombis are mere superstition!"

"To the uninitiated, yes, but a person can be suspended in a
catatonic deathlike trance with any of several tropical drugs. In
South America it is curare; in Hispaniola, datura is used."

"Or mancenillier," Smyth-Herleigh interjected.

"I see you know herbal medicine as well as Mamabin."

"Not really, but she made the sleep draft for me when I learned of
the Escape Commission's coming. I was a wild lad in the old days,
and took to the highway more for the adventure than for the profit. I
never killed anyone, despite the reports of my savagery. My main sin
seems to have been escaping from Newgate and cheating the
hangman. Out here I planned a new life."

"And you have it, sir."

"Thanks to you, yes. When I learned that a man near my age and
build was going to be hanged in Landsdown, I saw my chance to
throw the Escape Commission off my trail, so I took the draft and
had the slaves put my 'dead' body in place of Briddleton's during the
slaves' diversion on the Delta road. But how could you know it was
my face in the mask? I had to shave clean for the death mask. Is this

false beard so bad?"

"No," Cork said, "it's quite good, in fact. Until Tunxis returned, I had no inkling of a man named Black Jack Herleigh. But I did suspect that the affair had something to do with a run-away criminal, and both yourself and Tooks were new to the neighborhood. I decided on you, for Tooks, in his official capacity, could have made a mask of his own face and sent it along to Savannah without any hanging at all. You proved your mettle tonight when you gave Tooks the antidote for the death-sleep potion I put in his Knock."

"I thought Neela had done it to protect me."

"Your slaves think well of you, Smyth, and I suspect your attitude comes from having spent some time in chains yourself. If you perfect this new scheme of mine for rice production, you may well have no need for them. What the devil are you doing, Oaks?"

"I'm rubbing my shin where you tripped me."

"Sorry, old son, but I had to trip you. It was necessary to the charade."

I was truly touched until he gave me that smirk-a-mouth again.

"Of course, you can trot off to the swamps and have Mamabin fix you a poultice. And while you're there, have her give you new oleander leaves for your pillow. The old ones have scratched the back of your neck, and you are dreaming of the wrong things."

I decided to ignore him, but he is uncanny. How could he know that I had dreamed of my account books?

And there were celebrations, too, at the time of the centennial, back in 1876...

EDWARD D. HOCH
The Centennial Assassin

General Custer and 264 of his men had died at the Little Big Horn on Sunday. Now it was the following Saturday, and an air of gloom hung over Rodney Young's office in the White House. Usually he tried to leave early on Saturdays during the summer, looking forward to an afternoon of riding in the country, but this day there was no escaping the duties of office.

"A terrible thing to happen so close to the centennial celebration," he remarked to President Grant's private secretary, Leroy E. Cherage, who lounged in one of the big overstuffed chairs.

"Can't the army do anything about Sitting Bull and Crazy Horse?" Cherage asked without changing his position. He was a young man of French descent, one of a handful who had been brought in recently to replace the discredited former secretary, General Babcock. In an administration riddled with corruption that reached to the Cabinet itself, the collusion of General Babcock had been a personal embarrassment to the President. Thus his replacement with young men like Cherage, who offered no threat to anyone.

But Rodney Young personally found it difficult to work with them. His duties at the White House, as a glorified appointments secretary, were vague enough at best. Dealing with the likes of Cherage and others was almost more than he could manage. "I am certain the army will do what it can," he said, answering the young man's question. "But obviously not in time for Tuesday's centennial."

Leroy Cherage pressed his lips together. "Has word of the massacre reached the press as yet?"

"I fear it's only a matter of time. When the scouts reach Helena, in the Montana Territory, word will be telegraphed to Salt Lake City and then east. It's a wonder the army managed to notify us first—but then it still took six days." He played with an ink bottle on his desk, trying to form some plan of action. He hated this blot on the centennial festivities.

Rodney stood up suddenly. "I must see the President," he said with decision.

"At this hour? You know he is working on his memoirs."

"Yes," Rodney agreed, with a trace of annoyance in his voice. Even the impeachment and resignation of Secretary of War Belknap a few months earlier had not made an impact on Grant. At times it seemed he was more interested in reliving his wartime triumphs than in dealing with corruption and Indian attacks and the nation's one hundredth birthday. "Yes," he repeated. "But I'm going in to see him anyway."

He crossed the waiting room and entered the President's second-floor office adjoining the Cabinet room. Ulysses S. Grant looked up with a trace of annoyance. "What is it, Rodney? Can't you see I'm busy?" The odor of cigar smoke was heavy in the room.

"It's about the Custer affair, Mr. President."

Grant shot a glance at the door that led to the private telegraph room adjoining his office. It had been there since Lincoln's time, and that was how the word of Custer's tragedy had reached the White House. "What about it? I've already ordered the army to take appropriate measures."

Rodney cleared his throat. "The word of the massacre hasn't yet reached the public, sir. I was wondering if it might be delayed until Wednesday—until the day following the centennial celebration."

"How could we do that?"

"As I understand it, sir, the word is being carried by scouts to Helena. They're in army employ, and a telegraph message to one of the forts along the route could delay them for a matter of days."

"Do we have telegraph communications with forts in that area?"

Rodney pointed to the big map on the north wall of the office. "Here, Mr. President, at this settlement. Our message could intercept the riders there when they stop to change horses. I only ask for a few days' time, so as not to distress the nation in its moment of glory."

President Grant scratched his beard and considered the request. "Very well," he decided. "Do what you can to delay the news. It can do no harm to those poor fellows now."

"Thank you, sir." Rodney prepared to leave, then decided to press his luck on another bothersome point. "About the centennial, Mr. President—have you decided on your schedule for Tuesday as yet?"

Grant snorted. "I'll not ride the train to Philadelphia, if that's what you're asking."

"You've been invited to address the Centennial Exhibition—"

"I was there for opening day in May, and that's enough! Philadelphia is too damn hot in July. For that matter, Washington is also too damn hot in July."

"Surely you should do something to commemorate the day."

"I issued a proclamation suggesting public religious services, didn't I? Let the people go to church in the morning and watch fireworks in the evening. They don't want speeches from me." His voice took on a tone approaching bitterness. "They don't want anything but to get me out of here and put Hayes or Tilden in my place."

"You've served nearly two terms, sir," Rodney reminded him. "And with the scandals—"

"I know, I know. But don't ask me to go to Philadelphia." It was almost a plea.

"Very well, Mr. President." Rodney Young withdrew and closed the door. It was still four months to the election, and even longer before Grant's term officially ended. Rodney wondered if he'd be able to cope that long.

After sending off a coded telegraph message to the post commander in the Montana Territory, Rodney had just pulled down the cover of his rolltop desk when George Peters poked his head in from the Clerk's office to announce a visitor. "A young woman, sir. Miss Elizabeth Blazer."

"Elizabeth! Send her in, by all means." He could imagine no one else whose arrival would have delayed his afternoon in the country. But for Elizabeth Blazer he could wait.

She was a slim, attractive young woman with dark hair and pale skin and she swept into his office as if arriving to take command of a regiment. He had never known a woman quite so alive and sure of herself as Elizabeth Blazer, and the very sight of her stirred something deep within him.

"How are you, Elizabeth?" he greeted her, rising to take her hand.

"I'm well, Rod." She was the only one who ever called him that. "The White House seems a busy place for a Saturday."

"We're preparing for Tuesday," he replied, stretching the truth a bit. Elizabeth was deeply involved in centennial activities, working with the city of Philadelphia on its exhibition. The White House's participation—or lack of it—was a sore spot between them.

"Do you mean President Grant has had a change of heart about speaking at the centennial?" she asked.

"Not exactly. But we're busy on other aspects."

She seated herself in a chair opposite his desk, pulling up her long skirts to expose a glimpse of ankle. "Actually, I'm not here to badger you about that today, Rod. I have news for you that might be terribly urgent."

"What is it?"

"A woman came to me in Philadelphia with a story that President Grant's life is in danger."

"There are always such stories," he assured her. "Ever since Lincoln the people seem to dwell on the possibilities of assassination."

"She says he's to be killed before Tuesday—on the eve of the centennial celebration."

"There's no great danger of that," Rodney confided. "I doubt if he plans to stir out of the White House over the weekend, except possibly for church services."

"Those Methodists are like that," she said with an irreverent smile. "All the same, I think you should see this woman, Rod."

"See her?"

"I brought her with me to Washington."

"You take her story that seriously?"

"I remember Mr. Lincoln. President Grant is no Lincoln, but I don't want it to happen again." She shifted in her chair. "As I understand it, there is still no government agency charged with safeguarding the President's life."

"Congress doesn't seem to think one is needed. The Lincoln assassination was an aberration, the final gasp of that terrible war. It wouldn't happen again in a hundred years."

"You believe that, Rod? You believe there is no one in this country who would like Grant dead and the nation in disarray as the centennial approaches?"

"All right, perhaps I don't believe it. What should we do? The only police agency the Federal government has is the Secret Service, and their job is to deal with the flood of counterfeit money we've had since the war. They're hardly equipped to guard the President."

"Will you come listen to this woman's story, Rod?" Elizabeth pleaded. "She's waiting at my hotel."

He could see there was no escaping it. "I'll come. I have faith in your judgment."

She smiled slightly and rose from her chair. "Then let us go to meet Mrs. Ready."

They were staying at Willard's Hotel on Fourteenth Street, which had been the city's most popular meeting place since before the war.

Even now, on a Saturday afternoon, Rodney could hear the clamor of masculine voices from the bar off the lobby, and a haze of blue cigar smoke hung thick within.

But Elizabeth led him past the bar, where no woman ventured, and up the main staircase to the rooms above. Mrs. Ready was waiting there to receive them, and the first sight of her was a shock. Though her age might have been under sixty, her hands trembled with the feebleness of a much older woman. She needed a cane to stand and greet him, and he hastened to urge she be seated. Her eyes too, full of anxious uncertainty, reflected a troubled mind that had long ago seen its best days.

"Elizabeth told me of your warning, Mrs. Ready," Rodney said, seating himself gingerly on the edge of a chair opposite her. "It was noble of you to make the tiring trip from Philadelphia."

"I so fear for the President's life," she said in a voice stronger than he'd expected. "I must see him to warn him."

"I'm afraid a personal appointment would be impossible, because of the press of official business. You must understand. But I will certainly see that your message is delivered directly to him."

She seemed unsatisfied, but after a moment's hesitation she agreed. "Very well. Perhaps after you hear my story you will change your mind as to the seriousness of the threat."

"We are always concerned for the President's safety," he told her. "Just who do you think is going to kill him?"

"My son," she replied quietly.

"Your—"

"Did Elizabeth tell you who I am?"

"Only that your name is Mrs. Ready."

"Sarah Ready. But the *Mrs.* is only a convenience. I have never been married." She paused, trying to control the tremor in her right hand. "I was employed for a time by the late Horace Greeley."

"He was a great newspaperman."

"He supported your General Grant in the early years of his Presidency, but the corruption became too much for poor Horace to accept. That is why he ran against Grant on the Liberal Republican and Democratic tickets in seventy-two. You know what happened. The pressures of the campaign drove poor Horace to madness and death less than a month after the voting."

"You can't blame President Grant for that," Rodney said. "He had nothing but the deepest regard for Greeley."

She waved away his remark. "Be that as it may, there is one person who believes Grant caused poor Horace's terrible death. That person intends to have his revenge by assassinating the President."

"Your son?"

She nodded. "My son. Franklin Ready."

"Just why does he feel so strongly about it?"

She took a deep breath. "Franklin believes himself to be Horace Greeley's illegitimate son."

"You said—"

Sarah Ready hurried on. "You don't know what it is to bring up a boy without a father, without ever having had a proper husband. He was always questioning me, wanting to know *who*! I couldn't say that his father was a Greek sailor I'd met one night in New York. So finally one day I told him it was Horace. I told him I had been Horace Greeley's mistress."

"And he believed you?"

"Yes. I'd taken him to the *Tribune* office to meet Horace once, and naturally he made a fuss over Franklin. The boy remembered that, and when I told him Horace was his father, he was willing to believe it. He *wanted* to believe it."

"How long ago was that?"

"He was sixteen at the time. It was the year the war ended."

"So he'd be twenty-seven now?"

"Yes."

"And where is he?"

"I have no idea. After I left the *Tribune* we moved from New York to Philadelphia, where I could be near my sister. He left home when he was twenty and I haven't seen him since."

"Then why do you fear for Grant's life?"

"After Horace died I received a long rambling letter from my son. In it he made veiled threats against the President's life. Last week I received another letter—much more specific this time. He said he would kill President Grant on the eve of the centennial celebration, to punish all of America for what it did to his father."

"Couldn't you write and tell him the truth?"

"The letters bore no address, though the latest was mailed from here in Washington. That was why I went to Elizabeth."

"He's twenty-seven," Rodney mused. "And what does he look like?"

"When I last saw him, he was of medium build with dark hair and a close-cropped beard."

"A vague description at best. But we'll be watching for him, Mrs. Ready. If he turns up, we'll try not to harm him."

"I would like to give my warning personally to the President."

"As I said, that's impossible."

She studied him for a few moments, then turned away. "Very well."

"When will you be returning to Philadelphia?"

"I plan to remain here until after Monday. I want to be here if anything happens to him."

Rodney did not know if she meant her son or President Grant, and he didn't ask. He bowed slightly and left the room.

Elizabeth Blazer caught up with him outside. "Why couldn't the President see her? What would be the harm?"

"We have only her word that this son exists. She showed us no letter. Perhaps she is the only danger Grant faces."

"Do you believe that?"

"It's almost as easy to believe as a mad avenger who believes himself to be the illegitimate son of Horace Greeley."

"Then you'll do nothing?"

"On the contrary," Rodney assured her. "I'll do everything I can to safeguard the President, starting with a journey to Baltimore to-night."

On Sunday morning after church services he sought out President Grant in the oval library upstairs in the White House. Grant took the cigar from his mouth and said, "Well, Rodney. No riding this weekend?"

"I've been busy with other matters, sir."

"Young chap like you should marry and settle down."

"Mr. President—"

"Something on your mind? Here, let me pour us a little whiskey."

"It's a bit early in the day for me, sir."

"Is it?" He put down the half-empty decanter. "All right, out with it. What's bothering you?"

Rodney quickly told him of the meeting with Mrs. Ready. When he'd finished, Grant leaned back in his chair and said, "Obviously the woman is deranged."

"I agree that may be the case, but precautions should be taken nevertheless."

"Precautions? What sort of precautions?"

"If you'll pardon me, Mr. President—I spent last evening in Baltimore. I rode the train over and saw a man named Felix Woodward. Have you ever heard the name?"

Grant thought about it. "There was a Woodward under my command during the war—"

"No, this is a different one. I'd heard talk of him, but had never seen him before. His claim to fame is that he looks a great deal like you. Of course he wears his beard in the same manner to heighten the resemblance."

Grant snorted. "Many men look like me! With these chin whiskers who can tell us apart?"

Rodney hurried on. "What I want to do, sir, is to install Felix Woodward in the White House, just for tomorrow. Then if there is an assassination attempt—"

Grant's fist hit the table. "No! By God, Rodney, I won't have a double! If the Lord says it's my time to go, I'll be waiting. I never asked a man to shield me from Confederate guns, and I won't start now. You keep your Felix Woodward and I'll still be here to drink a little whiskey with you on the Fourth of July."

"I'm sure you will, sir. I only meant—"

"Why should poor Woodward endanger his life for me?"

"He has no family, sir. And he's suffering from an incurable disease."

But Grant was firm. "No, no! No double!"

"You understand the nation's position, sir? We've been without a vice president since Wilson's death last year. If anything happens to you, there'd only be an acting president—the president *pro tempore* of the Senate. That, coupled with the Custer tragedy, might be more than the nation could bear."

"You underestimate the American people," Grant grumbled. "Others have made that mistake in the past."

Rodney could see it was hopeless. "Woodward is here in Washington, sir—just in the event you change your mind."

"There will be no assassination attempt. Horace Greeley's ghost doesn't frighten me." Grant turned away, ending the interview.

Rodney went across the hall to his own little office and sat for a time staring out the window at the green of the White House lawn. Finally he opened the drawer of a wooden filing cabinet and removed a Model 1873 cavalry pistol he kept there. As he loaded it, he wondered if it was the type that General Custer had carried.

Rodney was at his desk early Monday morning, while Cherage and the other secretaries were trying out samples of the new instant coffee in the clerk's office. He liked the clerk, Peters, more than the others, but he had no time to linger over such frivolities this morning. The gun was ready in the top drawer of his desk as he glanced over the President's meager appointments list for July 3.

One that immediately struck his eye was an interview with a reporter from the Washington *Evening Star.* Arranged months earlier, it had completely escaped his mind until this moment. If the man was on schedule, he should be in the waiting room now.

Rodney walked across his office and opened the waiting-room door. The newspaper reporter was there, deep in conversation with Elizabeth Blazer. "I'm sorry to interrupt. You're from the *Evening Star?*"

The young clean-shaven man smiled. "That's right, sir. Thomas Gates, at your service."

Behind the reporter's back, Elizabeth was signaling him. He thought he knew why. "I have some bad news, Mr. Gates. It's impossible for the President to see you today."

"But the interview was arranged months ago!"

"Nevertheless—"

Then, as bad luck would have it, the door to the inner office opened and the President appeared. The young man jumped to his feet. "President Grant, I'm Gates of the *Evening Star,* here for the interview."

"Come in, then. I can only give you a few minutes."

Thomas Gates strode triumphantly into the President's office, leaving Rodney alone with Elizabeth Blazer. "You think he might be the assassin?" he asked her.

"He fits the general description of Mrs. Ready's son."

Rodney slipped the pistol from his desk drawer, tucking it into the waistband of his trousers. "I'll have to go in there," he said.

Elizabeth shook her head. "Grant is safe. If Gates was the assassin, he would have struck the first moment he was alone with the President. Why bother with an interview you'll never deliver to your paper?"

"A man believing he was Horace Greeley's son might bother," Rodney reminded her.

He knocked and entered the office. Thomas Gates was making notes in the visitor's chair and all seemed well. Rodney spoke to the President on a minor scheduling matter, then retreated to his own office.

"Didn't I tell you it was all right?" Elizabeth asked.

"It might not have been."

"What about your plan for a double?"

"Grant vetoed it. He said he went through the war without a stand-in, and he doesn't need one now."

"Have you told anyone else about the threat?"

"Not yet, but I may have to." He pulled a piece of notepaper toward him. "I should make a list."

He wrote down the name of Secretary of State Hamilton Fish, one of the few Cabinet members he trusted. Below it he put George Peters, the clerk. And Leroy E. Cherage. Though Rodney disliked the secretary, he would need him if the President was called away from the White House.

The door to the President's office opened and Thomas Gates stepped into the waiting room. "I have a deadline to make," he explained, hurrying past them.

Rodney went quickly to the President's door and looked in. "I'm still alive as you can see," the bearded man said, turning from the window. "Aren't you convinced yet that the woman's story is a hoax?"

"No, and I won't be until this day is done," Rodney told him.

"Call in the police or the army if it will make you feel any better."

"I believe I can protect you as well as they can."

"No one can protect me against a truly dedicated assassin." He picked up a book of Civil War history. "See that I'm not disturbed for a few hours, Rodney."

"Yes, Mr. President."

"Don't look so displeased. There is no one in Washington who'll want to see me anyway."

"Congress is in session," Rodney reminded him.

"Yes, yes, Congress." He glanced up. "Do any Congressmen know about General Custer yet?"

"Not to my knowledge. If all goes well, the news won't be made public until Wednesday. It will be on the front page of every newspaper in the country by Thursday morning."

"It's a problem to be faced." He sat down again at the presidential desk, resuming his writing, and Rodney left him alone.

Outside, in the doorway of his office, Elizabeth Blazer was waiting. "The President is all right?"

"Yes, he's all right." His mind turned to Mrs. Ready. "Do you think the old lady's still at her hotel?"

"Either there or searching the streets for her missing son."

"If there is a missing son." He sat down at the desk and added the name of Horace Greeley, with quotation marks around it, to the list he'd been making. "You know, I liked the idea of it being that reporter, Gates. Isn't it possible that Mrs. Ready's son, maddened by the wrong done his supposed father, might actually imagine himself to *be* Horace Greeley? In that case, the most likely place to find him would be on a newspaper."

"You could be a detective, Rod—one of those Pinkerton men."

Rodney started to reply when Cherage and another man came in through the clerk's office. "This is Mr. Simmons," the secretary said, "First Selectman of Berry Falls, Ohio. He's bringing a centennial gift to President Grant."

Rodney scanned the appointment book. "I have no such name listed."

"I'm sure President Grant would want to see someone from his home state."

Simmons was an older, bearded man, and it hardly seemed likely he could be the assassin. He spoke with a gruff voice as he explained the reason for his visit. "This piece of wood is from a hundred-year-old oak tree in our great state of Ohio. You'll notice President Grant's name and the centennial date have been carved onto it. I'm certain he'll want to have it."

Rodney thought he heard Elizabeth's sniff of disdain, but he didn't dare look. He excused himself and went to the door of the President's office. "Pardon me, Mr. President, but there's a special visitor from your home state."

The President stirred behind his desk and put down his pen. "Well, I suppose I must see him if he's from Ohio. Send him in."

Rodney motioned Simmons and Cherage into the office and went back across the waiting room to his own cubicle. "What about that Woodward?" Elizabeth asked. "Are you going to send him back to Baltimore?"

"He's already gone," Rodney said. "On the morning train." He was gazing at the paper where he'd written the list of names.

The door to President Grant's office opened after a few moments and Simmons emerged alone. "So pleased to meet you, sir," he said over his shoulder.

The President mumbled a reply as the politician from Ohio departed. Rodney glanced through the partly open office door and saw Leroy Cherage settling into the chair opposite the President's desk.

"I'd better be going," Elizabeth said.

Rodney glanced down at the paper again.

Horace Greeley.

He read over the list of names he'd written.

Hamilton Fish.

George Peters.

Leroy E. Cherage.

Horace Greeley.

His vision blurred for an instant and then cleared. It didn't make any sense, but there it was. "Come look at this," he said to Elizabeth. "I've just noticed the damnedest thing."

"What's that?"

He pointed to the names. "Look here."

Leroy E. Cherage.

Horace Greeley.

"Why, they're—"

"Anagrams! Mrs. Ready's son has been here in the White House all the time!"

He was reaching for his pistol when they heard the single shot from the President's office.

Rodney dashed across the waiting room and into the office. Leroy Cherage turned from the desk as he entered, revealing the slumped body in the President's chair. "You're too late!" Cherage said, with something like madness in his voice. "I've killed him! I've killed President Grant!"

The double-barreled derringer in his right hand was starting to rise again when, without thinking, Rodney shot him between the eyes.

At a few minutes after nine that evening President Ulysses S. Grant entered his White House office for the first time that day. Only Rodney and Elizabeth were present, and they stood up as he came in.

"I suppose you're to be congratulated, Rodney," the President said. "You were right about the attempt to assassinate me."

"I'm afraid it's no consolation to be right, sir, with Felix Woodward lying dead."

"You did your best, Rodney."

"If only I'd have seen that anagram a minute sooner!"

"The shock was even greater for me," Elizabeth Blazer confided to Grant. "I thought Cherage had killed you."

Grant glanced at Rodney. "Didn't even tell the girl, eh?"

"There was a possibility," Rodney said with some embarrassment, "that Elizabeth and Mrs. Ready were in the plot together. Elizabeth might have been the assassin." He felt himself blush and hurried on. "I didn't believe it for an instant, but I couldn't take the chance of telling her about the substitution."

"But—" Elizabeth looked from one to the other. "Then it wasn't true you refused to have a double, Mr. President?"

Grant snorted. "Of course I refused! Got talked into it by Julia, my wife! God, there were times when she shared a tent with me during the war—I had to listen to her now!"

"It's a good thing for the country that you did," Rodney said.

"What about Woodward's body—and Cherage's?"

"Woodward will be returned to Baltimore for burial. Cherage will go into an unmarked grave. I think it best, sir, if no one knows what happened here today—and that includes Mrs. Ready. It might give other people ideas."

Grant waved a hand. "Whatever you say, Rodney. I'm in your hands in this matter."

"I've already made arrangements, sir."

"Good!" He started for the door. "I'll be down the hall with Julia. Please join us."

When they were alone, Elizabeth said, "I'm glad you didn't tell me, Rod. When I think of that poor man, dying in Grant's place—"

"It was something he could do for his country," Rodney said.

"When I explained the problem, and the risks, and told him about General Custer, he was eager to do whatever he could. I don't think he had many months left anyway."

"If only we could have told Cherage the truth—that he wasn't Horace Greeley's son at all!"

"For someone like that it might not have made any difference. We couldn't risk it."

Elizabeth walked to the window. "Look, the celebration is starting early! There are fireworks over the Potomac."

He took her by the hand. "Let's go down the hall and watch them with the President and Mrs. Grant."

During the past decade much has been written about a "New Wave" in the science-fiction field, but the term is rarely heard in connection with mystery writing. Perhaps the reason is that "New Wave" writing implies an experimentation, a formlessness that by its very nature is foreign to the mystery field. Still, these final two stories show that experimentation is possible. First, Rich Rainey's tale of a man who might be mad. . .

RICH RAINEY
The Man in the White Room

The man tried to become part of the tree. His fingernails dug into the bark and his arms hugged the wide trunk as though it were a lost love. He tried to stop his heart from screaming but the roaring blood still echoed inside his brain. His gasping breath was so loud, so thunderous, he was certain it could be heard by his pursuers. All around him they were thrashing the woods, searching.

When he dared to open his eyes he saw a brilliant spotlight pierce the night. A sweeping arc of yellow light poured across the woodland floor. It was shining right on the spot where he stood. Guided by terror, his inner voice chanted: "If I get out of this, if only I get out of this . . . run, run, another country. Why didn't I leave, oh Jesus, what's happened to me? Let me be free. I gotta get out of here. . . "

The man is me and he didn't get out of it.

Three troopers converged on his hiding place. He broke cover and ran. But his legs were exhausted and no matter how much he wanted them to keep moving, they gave out. Then, as he fell, a heavy weight landed on the back of his neck. And though it was only a fist it brought the chase to an end.

Four walls. Four crazy walls padded. The guards wear chromium masks and say nothing to me, not wishing to provoke me. For I am in training and soon I will be a good man.

The young psychiatrist—"You can call me Robert"—wishes that I were an attractive redheaded woman since he is not being paid fifty dollars an hour to see me. But he is staff, I am a patient, and he must treat me. This treatment consists of his telling me about his fine new ranch home and what a large personal library he has. Then he tells me that someday I can be like him if I try hard enough.

In the beginning he asked me for motives. He looked for symbolism in the weapon I used, and he wrote down my answers in a black notebook. But there was no symbolism and our words were only so much babbling in the long run. "Why did you choose such an odd weapon, James? Surely you could have found something a lot simpler," he would ask. And I would shrug and say, "No reason. It was in my possession so I just used it. I didn't expect it to be traced to me." At times like this we both realized there would be no immediate change in my condition. For one thing, he wouldn't be satisfied until I conjured up a symbol for him. And another thing, in my mind I was aware of no psychotic condition. It just happened.

"You can call me Robert" would then slap me on the back, smile meaningfully, and leave me alone in the white room.

I see a girl, her long hair flowing. She is sitting by the river, waiting for me, sunlight coating her tanned perfect body. Quietly approaching her, she hasn't yet seen or heard me, my clasped fingers caress her eyes. Surprised, she laughs and we fall to the ground, listening to the flowing waters. And I am astounded that she is my wife, that with her I can forget about the world.

The house sat on a not too desolate hill. It always looked like summertime there. The grass was straw burned, the air was dry. It was one story high, with an aspiring chimney and loft. Basically one large room with slight indentations to separate kitchen from living room from bedroom. The fireplace was an accumulation of crumbling brick, filled with ashes from long ago.

In front of the porch steps, cranky and untrustworthy, a path beat out of the grass, dusty and almost straight. It ran for half a mile, interrupted by a forgotten one-lane road, then continued past a sandy stretch, a clump of forest, and then to the shore where the water roared.

A row of trees formed a barrier on the left side of the house, circling towards the rear. Tall spindly things, no kites. Whenever the wind struck a chord, the thin boughs danced.

We spent many nights with no lights, no humming lampposts, and in the darkness the house slept unseen, unknown. That was the reason we bought it. It was so alone. "There's no one around for miles," Sarah said when she first saw it. "Let's take it." It needed work but we planned to restore it when the local community college upped my teaching salary.

On the summer nights, when the house was too warm, we slept outside, near the caves just behind our land. Woodlore for the city dweller on the run. Time was different then. Two days was a week, who could tell. The air was cool, breezy. Firelight and lovemaking. A temporary paradise.

I see a girl, her long hair flowing. I see her coffin lowered into the ground.

It is a Thursday night. We've come into town to shop for a new quilt bedspread, one that will go with the brass bed Sarah picked up at a farmhouse auction.

There is some twenty feet between us. I am watching a merchant dress his window-front manikin. And Sarah is ahead of me, already at the next department store, waiting for me to catch up with her.

First there is the thud of the wheels as the long black car climbs up the curb, then the roar of its straining engine as it flies over the sidewalk, and then. . .

The driver doesn't know how much I love Sarah as the impact of the car forces her through the store window. And behind her the glass dances, all at once a million pieces. Thin lines of blood cross her pretty face. And the driver doesn't even know he's off the road.

Sarah is looking at my eyes. Her face is bewildered, frightened, fading. There is nothing I can do, nothing I can say, because she is dead.

Someone else calls the police, someone else calls the ambulance, because I am beyond all that, trying to reach Sarah to touch her one last time. But I can't reach her, just cut my hands on the glass, and when I see her slashed body under the chrome bumper I no longer want to reach her.

Next I am in the car with him. The radio is blaring, the air stinks of whiskey, and the driver is slumped over the steering wheel, passed out. There is an empty bottle on the floor. Several arms hold me, tear me away. It takes maybe three or four men. I am screaming because Sarah is dead, they are screaming because my hands are on the driver's throat.

I waited a month although I planned to let a longer period of time pass. But the dreams I had would not let me wait any longer. Two, three times a night, I would wake up, sitting straight up in the brass bed, looking for Sarah but only finding emptiness beside me. The house was no longer mine. It was haunted with the ghost of my wife.

And the daily newspaper told about the unfortunate accident on Main Street. Judge Parmonter, city court, lost control of his car due to a malfunction in the steering mechanism, and a young woman was crushed to death by the car. No mention of the empty bottle of whiskey, no mention of the drunken stupor the judge was in. No mention of anything but a sad mishap. The woman was survived by a husband and two distant cousins.

The life insurance policy, which we'd taken on Sarah's urging, came to twenty thousand dollars. I did not consider it a fair exchange at all. No payment could take away the image of myself standing helplessly on the sidewalk while Sarah entered another world.

The poor judge took a two-week leave of absence to get over his traumatic experience. He even tried to soothe his conscience by sending me a gilt-edged condolence card. I didn't read it. I wanted no excuse for his messed-up life.

One night, a month after the accident, the man drove his car to the judge's estate. It was in a secluded section of town just before the city limits. The man drove past the gate and parked his car about one hundred yards down the road. On the back seat of the car there was a mace. It was a foot-length lead pipe with two heavy chains fastened to it, each holding a spiked iron ball at the end of the links. The man picked up the mace and walked towards the house. He climbed a small brick wall and went directly to a window at the front of the house from which light escaped.

Inside the house, before a raging fire, Judge Parmonter sat in a soft leather chair, drinking from a long stemmed glass. The man watched Judge Parmonter for a couple of minutes, letting his emotions build until he no longer perceived the judge as a human being, just an object that had to be eliminated. The man heard a television blaring at high volume inside the house.

He circled the house, trying a number of doors until he found the right one. It was a back entrance. The lock was old, rusted, and unstable. He took out a screwdriver from his back pocket and unfastened the lock, prying it completely out of the door. He quietly entered the house and crossed the kitchen floor.

He looked at a luminous clock above the refrigerator. It was now one o'clock. Sign-off time. He walked down the hall, gently carrying the mace so the chains wouldn't make any noise. During the Star Spangled Banner the man approached the judge from the rear. Driven by blind hatred, by the ruin of his life, by circumstance, by a bedspread for Sarah, the man raised the mace high over his head and swung it hard through the air. Judge Parmonter looked up in time to see the spikes a split second before they crashed into his head. The man swung again and again, rearranging the judge's face until there was no longer any symmetry to it.

The man then turned off the television although he didn't know why. He stood facing the judge and felt sickened at what he had done. His eyes were repulsed by the still body in the chair and the blood-splashed mace in his hand. It slid out of his grasp and fell to the floor. He vomited, laid down on the floor and cried.

He heard a noise upstairs, footsteps, then a man's voice—"Sir, are you all right? I heard a loud crash. . . " The footsteps were closer, coming down the stairs.

The man panicked and ran out the back of the house. He was halfway to his car when he remembered the mace. In that instant he saw the future. They would suspect him, come after him and match his fingers to the mace. He ran back to the house, unsure of any plan, knowing only that the mace held his fate.

At the window again he saw a man in nightclothes, probably a servant, hanging up the phone, staring at the judge's body in horror. And the bloody mace was lying at the judge's feet. Brutal cold metal that would hang him. He had to get it, but how? Kill another man? He stood transfixed, paralyzed with fear. Then in the distance he heard the sirens. He ran into the woods.

When the man's family came to visit him he heard the psychiatrist tell them, "Sorry, there's still no change in his condition. But we have hopes for him. Sooner or later he'll respond to the treatment." Then the guards escorted the man and his family to the asylum garden. On the manicured lawn his parents and an assortment of in-laws talked to him.

Although the man had no smile on his face, no happy expression, the family took his silence as an answer to their prayers. At least he wasn't violent anymore. And it was easy to see that they wished it weren't like this, that they wished he'd been a baseball player after all, like any other normal person. What they do not realize is that in a place like this, nothing he says will matter because his fate is already decided. In ten years he will be a trustee. In fifteen he will be up for release. If only he would be more receptive.

"But he's been through so much. . . "

"Once you admit you have a problem then we are on the way to a solution. But you have to take the first step," the psychiatrist told me on his last visit.

He cannot understand that I do not have a condition. That it is all in black and white. My actions were justified. The judge gave up his right to live when he murdered Sarah because of his drunken way of life. And since he was an influential man this shortcoming of his was overlooked by the authorities. The responsibility was up to me and now it is all over.

The psychiatrist wants to go over the symbolism of the weapon again, so I tell him again. There was no symbolism in the mace. It is just a length of metal with two chains on the end. Attached to the chains are two iron balls with spikes. Very popular in Spain, where it came from. Very popular at my house where I kept it as an ornament. Given to me by a friend who picked it up when he was in the Naval service overseas. When he moved his family to another city in pursuit of a better job he asked me if I wanted it since he was going to throw it out. A simple neighborly gesture. He also gave me an old rocking chair which never killed anyone.

The psychiatrist does not accept this. It just doesn't make sense to him. And he is the one who will fix my mind? Maybe I should try and sell him a bridge.

In a way my white room is nice. Paid for in full by my insurance money, by my lawyer. If you have a lot of money and you kill someone you are temporarily insane. Traumatized. And a little white room will make you good as new. Say in fifteen years or so. If you are poor and you kill someone you are are a street viper, an animal. Then you are thrown into a gray room in a penitentiary. Somehow I am not crusading against this inequality.

Fifteen years is a long time though. Especially in a place like this. When they treat you as if you are mad, sooner or later you will act the part. And the thought of getting out of here doesn't exactly lift my spirits. Then I would be in a much larger asylum where judges get drunk, where napalm is manufactured like candy, where subliminal advertising criminals go for your mind, where the politicians deal any way but straight, where meaning has died along with Sarah.

So the man sits in the white room looking for a way out, but not really wanting it, because what is there to do once he's out? And his body and mind ache for Sarah but she is just an image frozen in shattered glass.

The man thinks of what it might be like if things didn't have to turn out like this. But the list of "ifs" is endless:

If his friend hadn't gone to Spain.

If Sarah didn't want a new quilt.

If the judge wasn't a drunk.

If he could have been close enough to save her.

If, after Sarah, he could find meaning somewhere else besides in a dictionary.

If only he had let the judge live.

The man starts to think hopefully of reincarnation. That maybe he will get a better shake in the next life. Or maybe he will run into Sarah on another plane.

And the man knows he has nothing left to live for, and that somehow he will die in the white room because he was born on the wrong side of time.

What are the limits of the form? Can a story be told through the random jottings in a writer's notebook, as Nabokov narrated Pale Fire *through the footnotes to a long, obscure poem? I offer no clues to the following, except to note the date of Richard Stone's death, as given in the first paragraph.*

LAURENCE SHEEHAN
"The Christmas Tree Lot Murders"

From the notebooks of Richard X. Stone (June 14, 1911 – Dec. 23, 1975), author of the more than eighty best-selling "Doctor Saint-John" mysteries:

Possible clues. Man's hands smell of fish. Lady's ring finger cut off (model after Doris). Tree bark. Discontinued automotive part. Traces of orange juice found in a houseplant.

Toward a theory of mystery fiction. Form of vicarious problem solving. Superior to cowboy western because covers sex. Needs of modern psyche. How different from ancient psyche. Detective heroes never burdened with family life, viz. Sam Spade, Father Brown, Dick Tracy, Hercule Poirot, my own Dr. Saint-John. How solve murders with wife like Doris on neck.

Book idea. *The Hung Jury.* Twelve people strangled in space of week, from all walks of life—rich and poor, black and white, some tall, some short, etc. (Make Mandy separate figure, not victim.) Dr. Saint-John called in, discovers all twelve victims once served on jury which convicted a man to death years before. Maybe Mandy could be widow of a victim of the original murderer, and now a comely social worker. Twist is the twelve jurors are not strangled by some revengeful friend or associate of the man who was convicted. Are killed by the lunatic judge in the trial! (Doesn't make sense.)

Clue. Birdshit on windshield. Might mean car parked under tree, or Doris's parrot loose in garage again. Also, man used word "windscreen" in conversation. Tip-off he's a Britisher (try to capture Brit. market with more focus on Anglo-Saxon type crimes). Saint-John makes a mental note, etc. Afterthought—why wouldn't he recognize bloke's accent? Maybe getting deaf after eighty-four books? Could start to wear gizmo in ear, for use as two-way radio as well as to hear what the hell people are saying to him.

Book idea. Holdup at fancy suburban cinema while a movie about a bank robbery is playing. Real shotgun fire outside lost in noise of sound track, lady cashier's screams for help lost in screams on screen (model cashier after Doris). Maybe actor playing robber in movie could be relative of actual robber of movie outside, while member of audience in moviehouse could be relative of Doris. N.G.

Book idea. *The Christmas Tree Lot Murders.* Great! Combines incongruous elements of joy at Noel, etc., with underlying violence of U.S. society, plus comment on commercialism. Woman's body found under twenty-dollar Scotch pine on Christmas Eve. But need plot. Setting is not plot. Setting is situation. Title is not plot. Title is title, name. Need plot. Question. What is plot? Plot is time, time is line made up of a series of clues, connected by color. Color is emotion. Time is clues linked by feelings (possible lecture material here).

Situation. Man wakes up in strange motel room. No idea what day it is. Takes his pills. Turns on TV and observes cartoons. Watches cartoons for hour and deduces it is Saturday A.M. Moments later, he takes a bath. Knock at door. Mandy.

Saint-John continuity. Suppose he goes deaf *and* blind at same time? How get around, etc. Perhaps hire young woman assistant.

Maybe start new series. Finish off Saint-John and explore new fictional territory. Maybe homosexual crime-stopper would capture largest possible market today. N.B.—query people at Random House on this. Who said great men never stop changing, no, men who change their minds never achieve greatness. One of those is right, can't remember, can't find my Bartlett's.

Difference between clue and sign. Walking slower, having trouble sleeping, getting busy signal when I call Mandy, these are *signs* of old age, not *clues.* Clues are footprints and stray hairs and such. Mystery is marriage. Mystery is living with someone daffy like Doris feeding the houseplants with orange juice. All she talks about is Vitamin C.

Question. What is scientific about science fiction? That which is fictitious about science! (No, doesn't work, didn't work when I said it at seminar in which Mandy enrolled, doesn't work now.)

Clues. Spotless kitchen. Vitamin jars. Tracks in the snow. Blood in the tracks. Christmas tree in the kitchen.

Book idea. Perhaps do mystery with light touch for a change, have some fellow go berserk in Dec., cutting down all neighbor's evergreens and hauling them into his house, setting fire to whole house with wife in bedroom, no, comedy wearing thin.

Setting. Man mournfully hums "The Girl That I Married" in

neighborhood bar at Xmas time, so dark in there he can hardly see swizzle stick. Invited to go singing carols with dubious bunch. Was supposed to meet Mandy but she has decided to spend holidays skiing with poet whose hands stink of fish. So goes caroling. Later body found under snow in Christmas tree lot. A fine Christmas for him! Saint-John called in, snoops around, determines wife hired hippie carolers high on dope to finish off her husband so she can take ocean cruises on his royalties. But Saint-John deeply moved by holiday spirit gets the goods on her, puts her behind bars, exposes the old fart for what she is, destroyer of the human spirit, eroder of the creative impulse, Prime Causer of headaches, decline in virility, etc.

Why mystery is superior to poetry. Poetry is largely the product of personality, thus arrogant hairy bastard youths able to enthrall audiences, women, etc. Whereas mystery is product of character, experience, study, diligence, intelligence, *tout avec la force morale et rationale,* that is why sometimes a bore.

Boils down to, do we admire Poe for his mysteries or his poetry? Ans. is his mysteries.

Question. What will they think of my Saint-John in 100, 200, 300 years? Will he hold up as universal figure? (R. House tells me in seventeen languages now, must show latest subsidiary rights rundown to Mandy if she ever returns my calls.) What if sales continue, enriching Doris but not me if I'm dead first?

Maybe dash off long poem, catch Mandy off balance by my control of that medium, my broad emotional range, woo her in a war of words, maybe then we'll spend week together, not at Stowe or Alta as with hotshot mad-for-skiing poet, but someplace warm.

Situation. Famous writer teaching seminar on "The Art of Murder" at local community college, dingy halls, rotten coffee, etc. "Coed" comes up to him after class, says, "I'm Amanda something." (What is her last name, no wonder having trouble working out this plot, with such leaky recall.) "I like what you said about the limitations of Ian Fleming."

Definition: Hero is man transformed by circumstances who transforms signs into clues. Hero knows his tea leaves, is laundry chute. Hero is artist on laundry chute of life (save).

Importance of fame, recognition, money, honors, not nec. in that order. All important. Next to Mandy, though, after a bath, pure soybeans.

Possible clues. No answer at blonde's apartment door. Check of my latest phone bill reveals seven person-to-person calls from Doris to a Dr. Linus Pauling. Who is he? My favorite driver (golf) missing from bag also. What is going on?

Situation (actually happened): Run into Mandy's skier friend at fish market. He is musing on his latest bit of verse whilst chopping mackerel. (Book idea: *Dead as a Mackerel*—the story of old man and young woman who plot death of awful poet, are caught red-handed and sent to experimental prison in Tahiti with beaches with signs saying NO DOGS.) I order half-lb. fresh cod.

Question. What is relation of art to life. Ans. Art builds on life, then walks off (good!).

Situation. Nearing Xmas. A young happy (like Mandy) back from Stowe or Alta, all Coppertoned and limping, even her buttocks are brown (how find out, I mean how get to see them?). Has broken up with fishmonger clod, wants Xmas tree for her condo, not a fake green plastic one, but real one. Invites creaking wreck to help her pick out. He agrees. Delirious he is. (Where is Saint-John—gone drinking wassail punch at all-male sauna bash, annual affair, can't be reached.) Off to Boy Scouts of America freezing cold tree lot. Old-timer spots excellent small apartment-type specimen fir right in first row. Mandy says she wants "Scottish pine." "Scotch pine," corrects worldly-wise older male companion blowing on numb fingers. He trudges to North Pole of lot where attendant suspects 1 or 2 S. pine may still be found.

On way, slips into meditation on career of President Poincaré of France, whom he has never read up on but admires for some strange reason. Rounds tree, then sniffs Doris's favorite perfume, mixture of Charlie and garlic juice.

Clue. Bloodied golf club.

Three possibilities. 1) He comes back with the tree. 2) He comes back with Doris. 3) He doesn't come back at all.

Mandy's possible reactions:

1) "You look *froze!*"

2) "Hello, Mrs. Stone." (Evenly—she says it "evenly.")

3) "Oh gosh I loved him secretly I loved him I loved him and his writing style but I kept it a secret from him for his own good, it was my secret and his style, he was my secret love, what does it matter now, etc."

Question. What is mystery? Better to ask—what isn't mystery? What isn't plot, clues, characters, tables of contents, oak tables, page numbers, indexes, and murders? What isn't?

The Yearbook of the Detective Story

Abbreviations: *EQMM* Ellery Queen's Mystery Magazine
AHMM Alfred Hitchcock's Mystery Magazine
MSMM Mike Shayne Mystery Magazine
MM Mystery Monthly

BIOGRAPHY
BILL PRONZINI

William John Pronzini was born in Petaluma, California, April 13, 1943. While still in his teens he worked as a sportswriter for his hometown newspaper. But it was not until the age of twenty-two, after two years of college and a brief, unsuccessful marriage, that he turned to fiction. He was already an avid collector of pulp magazines and mystery novels, so it was natural that his writing should be mostly in the suspense field. His first story, "You Don't Know What It's Like," appeared in *Shell Scott's Mystery Magazine* in 1966.

Following an assortment of jobs that included brief stints at warehousing, office typing, car parking, and even a part-time position as a civilian guard working with a U.S. Marshal, Pronzini became a full-time writer in 1969. Early the following year he left California with another young writer, Jeffrey M. Wallmann, and moved to the Mediterranean island of Majorca. They supported themselves by collaborating on specialty paperbacks and by publishing scores of short stories, separately and together, in the mystery, western, and science-fiction fields. Pronzini's first suspense novel, *The Stalker*, published by Random House in 1971, received an MWA Edgar nomination.

After thirteen months on Majorca, Pronzini moved to West Germany, where he lived for nearly three years and where, in 1972, he married Bruni Schier, a German kindergarten teacher he first met in Spain. Bill and Bruni currently reside in San Francisco. Always active in Mystery Writers of America, Pronzini presently serves as vice president of its Northern California chapter. He is also an active member of the Author's Guild, Writers Guild–West, and Western Writers of America.

In a field where collaborative efforts are few, Pronzini has produced a number of stories in collaboration with three different and highly individual writers—Jeff Wallmann, Barry Malzberg, and Michael Kurland. Pronzini has also adopted a number of pseudonymns: William Jeffrey (for early collaborative stories with Jeff Wallmann), Jack Foxx, and Alex Saxon. (Note the double x—for luck—in each of the last two.)

Along with some 170 short stories, Bill Pronzini's publishing credits include the following: *The Stalker* (Random House, 1971), *The Snatch* (Random House, 1971), *Panic!* (Random House, 1972), *The Vanished* (Random House, 1973), *Undercurrent* (Random House, 1973), *Snowbound* (Putnam, 1974), *Games* (Putnam, 1976), and *Blowback* (Random House, 1977). In collaboration with Barry Malzberg he has published *The Running of Beasts* (Putnam, 1976). Under the name of Jack Foxx there have been three novels to date, all published by Bobbs-Merrill: *The Jade Figurine* (1972), *Dead Run* (1975), and *Freebooty* (1976). A paperback novel, *A Run in Diamonds* (Pocket Books, 1973), was published under the Alex Saxon name. He has also edited an anthology of train-oriented suspense stories, *Midnight Specials* (Bobbs-Merrill, 1977), and co-edited with Joe Gores the MWA anthology *Tricks and Treats* (Doubleday, 1976). A new novel and an anthology of science fiction mystery stories, both in collaboration with Barry Malzberg, are scheduled for publication in 1977.

Four of Pronzini's novels have been purchased for movies and television, but to date none has been produced. Of his short stories and articles, thirty have been selected for inclusion in mystery, science fiction, "how-to-write," and Western Americana anthologies. This year marks his fifth appearance in *Best Detective Stories of the Year*. He has appeared three times previously under his own name and once, in 1973, under the William Jeffrey collaborative pseudonym.

About his series of novels featuring a nameless, pulp-collecting San Francisco private detective (*The Snatch*, *The Vanished*, *Undercurrent*, and *Blowback*), John Dickson Carr has written: "(Pronzini's) anonymous private investigator is an immensely likable addition to the roster. We welcome him with the heartiest handshake." And about his straight suspense fiction, the Hartford *Courant* has said: "You can always depend on Pronzini to author an . . . explosive novel of suspense that ties you down to the last page."

Whether writing about a private eye or simply about ordinary people trapped in a web of mounting terror, Bill Pronzini is, in the words of the Seattle *Post Intelligencer*, ". . . a kind of magician [who] builds his illusions, casts his spells, and creates his magic with words."

BIBLIOGRAPHY

I. Collections and Single Stories

    1. Alcott, Louisa May. *Plots and Counterplots*. New York: William Morrow & Co. A second collection of Alcott's "unknown thrillers," edited by Madeleine Stern and containing five stories, 1863–1869.

2. Allen, Grant. *An African Millionaire.* New York: Arno Press. First American edition of item #21 in *Queen's Quorum* (Ellery Queen's definitive listing of the 125 most important books of detective-crime short stories), a collection of twelve crime stories originally published in 1897. One of two first American editions of short-story collections in a forty-five-volume reprint series of classic mysteries. (See also 11 below.)

3. Asimov, Isaac. *More Tales of the Black Widowers.* New York: Doubleday & Co. Nine stories from *EQMM* and *Fantasy & Science Fiction,* plus three never before published.

4. Bailey, H.C. *Mr. Fortune: Eight of his Adventures.* New York: Garland Publishing, Inc. A new selection drawn from five prior collections, 1923 – 1936. One of two original titles in a fifty-volume reprint series of classic mysteries chosen by Barzun and Taylor. (See also 1, under Anthologies.)

5. Chester, S. Beach. *The Arsene Lepine-Herlock Soames Affair.* Boulder, Colorado (Box 4119): The Aspen Press. First U.S. publication of a 1912 parody novelette, introduced by Philip José Farmer.

6. Fish, Robert L. *Kek Huuygens, Smuggler.* Yonkers, New York (Box 334, East Station): The Mysterious Press. Seven stories about a modern smuggler, from various magazines, 1964 – 1974.

7. Futrelle, Jacques. *Great Cases of the Thinking Machine.* New York: Dover Publications. A sequel to Dover's 1973 collection, containing thirteen stories, many new to book publication.

8. Innes, Michael. *The Appleby File.* New York: Dodd, Mead & Co. Fifteen stories about Sir John Appleby, mainly from *EQMM*, but with a few appearing for the first time in America.

9. Morrison, Arthur. *Best Martin Hewitt Detective Stories.* New York: Dover Publications. Nine stories from *The Strand Magazine* and *The Windsor Magazine,* 1894 – 1896, with original illustrations.

10. Niven, Larry. *The Long Arm of Gil Hamilton.* New York: Ballantine Books. Three science fiction mysteries about a government sleuth.

11. Orczy, Baroness. *Lady Molly of Scotland Yard.* New York: Arno Press. First American edition of a 1910 collection of twelve detective stories.

12. Phillpotts, Eden. *My Adventure in the Flying Scotsman.* Boulder, Colardo (Box 4119): The Aspen Press. First American edition of item #13 in *Queen's Quorum,* a single short story about crime on a British railway, originally published in 1888.

13. Poe, Edgar Allan. *The Illustrated Edgar Allan Poe.* New York: Clarkson N. Potter. A new selection of twelve Poe tales and two poems, illustrated with montages by Satty.

14. Quinn, Seabury. *The Adventures of Jules de Grandin.* New York: Popular Library. Seven stories from *Weird Tales,* 1925 – 1927, about a popular occult sleuth, introduced by Lin Carter. First in a series which includes 15, 16, and 17, below, plus a novel, *The Devil's Bride.* The cases usually involve the supernatural.

15. ———. *The Casebook of Jules de Grandin.* New York: Popular Library.

Seven stories from *Weird Tales,* 1926–1929, introduced by Robert A.W. Lowndes.

16. ———. *The Hellfire Files of Jules de Grandin.* New York: Popular Library. Six stories from *Weird Tales,* 1926–1933.

17. ———. *The Skeleton Closet of Jules de Grandin.* New York: Popular Library. Six stories from *Weird Tales,* 1929–1930, introduced by Manly Wade Wellman.

18. Quiroga, Horacio. *The Decapitated Chicken and Other Stories.* Austin, Texas: University of Texas Press. First U.S. publication of twelve stories of horror and death, somewhat in the style of Poe, which appeared in South America between 1907 and 1935. Many concern animals, real or imagined, and only a few are criminous.

19. Rendell, Ruth. *The Fallen Curtain.* New York: Doubleday & Co. Eight stories from *EQMM,* including the Edgar-winning title story, plus three not previously published in the U.S.

20. Rohmer, Sax. *The Wrath of Fu Manchu.* New York: DAW Books. First American edition of a 1973 British collection containing four Fu Manchu stories and eight other mystery-crime tales, introduced by Robert E. Briney.

21. Todd, Peter. *The Adventures of Herlock Sholmes.* Yonkers, New York (Box 334, East Station): The Mysterious Press. First American publication of eighteen early Sherlockian parodies, introduced by Philip José Farmer.

22. van Gulik, Robert, trans. *Celebrated Cases of Judge Dee.* New York: Dover Publications. First American publication of *Dee Goong An,* the original Chinese collection upon which Gulik later based his own series of pastiches.

23. Zelazny, Roger. *My Name Is Legion.* New York: Ballantine Books. Three science fiction mysteries about a nameless private eye in a computer-run society.

II. Anthologies

1. Barzun, Jacques and Taylor, Wendell Hertig, eds. *Classic Stories of Crime and Detection.* New York: Garland Publishing, Inc. Fourteen stories published between 1900 and 1950.

2. Brown, Himan, ed. *Strange Tales from the CBS Radio Mystery Theater.* New York: Popular Library. Three novelettes, two of them supernatural, adapted from radio scripts.

3. Clute, Cedric E., Jr., and Lewin, Nicholas, eds. *Sleight of Crime.* Chicago: Henry Regnery. Sixteen stories about magicians and murder. (See also 17, below.)

4. Daniels, Les, ed. *Dying of Fright.* New York: Scribners. Twenty-five stories, mainly supernatural, but including a Carter Dickson mystery.

5. del Rey, Judy-Lynn, ed. *Stellar Short Novels.* New York: Ballantine Books. Three science fiction stories, one of them a locked room mystery by Andrew J. Offutt.

6. Eisenhower, Julie, ed. *Mystery and Suspense: Great Stories from The*

Saturday Evening Post. Indianapolis, Indiana: The Curtis Publishing Company. Sixteen stories, 1843–1966.

7. Gores, Joe and Pronzini, Bill, eds. *Tricks and Treats.* New York: Doubleday & Co. Thirty stories, including six never before published, in the annual anthology from Mystery Writers of America.

8. Greene, Hugh, ed. *The American Rivals of Sherlock Holmes.* New York: Pantheon. Thirteen detective stories, 1898–1915.

9. Haining, Peter, ed. *The Fantastic Pulps.* New York: St. Martin's Press. Twenty-one stories from the pulp magazines, with historical introductions by the editor. Mainly fantasy and horror, though a few crime stories by Hammett and others are included.

10. Hoch, Edward D., ed. *Best Detective Stories of the Year—1976.* New York: E.P. Dutton & Co. Seventeen of the best mystery-crime stories published during 1975, including the MWA Edgar winner.

11. Kahn, Joan, ed. *Some Things Weird & Wicked.* New York: Pantheon. Twelve stories, mainly supernatural.

12. Liebman, Arthur, ed. *Ms. Mysteries.* New York: Pocket Books. Nineteen mystery and horror stories by women writers, with female protagonists.

13. ———, ed. *Tales of Espionage and Intrigue.* New York: Richards Rosen Press. Thirteen stories, with introductions that give historical background for the settings of each story. Fourth in a series, "Masterworks of Mystery," mainly for school use.

14. Manley, Seon and Lewis, Gogo, eds. *Women of the Weird.* New York: Lothrop, Lee & Shepard. Eleven mystery and horror tales by women writers.

15. McCauley, Kirby, ed. *Frights.* New York: St. Martin's Press. Fourteen new stories of horror and suspense, mainly supernatural.

16. Parry, Michael, ed. *The Supernatural Solution.* New York: Taplinger Publishing Co. Nine mysteries solved by a variety of psychic sleuths.

17. Penzler, Otto, ed. *Whodunit? Houdini?* New York: Harper & Row. Thirteen mystery-suspense stories involving magicians.

18. Playboy. *Just My Luck.* Chicago: Playboy Press. Nine crime stories about swindlers and con men, reprinted from *Playboy,* 1959–1975.

19. Queen, Ellery, ed. *Ellery Queen's Anthology, Spring–Summer, 1976.* New York: Davis Publications, Inc. Fifteen stories in a semi-annual softcover anthology from *EQMM.* (Hardcover edition, *Ellery Queen's Giants of Mystery,* New York: Dial Press.)

20. ———, ed. *Ellery Queen's Anthology, Fall–Winter, 1976.* New York: Davis Publications, Inc. Nineteen stories in the semi-annual softcover anthology from *EQMM.* (Hardcover edition, *Ellery Queen's Magicians of Mystery,* New York: Dial Press.)

21. ———, ed. *Ellery Queen's Crime Wave.* New York: G.P. Putnam's Sons. The 30th annual hardcover anthology from *EQMM,* containing twenty-four stories from 1974 issues.

22. ———, ed. *Masterpieces of Mystery: The Grand Masters.* Des Moines, Iowa (1716 Locust Street): Meredith Corp. Fifteen stories by winners

of MWA's Grand Master Award. (One of a multi-volume series being sold by mail order. See also 23 and 24 below).

23. ———, ed. *Masterpieces of Mystery: The Prizewinners.* Des Moines, Iowa (1716 Locust Street): Meredith Corp. Twenty-one stories by Nobel and Pulitzer Prize winners.

24. ———, ed. *Masterpieces of Mystery: The Supersleuths.* Des Moines, Iowa (1716 Locust Street): Meredith Corp. Fourteen detective stories featuring sleuths voted the most popular by critics, readers, and writers.

25. Sullivan, Eleanor, ed. *Alfred Hitchcock's Anthology, 1977 Edition.* New York: Davis Publications, Inc. Thirty stories from *AHMM*, 1958–1969. First in a series of softcover annuals. (Hardcover edition, *Alfred Hitchcock Presents: Tales to Keep You Spellbound,* New York: Dial Press.)

III. Miscellaneous Nonfiction

1. Ball, John, ed. *The Mystery Story.* Del Mar, California (243 12th Street): Publisher's Inc. Sixteen new essays and a bibliography on various aspects of the mystery. A companion to the Mystery Library reprints of mystery classics in hardcover, a mail-order project of the University of California, San Diego.

2. Cawelti, John G. *Adventure, Mystery and Romance.* Chicago: University of Chicago Press. A study of "formula stories" as art and popular culture, with emphasis on the detective story.

3. Chandler, Raymond. *The Blue Dahlia.* Carbondale, Illinois: Southern Illinois University Press. First publication of Chandler's 1945 screenplay, with a memoir by producer John Houseman and an afterword by Matthew J. Bruccoli.

4. ———. *The Notebooks of Raymond Chandler and English Summer.* New York: The Ecco Press/Viking Press. Chandler's notebooks, plus his previously unpublished "gothic romance."

5. Copps, Dale. *The World's Greatest Sherlock Holmes Quiz.* New York: Berkley Publishing Corp. Short quizzes and puzzles.

6. Cox, J. Randolph. *New Nick Carter Weekly.* Fall River, Massachusetts (87 School Street): Edward T. LeBlanc. A bibliography of the early Nick Carter stories.

7. DeCamara, Mary P. and Yahes, Stephen. *Sir Arthur Conan Doyle's Sherlock Holmes: The Short Stories.* New York: Monarch Press/Simon & Schuster. A critical commentary and study guide designed for school use.

8. Harrison, Michael, ed. *Beyond Baker Street.* New York: Bobbs-Merrill. An anthology of twenty-five new Sherlockian essays.

9. Higham, Charles. *The Adventures of Conan Doyle.* New York: W.W. Norton & Co. A new biography of Sherlock Holmes's creator.

10. Lambert, Gavin. *The Dangerous Edge.* New York: Grossman/Viking Press. Biographical and critical studies of nine mystery-suspense masters, including Collins, Doyle, Chesterton, Buchan, Ambler,

Greene, Simenon, Chandler, and Hitchcock.

11. Landrum, Larry N., Browne, Pat, and Browne, Ray B., eds. *Dimensions of Detective Fiction*. Bowling Green, Ohio: Bowling Green University Press. Twenty-three essays on aspects of the mystery, mainly papers read at annual meetings of the Popular Culture Association.

12. MacShane, Frank. *The Life of Raymond Chandler*. New York: E.P. Dutton & Co. The first full-length biography of Chandler.

13. Murdoch, Derrick. *The Agatha Christie Mystery*. New York (Publishers Marketing Group, 1515 Broadway) and Toronto: Pagurian Press Limited. A biography, an assessment of Ms. Christie's work, and a complete list of her ninety-four books, nineteen films, and seventeen plays.

14. Norris, Luther, ed. *The Pontine Dossier*. Culver City, California (3844 Watseka Avenue): Luther Norris. The 1975–1976 edition of this annual, containing articles and stories related mainly to August Derleth's Solar Pons tales.

15. Ousby, Ian. *Bloodhounds of Heaven*. Cambridge, Massachusetts: Harvard University Press. A study of the detective as portrayed in English fiction from William Godwin to Arthur Conan Doyle.

16. Pointer, Michael. *The Sherlock Holmes File*. New York: Clarkson N. Potter. A study of actors who have portrayed Holmes on stage and screen, 175 illustrations.

17. Queen, Ellery, ed. *Ellery Queen's 1977 Mystery Calendar*. New York: Davis Publications, Inc. A calendar featuring brief biographies and photos of twenty-four leading mystery writers, and marking important dates in their careers.

18. Rosenblatt, Julia C. and Sonnenschmidt, Frederick H. *Dining with Sherlock Holmes*. New York: Bobbs-Merrill. A Baker Street cookbook.

19. Simenon, Georges. *Letter to My Mother*. New York: Harcourt Brace Jovanovich. A brief memoir by the creator of Inspector Maigret.

20. Smith, Myron J. *Cloak-and-Dagger Bibliography*. Metuchen, New Jersey (Box 656): Scarecrow Press. An annotated guide to over 1600 spy-intrigue novels published between 1937 and 1975.

21. Sons of the Copper Beeches. *More Leaves from the Copper Beeches*. Bryn Mawr, Pennsylvania (145 Stockton Road): James G. Jewell. Original articles and pastiches by members of a Sherlockian scion society.

22. Steinbrunner, Chris and Penzler, Otto, eds. *Encyclopedia of Mystery and Detection*. New York: McGraw-Hill Book Co. Articles on more than five hundred mystery writers, their characters and categories, with checklists of titles, extensive notes on film and television adaptations, and more than 300 illustrations. Despite some omissions, it is easily the most comprehensive reference work in the mystery field.

23. Treat, Lawrence, ed. *The Mystery Writer's Handbook*. Cincinnati, Ohio: Writer's Digest. Fully revised and rewritten edition of a handbook by members of Mystery Writers of America, first published in 1956.

24. Wynne, Nancy Blue. *An Agatha Christie Chronology*. New York: Ace Books. A catalogue of the novels and collections, with plot sum-

maries, omitting only the final novel and short story.
25. Young, Trudee. *Georges Simenon.* Metuchen, New Jersey (Box 656): Scarecrow Press. A checklist of all Maigret and other mystery novels and short stories, in French and in English translations.

AWARDS

Mystery Writers of America
  Best novel—Robert Parker, *Promised Land* (Houghton Mifflin)
  Best American first novel— James Patterson, *The Thomas Berryman Number* (Little, Brown)
  Best short story—Etta Revesz, *Like a Terrible Scream (EQMM)*
  Best paperback novel—Gregory Mcdonald, *Confess, Fletch* (Avon)
  Best biography and criticism—Chris Steinbrunner and Otto Penzler, editors-in-chief; Marvin Lachman and Charles Shibuk, senior editors—*Encyclopedia of Mystery and Detection* (McGraw-Hill)
Crime Writers Association (London)
  Gold Dagger—Ruth Rendell, *A Demon in My View* (London: Hutchinson)
  Silver Dagger—James McClure, *Rogue Eagle* (London: Macmillan)
  John Creasey Memorial Award (for the best first crime novel)—Patrick Alexander, *Death of a Thin-Skinned Animal* (London: Macmillan, New York: E. P. Dutton)

NECROLOGY

1. Barker, Ronald (1920–1976). Secretary of the British Publishers' Association and author of three mystery novels under his own name and three as "E. B. Roland," 1954–1962.
2. Bellah, James Warner (1899–1976). Novelist and screenwriter who published three mystery novels, 1936–1940.
3. Boland, John (1913–1976). British author of twenty-five mystery-crime novels, notably *The League of Gentlemen* (1958).
4. Britton, Anne (1930?–1976). British writer and editor, author of a Gothic mystery, *Storm Castle* (1967), under the name "Jan Andersen."
5. Cecil, Henry (1902–1976). Pen name of Henry Cecil Leon, British county court judge and author of some twenty-five legal mysteries, notably *No Bail for the Judge* (1952).
6. Christie, Agatha (1890–1976). Famed mystery writer, creator of Hercule Poirot and Miss Marple. Author of sixty-six mystery novels, notably *The Mysterious Affair at Styles* (1920), *The Murder of Roger Ackroyd* (1926), *The Murder at the Vicarage* (1930), *Murder on the Orient Express* (1934), *The A.B.C. Murders* (1935), *Death on the Nile* (1937), *And Then There Were None* (1939). This last was staged as *Ten Little Indians* and became one of her many successful plays, along with *Witness for the Prosecution* and the long-running London hit *The Mousetrap.* She also published seventeen collections of short stories, as well as roman-

tic novels under the name "Mary Westmacott." Her last books, *Curtain* (1975) and *Sleeping Murder* (1976), were written in the early 1940s and recount the final cases of Poirot and Miss Marple.

7. Curry, Thomas A. (1901?–1976). Prolific author of western and adventure novels who also published mysteries under the names "Tom Curry," "John Benton," and "Albert Jeffers," 1926–1947.

8. Disney, Doris Miles (1907–1976). Long-time mystery novelist, author of forty-seven books beginning with *A Compound for Death* (1943).

9. Gallico, Paul (1897–1976). Popular sportswriter and novelist. Some half-dozen of his forty-one books are crime-suspense, including *The Zoo Gang* (1971).

10. Hay, Jacob (?–1976). Short story writer, contributor to *EQMM* since 1961.

11. Knowlton, Don (1893?–1976). Former president of Hill & Knowlton public relations firm and widely published author. Contributor to *EQMM* since 1961.

12. Kyd, Thomas (1901–1976). Pseudonym of Alfred B. Harbage, distinguished Shakespearian scholar. Author of four detective novels, notably *Blood on the Bosom Devine* (1948).

13. Martin, Robert (1908–1976). Well-known pulp writer and author of more than twenty mystery novels under his own name and the pseudonym "Lee Roberts."

14. McDowell, Robert Emmett (?–1976). Pulp writer and author of seven books, 1954–1965, some about series sleuth Jonathan Knox.

15. Morgan, Bryan (1923?–1976). Author of books on British railways and at least one mystery novel, *The Business at Blanche Capel* (1954). Edited a 1975 anthology, *Crime on the Lines,* unpublished in the U.S.

16. Pangborn, Edgar (1909–1976). Noted science fiction writer and author of one mystery novel, *The Trial of Callista Blake* (1961). Contributor to *EQMM*, 1952–1962.

17. Pendower, Jacques (1899–1976). British author of some seventy mystery novels, largely unpublished in America, under his own name and as "T.C.R. Jacobs." A founder of the Crime Writers Association.

18. Schurmacher, Emile (1903?–1976). Newspaperman and author of seventeen nonfiction books, who published one suspense novel, *Assignment X: Top Secret,* in 1965.

19. Sullivan, Robert (1917–1976). Massachusetts Superior Court judge and author of two fact crime books, *The Disappearance of Dr. Parkman* (1969) and *Goodbye, Lizzie Borden* (1974).

20. Taylor, Phoebe Atwood (1909–1976). Creator of Cape Cod sleuth Asey Mayo who starred in twenty-two novels, 1931–1951. Under the name "Alice Tilton" she also created scholarly sleuth Leonidas Witherall, who appeared in eight novels during the same period.

21. Williams, John (1908–1976). British author of war histories and several fact crime books, including *Hume: Portrait of a Double Murderer.*

HONOR ROLL

(Starred stories are included in this volume)

Asimov, Isaac, "A Case of Income Tax Fraud," *EQMM*, November.
——, "The Winnowing," *Analog*, February.
Ball, John, "One for Virgil Tibbs," *EQMM*, February.
Beaird, Dick, "At the End of the Rainbow," *EQMM*, October.
Benjamin, Dorothy, "Sound of a Distant Echo," *EQMM*, September.
Blau, Kelly H., "The Scavengers," *EQMM*, December.
*Bloch, Robert, "Crook of the Month," *AHMM*, November.
——, "A Most Unusual Murder," *EQMM*, March.
Block, Lawrence, "The Dettweiler Solution," *AHMM*, September.
*——, "A Pair of Recycled Jeans," *AHMM*, August.
——, "Sometimes They Bite," *AHMM*, June.
Boland, John C., "Stand-in," *AHMM*, September.
Bradt, David, "A Kind of Madness," *EQMM*, November.
Breen, Jon L., "Adventure of the Disoriented Detective," *EQMM*, September.
——, "Craig Kennedy Up-to-Date," *The Pontine Dossier*, 1975–1976.
——, "The Flying Thief of Oz," *EQMM*, April.
Brewer, Gil, "The Thinking Child," *MM*, September.
Brittain, William, "Historical Errors," *AHMM*, February.
——, "One Big Happy Family," *AHMM*, September.
Brown, Marcia K., "Do Not Fold, Spindle, or Mutilate," *MSMM*, June.
Callahan, Barbara, "Lavender Lady," *EQMM*, April.
*——, "November Story," *EQMM*, December.
Carpenter, Duffy, "The Last Cigar," *EQMM*, July.
Catalan, Jacques, "The Prisoners," *EQMM*, October.
Cohen, Stanley, "A Game of Tennis," *MM*, July.
——, "Nadigo," *MM*, September.
Curtiss, Ursula, "The Pool Sharks," *EQMM*, October.
*Davidson, Avram, "Crazy Old Lady," *EQMM*, March.
de la Torre, Lillian, "The Aerostatick Globe," *EQMM*, June.
De Mille, Nelson, "The Mystery at Thorn Mansion," *MM*, December.
Deuel, Evelyn Groff, "Best-Laid Plans," *EQMM*, April.
Eckels, Robert Edward, "Attention to Detail," *EQMM*, *September.*
——, *"Judgment Postponed," AHMM*, December.
Ellin, Stanley, "Generation Gap," *EQMM*, September.
Ellison, Harlan, "Killing Bernstein," *MM*, June.
Feldhake, Susan C., "A Time for Everything," *AHMM*, September.
Fremlin, Celia, "Dangerous Sport," *EQMM*, September.
Garfield, Brian, "Joe Cutter's Game," *AHMM*, July.
Gores, Joe, "File #10: The Maimed and the Halt," *EQMM*, January.
Greenbaum, Everett, "Albion, Perfidious Albion," *AHMM*, June.
Greenwood, Robert, "Archetypes," *The Denver Quarterly*, Winter.

Parry, Henry T., "The Plum Point Ladies," *AHMM*, September.
Peirce, J.F., "Time Bomb," *EQMM*, October.
Pentecost, Hugh, "The Dark Plan," *EQMM*, February.
Perowne, Barry, "Raffles and the Dangerous Game," *EQMM*, June.
———, "Raffles on the Riviera," *EQMM*, September.
Pfeffer, Susan Beth, "In 125 Words or Less," *EQMM*, October.
Phaon, Jerrold, "The Outsider," *EQMM*, September.
*Porter, Joyce, "Dover Does Some Spadework," *EQMM*, October.
Powell, Talmage, "Death Pact," *MM*, July.
———, "A Time to Kill," *MSMM*, May.
Pronzini, Bill, "The Arrowmont Prison Riddle," *AHMM*, October.
*———, "Sweet Fever," *EQMM*, December.
———, and Kurland, Michael, "Vanishing Act," *AHMM*, January.
———, and Malzberg, Barry N., "A Matter of Survival," *AHMM*, December.
———, "Problems Solved," *EQMM*, June.
Rafferty, S.S., "Buzz 'em, Chick!" *EQMM*, June.
———, "The Christmas Masque," *EQMM*, December.
*———, "The Georgia Resurrection," *EQMM*, February.
———, "The Pennsylvania Thimblerig," *EQMM*, August.
———, "The Witch of New Hampshire," *EQMM*, May.
*Rainey, Rich, "The Man in the White Room," *MM*, September.
Rendell, Ruth, "A Drop Too Much," *EQMM*, August.
*———, "People Don't Do Such Things," *The Fallen Curtain*.
———, "The Vinegar Mother," *The Fallen Curtain*.
———, "You Can't Be Too Careful," *EQMM*, March.
*Revesz, Etta, "Like a Terrible Scream," *EQMM*, May.
Ritchie, Jack, "Kid Cardula," *AHMM*, June.
*———, "Next in Line," *AHMM*, April.
———, "Nobody Tells Me Anything," *EQMM*, October.
Romun, Isak, "Cora's Raid," *AHMM*, October.
*Runyon, Charles W., "Death Is My Passenger," *MSMM*, June.
Ryan, Donna, "Band of Fear," *Silver Foxes*, September.
Shea, Douglas, "Advice, Unlimited," *EQMM*, December.
*Sheehan, Laurence, "The Christmas Tree Lot Murders," *The Atlantic Monthly*, December.
Sisk, Frank, "Change of Identity," *AHMM*, November.
———, "Who Am I?" *AHMM*, October.
Slesar, Henry, "Hiding Out," *AHMM*, March.
Smith, Conrad S., "Steffi Duna, I Love You!" *EQMM*, May.
Smith, Pauline C., "The Dog," *MSMM*, May.
———, "Lost Child," *AHMM*, May.
———, "Painted in Crimson," *MSMM*, September.
———, "The Third Thursday," *MSMM*, October.
———, "The Triad," *AHMM*, June.
Smith, William I., "Everybody Calls Me Rocky," *EQMM*, August.
*Speed, Jane, "View from the Inside," *EQMM*, August.
Stevens, Hilary, "Eyewitness," *EQMM*, October.

About the Editor

Edward D. Hoch, winner of an Edgar award for his short story, "The Oblong Room," is a full-time writer, mainly of mystery fiction, and his stories appear regularly in the leading mystery magazines. He is probably best known for his creation of series-detective Nick Velvet, whose exploits have even been dramatized on French television. A collection entitled *The Thefts of Nick Velvet* was published by The Mysterious Press. His novels include *The Transvection Machine, The Fellowship of the Hand,* and *The Frankenstein Factory.* Mr. Hoch is married and lives with his wife in Rochester, New York.